MILES LEFT YET

Holly Schindler

Miles Left Yet

Published by Holly Schindler, LLC

Copyright © 2016 by Holly Schindler

Cover design by Holly Schindler
Interior design by Holly Schindler

Cover images by Marcus and photomelon, both courtesy of Fotolia

License Plate font by Dave Hansen, courtesy of FontSpace and Perfetto Brush Font by Davide Bassu, courtesy of Creative Market

Dedicated to those who are about to head out on a brand new adventure...

Mile

40,563

1.

"There she is!" Sarah shouted, laughing as she pointed at the 1965 Mustang that had been parked at the curb, a triumphant "Sold!" smeared across the window in white windshield marker.

Jim grabbed her hand and together, they raced the length of their front yard. Panting after the short jog, Jim threw open the passenger door to reveal that he'd placed three daisies tied with red ribbon on the white leather seat—an identical three daisies in red ribbon had been waiting for Sarah when Jim had picked her up for their first date on a night in April more than forty years before.

"God bless the Internet and VIN numbers," Jim joked. Because he'd found it—the car of their youth. Not just the same make and model—not just a '65 convertible. This was *her*—the exact car that had whisked Jim and Sarah off to a first summer of drive-in movies. The car whose stereo had played the first song they'd ever danced to, both doors open and the dome light shining like a moon as they'd swayed together in the parking lot of the college burger joint that had closed around them, lights out, chairs on the tables, a cloud of tired voices shouting, *Not one more Coke refill for you, not another plate of French fries, get out, get out, take it somewhere else.* The same windshield that had grown gray with steam at their favorite secluded make-out spot. The same car they'd later driven to the starlit lake, still shaking the rice from their hair, as they'd begun life as an official "we," the do-or-die kind.

And now, here, two days from their anniversary and one week until Jim's retirement, the Mustang was back. Jim had found her.

Not that it had turned out to be that hard, really. He'd anticipated a horrible search—a regular archaeological dig. But the old VIN, which he'd found on their carefully filed insurance papers in one of the you-never-know plastic tubs of paperwork Sarah had stacked in the attic, had instantly led him right back to the man Jim had sold the car to. Hard to forget the last name: Cherry. As in: cherry red, which was the color of the Mustang's paint. His kid—a sixteen-year-old girl—had been ecstatic when they'd shown up to take the car off Jim's hands. Bouncing around on her heels and clapping her hands, sending her permed hair flying all across her shoulders. It was 1985 then, and already the car was a classic. She'd rattled at breakneck speed about how jealous the kids at school would be. Cracked her gum to punctuate the end of each sentence.

Jim had felt a little guilty watching her drive away; maybe, he'd thought, he should have waited a few years to find out if his son, Carl, would want it. But then again, what kid ever prized the things that had been important to his dad? Wasn't that part of it, being young, being a teenager—rejecting everything your dad

3

had been? Going your own way, picking a new set of roads?

His heart had nearly stopped when Cherry—at that point bald and unsteady on his feet—had opened his garage door, and there she'd sat: Jim and Sarah's Mustang, looking no worse for the wear, really.

"I was afraid, at this point, she'd be in a junkyard somewhere," Jim had admitted.

"Lynn drove it a year," Cherry'd told him. "One year. Then her senior year boyfriend took her everywhere—even to school every morning. When she went away to college, she left it behind. Drove it here and there when she was home on break. I thought about selling it, I really did. But come on—a '65 Mustang. Sitting in the front seat, top down, wind in your hair, while 'American Pie' is playing. Doesn't get more quintessentially USA, now, does it?"

Cherry'd glanced at Jim and let out a low, long whistle. "Don't have to tell you, do I? Think I mighta just described your own life. Don't start thinking that'll make me go easy on the price, though."

Thirty—that was the amount they'd finally agreed on. It was still factory-original everything, Cherry'd bragged. With the exception of a few filters and hoses and the brake system's master cylinder, anyway. When he'd peeled back the tacky cow-print seat covers, exposing the original interior, Jim had nearly screamed with excitement. He'd sworn he could detect the faint smell of the perfume Sarah'd once worn.

The price might have pinched had Jim not begun to ascend his ladder of success relatively early on. A man could do that back in the era of Jim's young adulthood—could put his foot on the bottom rung of any business (in Jim's case, insurance sales) and climb every single working day, all the way up to district manager, then end (as Jim had) his thirty-year career as regional vice president, the high note he'd literally spent his adult life striving to hit. At Jim's stage of life, he honestly thought nothing of forking over thirty grand for another thirty years of good times—that was only a thousand a year. He and Sarah could easily spend just as much on dinner and movie tickets, not to mention golf fees. Didn't the car promise better, wilder times? The kind of times they deserved? Of course it did. He'd killed the engine when he'd arrived home and raced up the front yard, calling Sarah's name loud enough for the entire neighborhood to hear.

There were some signs, Jim slowly began to realize, that the Mustang hadn't been without a few hard days of her own—a hint of rust on the fenders, a dent in the chrome horse galloping across the grille. He felt sorry, staring at her there beside the curb, for having once abandoned her. And he wondered, oddly, if the poor car felt like a kid who'd been shoved into foster care, bouncing from one home to another, only to have his biological parents show up years later, arms outstretched, shouting, "Miss me?"

Sarah was still laughing, though. Clapping her hands and leaning into Jim, pressing her cheek against his chest. She wrapped her arms around Jim's waist and squeezed. "I feel eighteen just looking at it," she announced. "Don't you feel like the beginning just came back? Like we get to do it all again?"

Before he could answer, she was tugging her arms away, picking her daisies up out of her seat, sliding in.

Jim grinned, jingling the keys and racing to the driver's side. Because no matter how many dings and dents he and Sarah and the Mustang had collected over the years, Jim knew that as long as there was gas in the tank and the engine still purred, there were adventures to be had. As he cranked the ignition, his eye roved to the odometer. She hadn't yet broken forty-one thousand miles. Plenty of life left in her.

A gray ribbon of highway still stretched untraveled in front of them.

Mile

40,601

Two Years

Later

2.

Jim shifted and tapped the brake as he rounded the corner of the parking lot at the Granite Ridge Retirement Community.

Voices rustled like a breeze rattling tree limbs. But they always did at the Ridge—so many of them creating a sound so constant, Jim could, on occasion, grow deaf to their banter, just as he'd once been so accustomed to the sycamores outside his boyhood home he could overlook the sound of the wind combing through their leaves.

He honked in greeting as he passed by residents with dogs in tow, residents pushing visiting grandchildren in a nearby swing. As the engine rumbled close to their community garden, Jim's next-door neighbor and closest friend, Frank, turned to wave—raised his arm so high, he hiked one leg of his overalls, exposing his ankle. Jim brought the Mustang to a complete stop as Frank pulled himself away from the tomato stakes, his fist filled with swollen red fruit.

"My heirlooms came in," Frank said, rubbing the soil off with his handkerchief. He pushed a tomato under Jim's nose. "Have a taste," he insisted. They both took bites, chomping like they were apples just plucked from an orchard.

Jim admired Frank—liked the fact that dirt was still under his nails, no apologies. Was amazed that he could forecast weather based on the direction chimney smoke curled, that he could home-remedy just about anything. That he was still trampling through garden rows sunup to sundown at eighty-three.

But that was true of everyone at the Ridge, really. They'd refused to discard any part of themselves, to fold who they'd once been and place it in a trunk in the attic simply because they'd hit what younger generations might have referred to as their golden years. This was no rocking chair bunch. These were musicians who entertained the other residents—and, when asked, carted large black instrument cases to venues around town. These were photographers who adorned the hallways with artistic black and white portraits of fellow residents. These were energetic dancers who took to the floor not only to foxtrot but to West Coast swing—or square dance, depending on the tune. An astronaut who lived on the top floor—closest to the moon he had once visited—had set up a telescope behind the building, ready to demystify the stars for students who came by the busloads to hear him talk... ready, too, for anyone who might like to join him for a little night gazing.

There really were still plenty of stars to wish on. Plenty of wishes yet that had not been fulfilled. Plenty of new dance steps to learn and dishes to try and places to visit. The people at the Ridge had not come to put a period at the end of a sentence. They'd come to start a slew of new paragraphs.

"Well. I'll get out of your way," Frank told Jim, pointing down the usual path he drove the Mustang every Sunday, the laps he took around the building. "You gotta keep those juices flowing." And laughed because the tomato juices were rolling down his chin, too.

Those were Jim's own words, actually, what he always said he was doing every single week—*keeping the juices flowing and the mileage low*—as he steered around the edges of the Granite Ridge lot like a roller skater around a rink.

"Wanna go one more time around, old girl?" he asked Sarah. And before he could stop himself, he reached toward the passenger side. Instead of finding Sarah's knee, though, his fingers brushed an empty seat.

In reality, Jim was now a widower, and Sarah existed only as an image in his rearview. Literally. She was a Kodak picture (Jim's favorite of all her pictures), tucked into the corner of the mirror. An image—faded, turned slightly green, and curled from summer heat— that Jim talked to when he was behind the wheel.

Sarah'd died within a week of Jim finding their Mustang. As it turned out, that long gray ribbon of highway adventure was barely the length of the driveway at their house. But even their driveway belonged to someone else these days. And Jim had already lived at the Ridge for two years.

He'd loved his time at the Ridge. Loved the leisurely dinner conversation, the wild anecdotes and embellished stories that had left his stomach sore from all the laughing.

As good as it was, though, something was missing—it nagged at him in the quiet hours. It itched. It was a sore spot he couldn't quit poking at.

10

Jim edged the Mustang toward the Granite Ridge exit and paused, waiting to be overwhelmed by the urge to hit the road. He wasn't, though. He couldn't think of a single place he really wanted to go. Not with his partner in adventure gone.

Jim could never bring himself to get rid of the Mustang, either. But for far different reasons than Cherry had held onto it. It wasn't an investment, nor was it simply a slice of nostalgia. The car had been so easy to track it down, it was as though it was always meant to be. Like bumping into an old girlfriend only to learn you were both still single, the flame between you still flickering. If the car was supposed to come back to him, though, it couldn't have been just been to sit in storage.

He backed the Mustang into his garage unit. And he pulled himself out from behind the wheel.

He glanced through the open convertible top and winked at Sarah's picture. He knew that if Sarah had been there, she would have frowned in disapproval. *Really, Jim*, she would have said. *Two years in a garage. Two years?* Her voice would have gone up an entire octave on that last word. Her exasperation would have echoed through him.

"Don't look at me like that, old girl," he told the photo. "I'll figure it out. I promise." And he circled to the back of the car, where he began to tug a tarp on over the fender.

3.

Mildred jumped—as much as a person could jump when she was lying on her side—her eyes snapping open like just-let-go-of window shades. Her heart thumped harder than it ever did in her empty bed, her skin clammy against the thin material of her nightgown. Her breath wooshed like an ocean tide on fast-forward with her hand sandwiched between her ear and her pillow. Her thoughts whirled even faster as she tried to figure out what had startled her. She hadn't had a nightmare. But she was afraid, wide awake. What had happened?

Her ears perked like a worried cat's. The house she'd always lived in, from the cradle until that very moment, had collected its share of odd noises. It coughed, it rumbled, it muttered in rainstorms like it was grumbling a string of swear words, it squeaked. But then again, her right knee had developed a squeak, too. An actual, honest-to-God squeak, and every time she heard it (mostly as she was climbing the three front steps to her porch), her entire mind swelled with the image of a rusty hinge. All these sounds had been cataloged in her mind, the way a person always cataloged sounds when they lived alone. And in the mix of the familiar rumbling and grumbling and squeaking, she couldn't detect a single unusual out-of-place peep.

She sat up, swiveling her feet out of bed, and reached for the water glass on her nightstand. The water had barely touched her tongue when a knock exploded against her bedroom window.

She yelped and coughed simultaneously, and she wondered for a fleeting moment, as she wheezed and the water went down the wrong way, if it was possible to drown on a single mouthful of water. It would be, perhaps, the stupidest way to die ever: *Here lies Mildred Sudbury, who suffered a bad swallow.*

But it would also be far less frightening, in the end, than the other hundred possibilities that had suddenly revealed themselves, now that Mildred knew that this was also the sound that had yanked her from sleep. Someone had knocked on her bedroom window. Twice. And Mildred Sudbury had definitely passed the era of life when a young boy was likely to attempt waking his sweetheart by tossing pebbles in the direction of her bedroom.

Trembling, Mildred flicked on her nightstand lamp. The bushes beside the window rustled violently. Someone was out there—and they didn't want to be seen.

Her mouth suddenly turned so dry, it seemed ridiculous to her that she could have been thinking about the possibility of drowning only a minute ago. She snatched up her robe and cinched it around her waist, her heart beating like an after-school stampede through the Central High School corridors.

She swiveled, her silver pin curls catching the lamplight as she searched for a weapon. Her eyes scanned the bookcase, thinking she would have gladly given her eyeteeth for a marble bookend. Her landline phone? No. A wire hanger from her closet? How much damage did anyone other than Joan Crawford really think a wire hanger could do?

Frantic, Mildred lunged for the black instrument case on top of her hope chest and pulled out her flute. She'd show whoever it was that had decided to taunt her. In the dark, it would look as though she was wielding a metal club. And besides, death by blunt-force wind instrument would definitely be an even stupider demise than death by a mouthful of water. She'd go viral: *Retired schoolteacher kills intruder with a flute*. They'd make a movie about her: *Gutsy*, the picture would be called. Helen Mirren would play her.

She crept out of the master bedroom, the same room she had taken for her own when her mother had passed. And she began to inch her way toward her childhood-teenhood-adulthood bedroom, which she'd turned into an office after her mother's death. Where her pen had scratched happily, rhythmically (almost like feet during a game of hopscotch or jump-rope) as she'd graded decades of (sometimes delightful, sometimes incoherent) high school English papers. But the room had, since her retirement three weeks ago, begun to look like a paper in need of its own grading. It needed direction. Suggestions for revision. The room wasn't an office anymore. She had no need for one. "Office" had a giant red check mark next to it. An office wasn't the right answer. But what was?

"Hobby room," said the boy who dropped her avocados and whitening toothpaste into brown paper bags at Price Saver Grocery. "My grandma made a hobby room when Grandpa died and she was in the house alone."

"Volunteer," said the woman who zapped the bar codes on the back of Mildred's library books. "It'll give your days shape."

None of it seemed right. And honestly, Mildred didn't really want their help. She wanted the new direction of her life to hit her like she imaged inspiration had once struck Keats before beginning a new ode. So she'd pretended that her days were already filled. (What was that old coffee slogan? "Up to the rim with Brim!" Something like that.) At home, though, she straightened and re-straightened her shelves. She read a book a day. She organized her closet. She polished the silver, for the love of Pete. The second hands of her clocks moved like tranquilized turtles.

She knew there had to be more than this, than "retired." The very word irked her. Any other time in life was not marked by an *–ed*. "I'm a teacher," people said. Or "A college student." "A dentist." "A chef." "I paint houses." "I fly jets." "I care for children." All present tenses. Suddenly, here she was, an *–ed*.

The only other *–ed*s she'd ever seen were in obituaries, which she'd begun to read with regularity. A morbid fascination that allowed her some way to measure her own accomplishments. What really pinched her were the lists of "survived"s (another past tense), as in: "She is survived by her three children, seven grandchildren, and twenty-one great-grandchildren."

This was a weight, too, nearly as heavy as her unfilled hours, her directionless days. Maybe she'd missed something by not having a family. Every item in the list of "Not Done" was always a missed opportunity. But a single woman in her sixties couldn't exactly decide to just go get herself a baby, now, could she? That unused office couldn't exactly become a nursery.

Mildred glared at the office door looming ahead of her as though it were an impatient student growing increasingly annoyed at how long it was taking Ms. Sudbury to answer his question. *You just wait your turn. You'll get your new purpose after I get mine. You're second in line. Besides, I'm about to kill an intruder. Priorities, dear, priorities.*

She inched down the hall and stood at the edge of the living room with the flute raised like a bat, her eyes roving across the shadows.

Another unsettling rattle exploded against the sliding glass back door: *rat-a-rap-rap.* A knock, a definite knock.

No—not a knock. A threat.

Mildred lurched for the wall phone between the living room and the kitchen. And dialed 9-1-1.

It took fifteen minutes for the police officer to show up. *Fifteen minutes*, Mildred thought bitterly as the doorbell finally rang, a jagged frown etched into her face. Enough time to be raped and murdered and then murdered again. It only took ten seconds to pour an entire gallon of milk down the sink. Isn't that about how much blood was in the human body?

Her hand rested on the deadbolt. What if it hadn't taken the police fifteen minutes? What if they were still on their way? What if this was the same person who had been in the bushes beneath her bedroom window? What if he'd been out there all this time, savoring the taste of her fear?

"Who is it?" she shouted.

"Officer Prescott."

Mildred flipped the deadbolt and cracked the door, the chain still attached. A badge slipped through the space.

Mildred wasn't stupid. She'd been around for decades of crime shows—the *Dragnet*s and the *Adam-12*s and the *Columbo*s and the *Hill Street Blues*es and the eleven thousand *Law and Order* spin-offs. If this were a prime time show, that badge would be fake, and tomorrow morning, someone in a khaki trench coat would be standing over her cold body shaking his head. *Here lies Mildred Sudbury on her living room floor, but don't worry, in thirty minutes we'll know what happened here. Her murderer will be in the slammer, and you'll have forgotten all about her by the time next week's episode airs.*

But as much as prime time TV had warned Mildred about situations such as these, at some point in life, trust, which was as sturdy as a tightrope, had to enter into the equation. If prime time really wanted to help a girl out, Mildred thought as she unlatched the chain lock, it would add creepy music to real life every time danger appeared. That way, she'd know for sure if the person who had just crossed her path was out to turn her skull into a planter, with petunias coming out the eye sockets.

The easy way the officer slipped through her front door made Mildred's frown deepen, her heart pick up the pace. He acted like he was planning his midnight snack—hoping to hurry through Mildred's trivial business so he could make it to his favorite burger joint, scheduled to close in twenty minutes. So what if this man wasn't planning to try out his new Ginsu knives on her? Now he was going to placate her. Didn't that cut in its own way?

Mildred met his condescension with a teacherly size-up: She crossed her arms over her chest and raked his figure with her eyes. She took note of the balding crown of his head, the thick black hairs growing like vines around a wedding band, and a gut holding the kind of extra weight men seemed to acquire after their second child.

"So—what's the disturbance," he asked, halfway bored. "Ms.—"

"Sudbury," Mildred snapped.

The officer perked, his eyes flying wide. "Sudbury?" he repeated. There was something about his face then—the openness of it, maybe. But Mildred saw his younger self—and recognized him.

"Chad Prescott," she blurted.

"Yes!" he shouted, pleased she remembered him. She couldn't quite place the year, but guessed somewhere between '89 and '92. Names were a kind of fashion, too—a sweater a child wore through life. Chads had disappeared; Chads weren't in high school hallways anymore. They were losing their hair and had children of their own.

Then again, Mildreds were not in high school corridors, either. Mildreds had become *–ed*s.

"Is somebody bothering you, Ms. Sudbury?" he asked, his voice high-pitched.

Mildred stiffened. Forty years ago, in the same situation, the police officer's tone would have been low, manly: *I'll rescue you from the train tracks, you damsel in distress! Look how virile I am! Let me take you out for a shrimp cocktail and tell you all about me!* Now, the tone Officer Prescott chose was squeaky, pacifying. It was the tone of veterinarians and pediatricians: *Oh, you poor sweet thing. Let me take care of you.* It didn't exactly make her feel grateful. Instead, she felt like kicking Chad in the groin.

"Did you see him?" Chad gasped. "He didn't actually get in, did he, Ms. Sudbury?"

"No—no," Mildred answered, waving her hands for emphasis and realizing, at the same time, that she was still holding her flute. She cleared her throat, placed the instrument on the coffee table. The flute seemed silly now. But that's what second thoughts did, really. Turned so many good ideas into silly, empty gestures.

Chad put his hand on his chest and heaved out a long, relieved exhale. As he glanced about the living room, though, his face twisted with concern again. "Ms. Sudbury, are you all alone here?"

Mildred flinched. She pictured her obituary: *Mildred Sudbury is survived by nobody, nada, zippo. An unused office will be erected in her memory.* "I'm fine here alone."

"Stuff goes on around here, though."

"What do you mean, 'stuff'?" Mildred inquired, in a tone that was instantly familiar to her. She suspected she had used it on Chad before—for some reason, she felt it was for losing his classroom copy of *Lord of the Flies.*

"The neighborhood's changing. Surely you've noticed."

She hadn't, actually. At least, not in a way that had caused her any alarm. Her neighborhood had already changed a hundred times over. Before Mildred was even born, the coal chutes on houses had been closed forever with the switch to natural gas. By the time she got her driver's license, carports had popped up in backyards because no family Plymouth could fit in Model T-sized garages. Children grew and moved. Parents aged and moved. New neighbors, new generations, new noises. Gas-powered lawn mowers replaced reel mowers. Mailmen drove trucks instead of delivering by foot. The milkman of her early childhood was long gone. Women wore pants to work. Cable lines crisscrossed over the streets. Laundry was rarely dried on a clothesline. Music bleeding through living room windows was no longer big band; no more "In the Mood." What the world *did* always seem to be in the mood for was change—it was in a constant state of flux. Mildred's neighborhood had always simply changed along with it.

"The whole area's almost entirely rentals," Chad informed her. "Not that renters are bad, it's just—they don't seem to care as much as people who own, and we've had some—activity—if you know what I mean."

Mildred didn't, but she didn't want to ask, either—mostly because she didn't particularly like the roles they were suddenly taking on, the shift of power, the black uniform and the gun vs. her flimsy robe, which was something else that had changed, too. Women didn't wear robes anymore when they stepped outside to pick up their paper from the driveway each morning. Come to think of it, she wasn't sure when the last time was that she'd seen one of her neighbors come out to pick up a printed paper. She suddenly felt like that old Model T garage at the side of her own house, no longer the right size to fit with the modern world.

"Drugs," Chad explained. "A couple of blocks over, but still—they were selling out of the house. Worst part was how obvious the whole thing was—people coming and going all night long, 'visiting' for five minutes. Long enough to make a sale and—*vamoose!*" He grinned.

Clearing his throat when Mildred didn't grin back, he added, "I don't think it's over, though."

"But you arrested them," Mildred protested. "Right?" How could she have been so oblivious, lost in her world of silverware and library visits? How could Ms. Sudbury, with the eyes in the back of her head, *don't even think about cheating because she'll know crack off the bat*, not know that something criminal had moved so close? Had she lost powers of observation along with her present tense? Was she no longer the same Ms. Sudbury?

"Ms. Sudbury?" Chad pressed. "Did you hear me? I said it's not over. That's not the only house. But there's not enough evidence for us..."

Mildred mumbled incoherently. This wasn't who she thought her neighbors were at all. How could she have been so wrong? Only once, she remembered. Only once before had she ever been wrong about anyone. The thought scratched against her like grass blades against bare feet, making her itchy and uncomfortable.

"Ms. Sudbury?" Chad tried again. "I know you'll make the right decision. About whether to stay here alone. Ms. Sudbury doesn't make mistakes."

Chad edged toward the front door. He wanted to check the bushes, he was saying. Wanted to make sure her windows were all locked tight before he left.

"Once," Mildred said.

Chad stopped in the middle of the front hallway, turned, raised his eyebrows. "Sorry?" he asked, wrongly assuming she was talking to him.

"Once," she repeated. "I made a mistake once."

4.

Inside her new apartment at Granite Ridge, Norma watched as her only daughter, Elaine, waded deeper into yet another round of Things My Mom Does Not Know, Poor Norma and Her Old-Fashioned Ways.

Elaine had always been built like a football player—day one, the first time she'd seen her, Norma'd thought, *A miniature little defensive lineman*—but she was currently sweating through the relatively simple task of moving an armchair. Beads of sweat popped across her face, down her neck, and around her arms. Her face was turning a shiny fuchsia, too, reminding Norma of those old anodized aluminum tumblers Elaine had loved, the ones they'd used on the patio for lemonade in the summer. Norma wondered how it was possible for Elaine to remember the exact spot she'd placed its wooden feet a week ago, the exact angle of the chair. But somehow, she scooted it straight into position beside the east window, as though there were markers on the carpet.

"There," she said happily, dusting her hands off and propping her fists on her hips. Just like she had when she was four years old, her plump little fingers on the hips of her favorite striped green dress, a scowl on her face as she shook her head no—to whatever Norma'd just suggested.

"Really, Mother," Elaine chastised. "This spot is so much better for your eyes. Here where you can get plenty of sun. Why would you move your reading chair *out* of the sun?"

Because I read the morning paper in that chair—and the sun rises in that window in all its glare-filled glory, Norma wanted to say, but she swallowed her words.

Elaine flittered about the apartment—as much as a defensive lineman could flitter, anyway—putting their family portrait on the mantel instead of on the spinet piano Norma's grandmother had purchased for her when she was ten, the pair of silver candlesticks (which had once been a wedding present, but had become, according to Elaine, an antique family heirloom) on the coffee table instead of the mantel.

Antique, Norma repeated to herself, somewhat bitterly. An antique was something she and Charlie had gone shopping for on the weekends, picking up bits and pieces to add to their home. An antique had to be at least a hundred years old. Norma's candlesticks were *vintage*; they were *collectible*. They were not antiques.

Barbara, the granddaughter named after Norma's mother, climbed onto the small floral couch and punched at the buttons on the TV remote. The room filled with the *boings* and the *ouings* and the *splats* that accompanied cartoons. Barbara let out a belly laugh, crossing her legs and propping her head on her hand and her elbow on her knee. *She looks posed*, Norma thought as she lowered herself into her repositioned floral chair.

She still could have said something about the sunrise and the paper—in fact, Norma quietly composed a long and winding rebuttal about that very subject in her head. It sounded loving, motherly, but also on-target and forceful, like something Gloria Stivic would have proclaimed on *All in the Family* or Julia Sugarbaker would have spouted on *Designing Women*.

Where are women like that now? Norma wondered as she took solace in the fact that the speech in her head was spot-on—even though she would never say anything, not to Elaine.

By now, with sixty-five years under her belt, Norma was an expert at knowing what every specific stage of life called for. What a woman was to acquire and dispose of, decade by decade. This era—her sixties—called for Norma to let Elaine maintain some modicum of control over her own era—her late thirties (a period that Norma often thought of as the "pre"s: pre-menopausal, pre-midlife-crisis, pre-retirement, pre-grays, pre-wrinkles). Money was a funny thing, after all, and nothing could emasculate a person like having none.

Elaine and her husband were drowning, as they had been for the past four years or so; rather than helping each other, though, they had fallen into the habit of taking turns pushing each other's heads under the surface of their deepening misery. *Yes*, Norma had often thought, *that's exactly right—they look like they're involved in some wrestling game in a pool, but without the laughter: Back and forth, Elaine shoving Nathan down and pushing against his shoulders to break the surface and get a deep breath, then Nathan doing the same. Her against him, him against her, when they* should *have teamed up, joining forces to look for a life raft...*

It had all started when Nathan lost his position as a hospital pharmacist. He sent out an entire stream of résumés. He interviewed. He pleaded. And he wound up with a pharmacy position at Walgreens, the one with the 24-hour drive-thru window, working the kind of hours that meant (according to Elaine) the only way he would have any one-on-one interaction with Barbara was via Skype. Then Elaine was put on academic probation after a rather tragic semester in her nursing program that had included a D+ in chemistry. Upset at the wasted tuition money, Nathan began lobbing insults, almost gleefully, like a boy with a slingshot. Determined to prove her husband's new salary stunk, Elaine started charging new draperies and vases and throw rugs, exotic coffee blends for neighbors who happened by for a chat. ("If you want our life to look a certain way, it takes money! It wasn't like I had the cash to buy that stuff. Of course I had to charge it!" Norma'd heard Elaine shout in the background when Barbara called her on Sunday afternoons.) As their misfortunes accumulated, Nathan wrecked their 2009 minivan. Elaine called Norma from a curb behind the collision center at the Ford dealership, blubbering, desperate, and ashamed.

"Forget the car," Norma had instructed, even though the voice in her head yammered on about the ridiculousness of owning a van when they only had one child to transport to soccer games and ballet lessons. (And while she was at it, what were they doing charging up a bunch of ballet lessons, anyway? Why hadn't they just let her buy them for Barbara like she'd offered? Why had they let everything get so desperately *bad*?)

"This ends right now," Norma'd said, sandwiching the cordless receiver between her shoulder and her ear, squatting to look under her bed for her other brown loafer. She needed to get to a realtor. She moved with the same quick sureness that had once marked trips to various school offices, as she'd delivered Elaine's forgotten lunches or history papers. Norma'd had no emotional ties to bologna sandwiches or clumsily typed pages in plastic sleeves; it was Elaine she had the attachment to. (Even her insolence, when she was young, had been somewhat endearing. Norma had thought of it as a fire that would blaze a trail. *Watch out*, the world would say, *here comes that Elaine Johnson. Respect her like you would a tornado—get out of the way or get hurt*.)

Before she'd even hung up the phone, Norma'd already felt an odd, sudden detachment to the place she'd called home for the bulk of her life. The place she'd spent decades decorating with her antiques into a Goldilocks *and this is just right* kind of precision. At that moment, as she'd begun to plot the sale, she'd known, too, with only the slightest of pangs, that her house wasn't important—no more than those bologna sandwiches had been. The important thing was saving Elaine. No—more than that, it was what this moment in her life called for: making sure her daughter and her own family had a home.

So she'd sold her home of forty years—*undersold*, that was the word her real estate agent had used. But Norma had insisted on a price that would ensure a quick sale. She'd used the money to pay off Elaine's mortgage. With no real joy, she'd moved into Granite Ridge. Like so many other women of her generation stuck rescuing adult children from the never-ending recession and lack of opportunity, it appeared (for all intents and purposes) that Norma had been caught in a web of eminent downsizing.

The truth was, Charlie had left her with enough

to buy ten houses. Perhaps just knowing that Norma had so easily given up their prized house would have given poor Charlie heart failure all over again.

But maybe, she'd reminded herself, this whole Elaine thing was also a way to find out for sure if this stage of life really did call for (as she'd begun to fear) giving up on friendship. And by friendship, she in no way meant being polite neighbors who chatted at the chain-link fence. She meant real, honest, deep friendship—the kind that Norma had known in the pigtail and saddle shoes-wearing era of life. Had that truly faded away forever, just like her freckles? Was she left now with only nodding at vaguely familiar faces over a grocery store checkout lane conveyor belt? The only place to find out, Norma'd thought, was at a place like the Ridge. *An old folks' home*, the little girl still inside of her had said, wrinkling her nose. *Yes*, the present-day Norma had answered. *How wonderful. Young people have such a funny smell.* And she'd chuckled to herself.

Norma had then given Elaine a Julia Sugarbaker-style speech (for real that time), her voice rising and falling with emphasis. A one-time deal, she'd proclaimed. That was it. Elaine and company had a house. Which meant they could put mortgage payments toward repairing their car and paying off debts. *No more blubbering curbside phone calls, Elaine.* Worry had crawled up to the edge of Norma's heart and spilled out, overflowing just as it always overflowed where Elaine was concerned. Her fears, like those most mothers carried for their children, had fumes that she could choke on.

Elaine had appeared appropriately stricken as she'd accepted her mother's rescue. In retaliation, she'd taken it upon herself to show Norma her own faults, as though to remind her that no one was perfect;

everyone screwed up. *Look here, Mom, you can't even decorate your apartment!*

Yes, in this era of her own life, Norma's job was to allow Elaine to correct her. To let Elaine to feel, during her visits, that she was, in fact, quite a capable woman, despite having to be rescued—every bit as capable as her mother. No. More capable. When Elaine was gone, it was easy enough to put her life back in the order Norma liked, her own lived-in vision of perfect, with slightly crooked window shades and the bed pillows in the wrong order and the family picture on the piano.

Norma caught sight of her own reflection in the window next to her chair. She was no defensive lineman. That was something Elaine had inherited from Charlie's side. What Norma *did* see was a Gorilla Glue woman—made of the tough stuff that had always held her family together.

She was still attractive. Not in the way of twenty-year-olds, and not in the way of some aging actress, either, with her body parts shoved and bound to prove her own desirability. She was fleshy. Sturdy. Which in itself had once been a kind of prettiness. (Hadn't Lauren Hutton and Christie Brinkley and Cindy Crawford presented an almost athletic attractiveness?) Her skin was smooth, her complexion ruddy and healthy, and her hair had never gone completely gray—some would pay a small fortune to get the natural frost job streaking through her auburn hair.

Elaine, though, saw *mother*, saw *rescue net,* saw *the woman who knows I sucked my thumb until third grade and sneaked Camels through high school and loved my first boyfriend more than any of the others, even Nathan*; and Barbara saw *Grandmother*, saw *singer of silly old songs*, and the Social Security office saw *widow of Charles Johnson*, and no one, other than Norma, would ever look at her and think, *Gorilla Glue*.

That last thought upset her; she needed to get away for a minute.

Standing, she called to Barbara, "Let's go for a walk, pretty girl."

They skipped (correction: Barbara skipped, while Norma walked with her distinctive, purpose-driven long strides) down the lushly carpeted hallway. At the elevator, Barbara lunged forward to push the large green button, prompting the doors to slide open. (*An elevator to simply go down one floor*, Norma sighed to herself. *Don't they know a Gorilla Glue woman can get down a flight of steps as easily as a first grader can play hide-and-seek for hours, racing across an entire neighborhood of backyards in search of just the right never-find-me-in-a-million-years hiding spot?*) The elevator let out a polite ding to announce their arrival, and together, they headed out the back door, into the courtyard.

The Granite Ridge Retirement Community for Active Seniors was an *Architectural Digest* award-winning complex. It was also arranged for comfort. Ease of living in awe-inspiring surroundings. This was no nursing home filled with bedridden slobberers, but a facility with chandeliers and a library and a pool, a theater room for movies, and activity areas for card nights and dance lessons and art classes.

Residents took group vacations to the Caribbean—at least, that's what the activities director told Norma. Immediately, Norma's eyes had swelled and she'd thought, *The Caribbean!* A woman didn't go on many vacations when she was married to Charlie the workhorse with the never-ending stream of improvement ideas for their family business.

She'd pictured herself walking the beach in a giant floral caftan, her forearms concealed by a stack of plastic bracelets, a Carmen Miranda-style basket of fruit propped on her head. Seemed an awfully long way to go for a daiquiri, but then again, when had Norma ever indulged in such frivolities? When had she ever dared be gone so long, completely out of reach? It seemed rife with decadence.

The air of the courtyard gurgled with the noises of the nearby sculptural water fountain. Wrought iron balconies displayed lush plants grown by lifelong gardeners with green thumbs. A wind chime clinked musically in the slight breeze; jagged, abstract metal pieces reflected the mid-June Missouri sunlight. Norma had heard an artist lived up there. Not that she had ventured from her own room long enough to meet him.

Norma was moving at a nice clip, stepping off one of the many stone patio areas and rounding the corner of the building, toward the manicured lawn that separated Granite Ridge from the nearby golf course.

"We shouldn't go too far," Barbara warned her, fidgeting in the sun. "Or stay too long. Without telling Mom."

Sadness clamped onto Norma like clip-on earrings worn too long. Poor Barbara. Her childhood was nothing like the one Norma had known.

Looking back, Norma's youth had been carved out of pure, undeniable freedom. Everything about it— the look of it, the pace of it...she swore, thinking back, that it had even *smelled* differently. Her childhood had smelled like independence. Hadn't it? Hadn't Norma's neighborhood sidewalks stretched like arrows pointing straight to the opposite side of the world? The kid side? A side that did not smell of adult things—her mother's stewed tomatoes or her father's aftershave, the Oxydol green bleaching crystals in the laundry room, the Simoniz car wax in the garage. A side of the world that smelled instead of bubble gum and grass stains and mischief. Norma's childhood world had been filled with its own music, too, and every object she encountered was an instrument: metal roller skates that ground against concrete, bicycle bells that clanged at the end of sidewalk races. And laughter—it had been melodic, ringing out against high-pitched voices beneath streetlights on a summer evening.

The kid side of the world (which had, in Norma's mind, been the *real* world) had felt as open as the Kansas horizon. And it had been Norma's job to acquaint herself with every inch of it. Each morning brought a new possibility for adventure. She'd slurp her oatmeal, toss her bowl in her mother's Palmolive suds, and be out the door, never expected to return again until dinnertime. In the freckle-faced pigtail era of Norma's life, she'd done so much walking and skipping and jumping and climbing that by the time the evening called her and all her friends home to dinner, her feet had throbbed inside her saddle shoes—and she'd found herself hungry enough to eat anything on her plate. Even liver and onions.

Now, though, Barbara trotted along, swiveling her dimpled chin over her shoulder every now and again in order to make sure that her grandmother was still within arm's reach. With her perfectly wavy blond hair and pretty pink wrinkle-free skirt, she looked more like a cover of *American Girl* magazine than a real kid. Real kids, Norma thought, were supposed to have Band-Aids on their knees and tell fibs and dare each other to eat crickets and bloody their knuckles in fights and lose a few toenails racing toward home base and kiss and make up and then shrug at the dinner table when asked what went on that day and say, "Not much."

"Look, Grandma," Barbara said, squatting and picking up a stone lining one of Granite Ridge's many small decorative gardens. "What does this one look like?"

"A human kneecap," Norma blurted.

Barbara's eyes widened; it was too gruesome an answer for a seven-year-old, Norma knew—at least, too gruesome for the seven-year-olds the world was churning out these days, suspicious of everything from car salesmen to caterpillars. Norma swore Barbara's first words had been "stranger danger." She had never been alone. Not once in seven years. She was escorted to friends' houses and her hand was held as she walked across intersections and she was buckled into her car seat before being driven to the school bus stop each morning. Barbara was a girl who trusted fences. Norma figured that by the time she sent her own children to school, Barbara would be putting stun guns in the front pockets of their backpacks. Norma pictured this future morning ritual without a drop of sarcasm.

No, "human kneecap" was certainly not an answer for today's child. But she couldn't help herself. The kid needed a couple of scars. She needed to try on a few swear words. Not always answer when her mother called. Norma didn't get this porcelain generation, these children who were never allowed—or even seemed to have much desire—to investigate the kid side of the world all on their own.

Barbara skittered backward like an abused cat when one of the nearby garage doors rattled open. Norma glanced sideways as a man lunged under the still-rising door and immediately began to tug at the elastic edges of a blue cloth car cover, exposing a vintage red Mustang.

A car covered in a garage? Talk about overkill. What was he protecting it from?

Norma took a few steps closer as a way to offer a hello; the man turned at the clicking sound of her sandals, making Barbara skitter again. She was especially distrustful of men, poor Barbara.

"Lovely day for a walk, ladies." Jim Avers, Norma's neighbor, smiled at the two of them. It was a strained smile, though. Like something was bothering him. Like maybe he wanted to get away—at least for a few hours. Surely that was the reason for freeing his car.

"Or a ride," Norma added.

"Nope, no ride," Jim corrected. "Just sitting in her for a little while."

Obviously, Jim Avers did not have the same expertise Norma had acquired; he had not mastered understanding the requirements of each new era of life. Just as the pigtail stage had mandated wearing saddle shoes to explore the sidewalks, Norma was well aware that this stage called for—among other things—giving up a car. In fact, the hassle of owning a car seemed absurd; the Ridge had both a van to take residents out on pre-arranged group outings and a private car to transport them individually—and not just to the airport or the doctor, which the outside world often seemed to think of as the top two destinations for anyone over sixty. They had a chauffeur to carry them off to Saturday night dates and the movies and the university to hear a new lecture and literally anywhere else their hearts desired. Norma couldn't understand why Jim hadn't gratefully tossed his keys into the proverbial ocean. Especially if he wasn't all that interested in driving. What was the point? Besides, it seemed so out of character for anyone who lived at the Ridge. They could all now afford the fairly steep monthly rent because, for the most part, they'd also spent their lives avoiding frequent money-dumps on unnecessary items.

"You ever going to get your red thing out?" Norma blurted.

Jim let go of the section of tarp he was attempting to free from the front bumper. He pressed his hands against his knees and straightened up. Immediately, Norma's eyes trailed down his legs, toward his feet. Jim Avers wore spotless white plain Jane (or was it plain John on a man?) sneakers and long white athletic socks. A sight that instantly got Norma's hackles up, for a reason she couldn't quite pinpoint. Maybe Barbara's distrust was spreading—like contact dermatitis.

Slowly, the surprised expression on Jim's face gave way to a grin.

Norma flashed a grin back. *Saucy.* Hers was a saucy grin.

"Pretty racy language there, company considered," he told her, pointing at Barbara.

Norma stood silently, staring directly at him. She wouldn't have said it if she'd thought there was the slightest chance of her granddaughter recognizing it as a double entendre. Besides, she was sick of vanilla-flavored polite interactions. She'd begun to feel as though learning to be polite was just a way to beat the true individuality out of a girl.

Jim tipped an imaginary hat. He whistled as he returned to the task of tarp removal, his white sneakers flashing with every step.

Above, a window wooshed open. "Mother!" Elaine screeched.

Norma swiveled her head to look upward. "What is it?"

"I need to talk to you!" Elaine's round face disappeared; the window slammed so hard, Norma half-expected cracks to wiggle their way through every pane.

"Shoot me now," Norma murmured.

"What, Grandma?" Barbara asked, her sweet rosy cheeks tilting as she cocked her head to the side.

34

Norma shook her own head. "Nothing, pretty girl. Just singing," she lied.

Barbara reached her hand out for Norma to take. It reminded Norma of the way the Golden Retriever she and Charlie'd had at the beginning of their marriage had come to her with his collar clamped between his teeth, begging to be taken around the block.

"We'd better go," Barbara insisted. "Mom's waiting."

Norma grunted; together, they returned to the apartment. Maybe, Norma mused, the quicker she dealt with Elaine's newest nitpick, the quicker she would leave and life could get back to its new normal. Not that Norma really knew, exactly, what that was yet.

"Mother!" Elaine moaned, her head buried deep inside the refrigerator. "What are all of these Styrofoam plates? Why do you have so many leftovers?"

"Guess I need to clean out the fridge," Norma sighed, eyeing the keys that Elaine had placed on the counter. Elaine kept her keys on a long rope that had the name of Barbara's elementary school embroidered into it. *Lanyard*—that was the word that Elaine used. As Norma stared, though, with Elaine's screechy voice filling the apartment, *noose* was the word that came to her mind instead.

"But do they give you enormous portions? Why do you need to take so much back from the dining room?"

"No, those were delivered," Norma muttered, her eyes tracing the jagged teeth along the edge of Elaine's house keys. Norma had bought those keys. She and Charlie had, anyway. She remembered the happy way her own keys had jingled in her purse, the delight she'd once felt tearing a page out of her mortgage payment book each month.

"Delivered?" Elaine repeated, her voice fraying

as she pulled herself out of the fridge. She tilted the Styrofoam container, getting a better look at the way Norma's name and apartment number had been written across the top in Sharpie marker. "Don't you ever eat in the dining room?"

Norma felt as though she'd just been handcuffed and shoved into a police lineup, sure to be identified as the guilty party. But guilty of what?

Pulling her eyes from the lanyard-slash-noose, Norma looked straight into Elaine's creased face. Her daughter's hair wasn't as puffy as it had been when she'd arrived with Barbara in tow. Now that it drooped, Norma could see the dark roots. Part of Norma wanted to tell thirty-eight-year-old Elaine that in another minute and a half, her roots would be gray. She wanted to ask her if she truly wanted to spend that precious minute and a half micro-managing her mother's life. Weren't there other things that interested Elaine? Wasn't there something in her life that fulfilled her, or made her giggle, or let her, in the midst of her generally crappy financial situation, feel good about herself? Couldn't they just agree that Norma was as stupid for eating alone in her apartment as Elaine had been for buying curtains online that she couldn't afford—and that the two of them together were also just as stupid as Nathan for taking a job below his qualifications and experience? A three-way tie.

"We're going to dinner," Elaine declared, tossing the container into the fridge.

Barbara perked. "Do they have hot dogs here?" she asked. Hot dogs were birthday food in her house. These days, they really did cost as much as some of the lesser cuts of steak.

"Oh, no—" Norma started. "You two have things to do. Some other time—"

"That's missing the whole point of being here, if

you don't go down to dinner, Mother," Elaine informed her. "There has to be two weeks' worth of food in these containers. Two weeks! That's how long you've been here. You haven't once gone down to the dining room to eat? Companionship. Studies prove that life for the elderly improves—"

"The elderly!" Norma blurted. "Watch your language! Don't think you're too old to get your mouth washed out."

Elaine ignored her. "How many people, Mother?"

"How many people what?" Norma challenged, getting that cuffed-and-in-a-lineup feeling again.

"How many people have you met?" Elaine barked, in a tone that accused Norma of evading her question on purpose, like a child trying to sidestep well-deserved punishment.

"Lots."

"Such as?"

"Jim!" Norma shouted. "Linda!"

"Your next-door neighbor—whose name is right there beside your own mail slot, I might add—and the activities director," Elaine grumbled, slamming the refrigerator door and crossing her arms over her chest. "Who else?"

Norma glared. She needed to work up to it. She'd get there in her own time.

"Put your lipstick on, Mother," Elaine sighed. "We're all going to dinner."

Sullenly, Norma stomped back toward her favorite chair and began to wiggle her toes inside her sandals. She figured that at some point, Elaine had to notice that her feet worked just fine—every bit as capable as they'd been in saddle shoes. She could still walk every single inch of sidewalk the world had to offer.

5.

"God's a damned sadist," Jim grumbled, tilting the rearview so he could get a better look at Sarah's picture.

If he'd dared to make such a statement in public while Sarah was still alive, Jim would have been begging to get off the basement couch. Everyone had one, covered in cat scratches and Kool-Aid stains. After a long, miserable night, he'd be teasing Sarah, chasing after her apron strings, tickling that extra-sensitive spot behind her right ear, trying to tug out the smile that said he was no longer banished to the scratchy, half-bald upholstery that smelled like the upset stomach their son'd had ten years earlier.

As it was, though, Sarah just continued to smile at him from the rearview. Her faded picture showed her sitting in the Mustang's passenger seat, her elbow propped casually on the rolled-down window. Green eyes hidden by enormous sunglasses. Hair mostly hidden by the scarf draped over her head and knotted beneath her chin. A single curl flying out from under the scarf revealed it had been tinted lavender.

Sarah had never truly been vain about anything other than her hair. Her smooth skin had been a tribute to shade trees and straw hats and long-sleeved shirts. But her hair had grayed early, and she'd begun to dye it the moment the very first couple of wiry white strands made their appearance. Shortly before this picture was taken, the boxed home color she'd used had turned it a light shade of purple. He'd made the mistake of teasing her about it, asking if she'd had a run-in with a rogue grape Popsicle. He'd slept with her shoulder blades in his face for four days (and it might have gone on longer if Sarah hadn't felt she needed to get over it in time for their anniversary). It was true—a woman's hair really was her crowning glory.

"I'm telling you," Jim informed the picture, "God's at it again. Frank this time. You remember Frank. I told you about him. My next-door neighbor. I knew it the minute I saw his empty chair at breakfast."

Jim placed his hand on top of the steering wheel. "Oh, Sarah, come on, now," he moaned, as though the woman in the photo had stopped smiling long enough to disagree with him, tell him Frank being gone from breakfast didn't have to signal anything tragic, only that the man had overslept, maybe, or taken a longer than usual shower, or decided to watch morning TV in his pajamas. "Frank was a farmer," Jim argued back. "Owned a respectable fifty acres just outside of Rogersville until the year he moved into the Ridge. Still rose with the chickens—even though there weren't any chickens anymore. Frank not showing up on time—it meant, well. You know what it had to mean."

He reached into the glove compartment to retrieve a smorgasbord of pills in brown vials. The same smorgasbord he kept hidden away from everyone. And began to pop them, one after another.

Frank was gone. People in Jim's life had a tendency to leave just that way—here one moment and so long-gone the next, he almost had to remind himself he hadn't just dreamed them up, that they had in fact been very real, not some sort of imaginary playmates. Yes, to begin with, there a person would be, laughing and leaning back into a favorite chair with no hurry, just swinging a foot, leisurely. *La-di-da, tomorrow we might do something fun like maybe take a drive, do you remember when that used to be the thing to do on a Sunday afternoon, when that was entertainment? When the days were so long, and there was no rush? There's no rush now, none at all, let's plan on that tomorrow. Let's take a drive. Who knows where we'll wind up.*

Jim would relax into that notion, into the idea that he and his special someone—his friend or his wife—had gobs of time. He'd sink deep into it, like Frank had once described sinking into the goose down mattress on his grandfather's farm. And then—*poof!* It was as if God had flicked a light switch, turning off his special-someone and leaving Jim alone in the dark. No warning, no preparation, no time to say goodbye. And the last thing Jim ever said to them was something stupid, something about the laundry, or fertilizer, or "uh-huh." How cruel was that? *Uh-huh* was the last word he'd ever said to his wife, and he'd only half-listened to what she'd said before because he was falling asleep, and the next time he'd rolled over, she was stiff and cold and dead.

"God," Jim declared, "can be a real jerk. Apparently, no one ever taught the guy to play fair."

He sighed, squeezing the steering wheel in his fists. "I wonder if his boys will even want those seeds. Heirloom tomatoes, grown by his family now for a hundred and fifty years. And all those things he knew—weather predictions and what teas could cure what ailment. It all died the moment he did, I'm afraid. Those boys won't even take the time to find out how valuable those seeds are, won't care that they could make some money online. They'll see it all as trash."

Jim's stomach sank as he wondered how his own son would handle his belongings when he met the same fate. He mulled it over, squinting through the windshield. He'd been squinting for years, actually—ever since glasses were prescribed—because he'd never liked the artificial sharpness of the world when he wore them. He preferred instead the imperfect blur of his own eyes. But he hated the fact that his vision never did get quite so hazy that he didn't have to see Carl sprinting in the opposite direction. That son of his had never been able to get away from him fast enough. Even at Sarah's funeral, he'd shaken Jim's hand and herded his wife and son for their car, *hurry, hurry, hurry.* Jim was tired of the constant feeling of chasing Carl. Of feeling like Carl was always in the process of slipping away—now that he really thought about it, Jim realized the sensation was an old one. It had been with him since Carl was barely seven.

"He probably won't even show up for my funeral," Jim grumbled. "Just hire some bulldozing company to reach through my apartment window with a giant claw and scoop everything out, drop it into a Dumpster in the parking lot. Call the VA, let them bury me. Handle it all like entries on a weekend honey-do list, right between returning the library books and fixing the broken hinge on the back screen door."

Still, Sarah stared at him. She would be forever happy in that photo, which Jim had taken on a drive to the hotel room where they would spend their second anniversary. At least, that's what Sarah's curly handwriting proclaimed on the back of the Kodak paper. Back then, hotel rooms were getaways for hours of uninterrupted lovemaking. Once Jim had started working insurance, though, and he was on the road by himself, hotels began to feel like punishment, like being banished to a quiet, empty corner. A corner that often smelled like cigarette smoke and pizza crusts and someone else's lovemaking.

"It was the biggest part of the job back then, remember?" he asked the picture, hoping that saying some of this out loud would bring something back—some tucked-away memory that would lead him to the just-right thing Sarah would have said herself, the comfort she would have offered him after Frank's passing, had she still been around.

"Getting out on the road," Jim went on, "schmoozing and pitching new insurance policies to old business clients, finding new clients to visit on a regular basis. Back then, it took a handshake and looking a man directly in the eye to close a sale. Nothing ever got accomplished with a cold call back in those days. Other than getting to know the exact pitch of a dial tone after a rotary receiver had been slammed down.

"I was tortured by those hotel rooms," he confessed. "When we were together—on vacation, our honeymoon—I never really noticed them. But when you're alone, and there's no one to talk to, all you *do* is look at the room...Oh, sure, they got better over the years. By the end, when I wasn't just meeting clients but my own sales teams, they were downright posh. But a hotel room is always just a hotel room, no matter how fancy the shower head.

"When you're alone, hotels all have the personality of the prettiest girl in high school. You know the kind. The girl who was so attractive, the whole world kept thundering right up to her door, everyone racing each other to be the first to get close to her. And all that attention only taught her that she had no need to become well-read or develop a sense of humor—no need to ever become something other than pretty.

"Naw, a hotel room didn't need to be a home; a pretty girl didn't need to be interesting. So they weren't.

"But then there was you, old girl," Jim told Sarah's photo. "And you knew. I'm not sure how, because I never really said anything about it. But you did—you knew it was torture. So you packed my suitcase to make it all a little less unbearable. Oh, I looked forward to that," he whispered. "The way you never failed to pack a joke. A laugh. A handful of black licorice but no socks. Or your own frilly-edged handkerchiefs instead of my plain white squares.

"My favorite, though," he went on, "my favorite was Chicago. August, 1975. Five o'clock—it had rained earlier that day, and when the dark clouds rolled away, the puddles started to evaporate, making the whole world muggy and full of the kind of heat that made everyone irritable. The trip so far had been an utter failure. Can't exactly sell anything when you're cranky and upset.

"So there I was, figuring I could either go home empty-handed or extend the stay another day. And right then, I was so perturbed, I really didn't know which scenario was the worst one. I stomped into the room, my shirt glued to my skin, and I came at my suitcase like I'd rather tear it apart than open it. I just needed a shower—just five damn minutes of cooling off.

"But then I found it, underneath all the shirts, between my boxers and my dress slacks: a piece of your pink lingerie. And your note: 'Smell me if you can't have me, darlin'. Just wait till you get back.'

"The room felt like a home in that instant. *That's*

my girl, I thought. *She's got looks and a personality to boot. Jackpot."*

Jim paused to relive the heat, the frustration, the way he'd hated the entire world until the moment that he'd found her note. "Good thing memories can't wear out with use, like socks or 45 records."

He sighed, remembering the reason he'd come down to talk to Sarah in the first place. "It's especially good since memories are what I've got left. No more wife, no more neighbor-slash-friend. That's God's sick sense of humor," he told Sarah's picture.

"Oh, don't shake your head at me, old girl," he muttered, because that's what she would have done right then. Shaken her head at the idea of God having some sort of special vendetta against him.

Jim climbed from their car, slammed the door, and started tugging the tarp back over it.

He glanced down at the hood, finding his stark white head of hair reflected in the shiny surface. "My red thing," he said, and chuckled.

Back in his apartment, Jim placed two just-picked red tomatoes on his small kitchen table. He would look up how to harvest the seeds. He'd preserve them himself, he thought. It should have made him feel better, but the silence bleeding through Frank's old wall tortured Jim. At least, it tortured him until his stomach began to growl angrily, insistently, stealing his attention. Regardless of what his stomach said, Jim still really wasn't in the mood to eat. But he'd become his own policeman since Sarah's passing, and knew he needed to at least attempt one decent meal. His watch confirmed dinner was being served in the dining room. So he combed his hair and left his apartment again, his white sneakers sinking deep into the plush burgundy carpet as he made his way down the hallway.

At the other end, a woman raised her arm and began to wave.

Jim instantly recognized the wide hips and that overly-full-of-herself sashay: Linda the activities director. Instead of groaning, Jim put on a smile. It was time, he told himself, to return to the Jim he'd always projected to the world of Granite Ridge: Good old Jim. Funny Jim. Easy Jim. Jim who could make anybody laugh and feel relaxed and confident. *That* Jim.

"Can I count on you to join us for exercise tomorrow morning?" Linda asked.

"Lady," Jim replied, falling into the good-natured daily script he'd written for himself, "I am never going to join your ball-throwing, jumping ridiculousness." In truth, exercise at the Ridge involved far more than sitting in chairs and catching beach balls. They did senior yoga; they'd trained for 5K runs. "Unless," he quickly added, "you've got that new neighbor of mine—Norma Johnson, I think is her name—signed up. Now there's a woman I just might learn to exercise for." He felt his head jerk backward in surprise, not entirely sure where that last bit had come from.

Linda giggled. But it was a fake giggle, a giggle that said, *Yeah, right.* Jim felt her giggle twisting into him like a corkscrew. Linda was only vaguely familiar with the life stories of the residents; she didn't know Sarah was living these days in Jim's rearview mirror—but she obviously thought love was.

Love, for Linda, was a commodity to be sold to the eighteen-to-twenty-four-year-old market, in the form of pop songs and pretty dresses and dinner dates and romance novels and rom-com movies. Flirting and new crushes were something Jim, at sixty-seven, had outgrown. Of all things. The woman in front of him thought he'd outgrown love.

But he had no time to be offended; he was back to being good old Jim. So he simply smiled and tipped his imaginary hat and hurried on.

"We're having a resident meeting next week!" Linda called after him. "I want to see you there. I need your input! Jim! You promised you'd give me feedback on future activities and events!"

Jim shook his head as he raced past Linda, down to the first floor, past the library and an activity area being set up for some kind of movie marathon. He entered the elegant dining room, bathed in light from the crystal chandelier, and started toward his usual spot at the large table closest to the kitchen door.

His own chair sat empty, waiting for him in the midst of his usual dinner gang: a balding ex-lawyer, a used-to-be-pediatrician in a red bow tie, and a would-be artist who still, Jim often said, painted bananas and bad trees—and had missed, in his clean-up for dinner, a yellow slash of acrylic along his jawbone.

Frank's chair was empty, too. But the dinner salad at his place setting had been topped with tomatoes. Jim wasn't sure if that dinner salad was a tribute, or if everyone else at the table was actually waiting for Frank. How could they not know that Frank was gone?

Jim scanned the room, eyeing the cloth linens and the silver on each table. The upright piano sat empty in the back corner, the wooden cover down over the keys. Jim shivered. Today, he swore the cover looked like a closed casket.

He'd barely gotten out a full sigh when he saw

her seated near the doorway: Norma Johnson. "Red thing" Norma Johnson. His other next-door neighbor. Looking lovely in a coral-colored, long-sleeved blouse that complemented the frosted auburn hair she wore in a bob angled down under her chin. There was a sharpness in her face, an intelligence in her eyes, and a tightness around her mouth that could be taken for a wordless warning. Like she was telling the world, every single time she ventured out, that she had a new pair of scissors in her pocket and would just as soon cut everyone in front of her to pieces than deal one more second with their stupidity. She was no one to mess with, this Norma Johnson. Jim liked that.

Right now, though, Norma's shoulders also had a kind of wilted appearance. Droopy. Norma's posture looked droopy. Norma reached for a small cup of salad dressing, but the woman beside her eyed her in such a way that Norma left it right there, in the middle of the table.

Jim let a crooked grin etch itself into his cheek. The eyes on the younger woman beside Norma were different—duller—but the chin and nose were the same. He had them pegged, easier than pegging a potential client at a cocktail party: *mother and daughter...and granddaughter, too*, he surmised, watching the pretty little blond girl who shared their table devour a hot dog blanketed in a giant stripe of ketchup.

"Well, well, well," Jim said as he sauntered up to the table. "If it isn't old Normal."

She flinched at the nickname Jim tossed out. Flinched against the easy way he'd said it, as though he'd been using it every day for the past two weeks. In truth, he'd never even used her given first name, not out loud, not since the day she'd moved in, when Linda'd introduced her to everyone at dinner, and Norma had nodded at them all and placed an order like she was at a takeout Chinese dive, waiting impatiently for her Styrofoam container to be handed through the kitchen window so she could sprint back up to her room. It was the last time she'd even bothered to come down to the dining room for supper—until now.

"Norma," the woman at her side corrected, over-emphasizing the name in a too-loud tone, as though she thought Jim had turned the volume down on his hearing aid.

Jim pulled at his earlobe to point out that he wasn't wearing any such aid, and to tell her, at the same time, that aids weren't necessary.

He squinted at the daughter, taking her in, sizing her up. The at-home bleach job was too harsh, slightly orange. And her clothes, while clean and tasteful, were far from expensive. And the lines on her face—between her eyebrows, around the corners of her mouth—those weren't laugh lines; they were frown lines.

Norma's face was smooth, though. The kind of smooth that accompanied a worry-free life. And the only way, in Jim's experience, a person made it this far being worry-free was with money. Maybe money didn't buy a person happiness, but it sure bought them a good night's sleep.

The daughter was struggling financially—a struggle that was sure to be more profound for a girl who'd spent her childhood counting on having everything she needed and most of the things she wanted. Shiny packages on birthdays and Christmases. He wondered how often Norma had stepped in to help her daughter. Maybe moving to the Ridge was Norma's attempt to escape the constant pull on her purse strings. It wasn't hard to imagine—there was a definite push and pull going on between the two grown women. Yes, Jim knew people—you could take the salesman out of the job, but you could never take the job out of the salesman, he thought, sliding into the chair on the opposite side of the table from Norma.

"Jim," he introduced himself to the younger woman.

"Elaine," she said. "And Barbara," she added, nodding at the girl who had begun to fidget now that she was seated beside a stranger. Without apology, she stood, carried her plate to the empty seat at her mother's side, and resumed scarfing down her hot dog.

At her age, he suspected, he would have acquired the kind of social graces that would have allowed him to come up with an excuse to change seats. Would have held his plate toward his mother and asked for another helping. This girl moved unapologetically, as though there was never any need for her to think of another person's feelings—certainly not the feelings of some old fossil like Jim. She moved with an air of acquired superiority, and when she crammed the last of her hot dog into her face, her eyes danced about the dining room as though all activity should stop until someone brought out another hot dog for her on a small silver platter.

You're just in a bad mood today, Jim told himself. *You're seeing things that aren't there. Reading something negative into everything.*

But he wasn't so sure that was true.

"So," Jim said, leaning deep into his chair. "You order our drinks yet?"

"Our?" Norma questioned, eyeing him like she'd eye a stain on her favorite shirt.

"Sure," he said. "Our vodka tonics."

"Vodka?" Elaine repeated.

"Oh, yeah. Normal here can't get enough of them. Dangerous woman when she gets a few in her. Let me tell you, the other night—"

"Wait. Wait," Elaine said. "You two really do

know each other? I mean, you spend time together?"

Jim scanned their faces—shock on Elaine's face and hope on Norma's. The truth was, Jim knew that Norma had won the Intensely Private Award of the Millennium; she'd spent the past two weeks darting out of her room for mere snatches of time, grabbing a copy of the paper or a morning muffin or a book from the library, and immediately darting back. But that, Jim knew without a drop of doubt, was not the answer either one of them wanted him to give.

"What've you been doing, giving your girl the old healthy grandma routine?" Jim asked, reaching across the table to nudge Norma's arm playfully.

"Healthy grandma," Elaine repeated, squinting until her eyes looked more like buttonholes.

"Yeah—I'm sorry. What'd you say your name was again?" he asked, in a way that made Elaine flinch and Norma turn to hide her smile.

"Elaine," she said slowly.

"Right. Elaine. Sorry. I guess our kids just haven't come up in conversation."

"They haven't," Elaine muttered, glancing at her mother.

Norma held Jim's gaze.

"Nah—but neither do parents when you're young, right? Same difference," Jim explained, motioning toward the new waitress—Hannah, with the flushed cheeks and the general air of fear and hesitation that indicated she was certain she was screwing up, but didn't quite know how.

"Two vodka tonics," he ordered. "And this time, only one for Normal."

Hannah's eyes swelled until she reminded Jim of the paintings of kids on velvet that Sarah had hung in the rec room forty years ago. She was young. Really young. Elaine could have been her mother.

50

"I—don't—I—"

Jim held up a hand, cutting her off. Liquor was reserved for candlelight dinners, holidays, and birthday celebrations. And the girl, in all her nervous, awkward wonder, was surely too young to serve it, anyway.

"Just tell Kathy in the kitchen. Tell her it's for Jim." And he winked. Kathy would get it. She'd make a couple of club sodas, lime slices dangling like lip piercings from the rims of two squat crystal glasses. They'd look the part.

Hannah nodded, tripping on her shoelace as she hurried away.

"Seriously," Jim told Elaine. "I can't tell you how glad I am that your mom's moved in. She's really livened this place up."

"I thought—all those leftovers, those dinners you said you had delivered." An embarrassed blush flamed across Elaine's face. "You acted like you were *alone* in your apartment," Elaine protested.

Norma cleared her throat, shrugged. "Well, dear, you didn't exactly give me a chance to prove you wrong." She winked at Jim with her left eye. Elaine was seated to her right—where she'd never be able to see it.

"I'm not sure about—all this drinking—"

"Oh, come on, now, Elaine," Jim said. "This isn't a frat house. All I'm saying is that your mom here is doing just fine. No need to worry."

"Huh," Elaine said, dropping against the back of her chair. "I had no idea."

"Yeah, well, you didn't want your mom here to know everything you did on a Saturday night when you were seventeen, right?" Jim asked through a kind grin.

"I suppose I—might not've," Elaine admitted, looking at her mother in a new way. The air lightened between them, as though Elaine had just stopped squeezing her mother's wrists in her fists.

"I'm sure your own life is waiting on you. Now that you've had your dinner," Jim told Elaine, in the kind of flat, final voice that made her push her chair back and stand.

"Well, Mother, I—" Elaine paused to kiss the top of Norma's head. "We'll be back to visit soon."

"Bye, Grandma," Barbara offered, climbing down from her own chair and skittering along after her mother.

"Bye, pretty girl," Norma said softly.

Norma nodded slowly at Jim as Elaine's feet softly pattered away.

"Smooth," Norma told him. "Very smooth."

"Like silk," Jim said proudly.

"Or bathtub slime," Norma muttered.

Jim chuckled as their club sodas arrived.

Hannah sloshed liquid onto the table, muttered an apology, and wiped her wet fingers on her apron.

"Not the way you should be talking to someone who just saved you, Normal," he added.

Norma shoved the lime slice from the edge of the glass into her drink, took a sip, and grimaced, as though disappointed to find not a drop of vodka in it.

"Seems to me that you owe me one," Jim added, as his usual Monday dinner—meatloaf, garlic mashed potatoes, French-cut green beans, a dinner roll, and apple pie—slid into place beneath his nose.

"I owe you?" Norma frowned as she pushed her own dinner plate to the side.

"Sure. I saved you from daughter overload. Now, you owe me."

"What are you after?"

"There's a candlelight dinner next Friday," Jim said, running a forkful of mashed potatoes through meatloaf grease. "You're my date."

Norma flinched slightly. "Haven't you noticed

where we're sitting?" she asked. "I'm retired. I don't do business deals anymore."

"In that case," Jim said, leaning to the side. He cupped his hand around his mouth and hollered, "Elaine!" He balled his napkin and started to rise from his chair, as though planning to catch her before she was out the door.

"Yes," Norma hissed, reaching across the table to shove him back into his seat. "Yes to the candlelight dinner."

6.

"**B**oys are everywhere," Mildred muttered to herself, disgustedly and repeatedly the day after her late-night reunion with Chad Prescott. They whizzed past her on their skateboards as she crossed her street to retrieve her mail; others traveled in clumps as they sauntered past her house shirtless, shorts riding low enough on their hips to expose the elastic waistbands of their underwear. Curse words made dark, threatening clouds around their heads; every few steps, one of them would swivel his neck and spit onto the pavement for emphasis.

Before Chad's visit, the boys in her neighborhood were simply mischief-makers. Nothing to fear. After all, Mildred had known generations of them. They'd started out sweetly, blushing and sweating inside their woolen class sweaters as they stood in front of her massive oak desk (it seemed to her that teacher desks had once been as big as Edsels).

Over time, the boys in her room had grown rougher; they'd eyed her with resentment when she punished them. But they'd accepted her discipline, too. Even last year, boys were pulling themselves from student desks and complying when she handed them passes to go to the principal's office. They were answering when she asked them questions about their reading assignments. They'd even sat up straight when she asked them to—grumbling the entire time, of course. Still, though, they did as they were told. She had never, not once, ever feared the kind of retribution she'd begun to see on TV—teachers' bodies riddled with gunshot, found rotting in the woods outside their schools.

Mostly, Mildred had known she'd never have to worry about the boys in her classrooms because she listened to them. Every crazy answer to what the Robert Frost poem *really* meant. She'd praised their essays for original thought. She'd found their uniqueness and she'd tugged at it, like a sweater buried deeply and crammed tightly into a drawer. Tugged and tugged until it finally popped free.

Yes, Ms. Sudbury had listened. She'd viewed her boys as real people, not as problems in the making. Not as criminals up to no good. And in the modern high school, that had earned her a degree of respect. Boys listened back because she'd listened to them first; she saw them all as she'd seen their grandfathers and fathers—teenagers testing the boundaries, good people on the inside underneath their disinterested slouch.

But now that Chad had divulged the truth about her neighborhood, the boys were starting to look different. She spent the better chunk of that first day after Chad's visit peering through the part in her front curtains watching for them. And when they paraded down her street, they just looked dirty to her, in every sense of the word. Their skin, tanned already from the early weeks of a lazy summer, glistened with sweat. Mildred pegged them as aimless and resentful of any real job that happened to drift their way.

Mildred's skin tightened on the back of her neck as she watched them, cackling and grimy and half-naked. She wondered which one of them had knocked on her bedroom window. And she wondered why. To simply torture the poor old lady? To run her off? Was that what they wanted? Or were their minds impossible to read because they didn't even know what they would be doing from one minute to the next? The longer Mildred stared, the more they seemed like hair triggers just waiting to be brushed the wrong way.

She wondered if this was how it would always be. If she would spend the rest of her days cowering inside her old house, ducking and covering just as she'd once made her students during storm drills. Only, when would this storm end? How would it end? The odds, Mildred suddenly felt, were against her. The building she'd called home for the entirety of her sixty-two years felt as flimsy as the tar paper shacks she had shown her students pictures of while they'd read *The Grapes of Wrath*.

Until the ad. The blissful, glorious ad for the Granite Ridge Retirement Community. It aired at a quarter to two in the morning, as Mildred sat on her sofa and ate peanut butter from the jar with a spoon, too afraid to sleep. Granite Ridge appeared on her TV screen as a beautiful place filled with people just like her—no sloppily dressed, angry, dirty, frightening boys. It was also a place that would surely have lots and lots of locks, Mildred thought, with the same kind of ache in her chest she'd once gotten as she'd stood outside dress shops as a young girl, staring at outfits not sewn by her mother. Shiny, beautiful locks and lots of people. Neighbors and front-desk workers and groundskeepers and gates. Yes, there was surely a gorgeous gated entrance—the kind a person had to have a code to enter.

"Granite Ridge," the text flashing on her TV screen proclaimed, "A stone's throw from... companionship...adventure...good times..."

I want, Mildred thought. For the first time in a long time. *I want.*

But there was so much stuff, Mildred thought sadly, her half-smile fading completely and the peanut butter feeling like glue in the back of her throat. Ceramic living room tchotchkes glistened in the bluish light from the TV. The house was crammed with the collections of two full lifetimes—hers and her mother's both.

"...no more household chores..." the text on the TV proclaimed. "...freedom to come and go as you please...live in luxury..."

The TV was practically purring at that point—or was that Mildred?

"...become a Granite Ridger."

Yes! I will! I want! the voice in Mildred's head barked.

Suddenly anxious to respond to the demanding voice (it wasn't just shouting by then, but stomping its feet, knocking against her heart far more insistently than that troublemaker boy had against her window the night before), Mildred jumped to her feet. Out of habit, she immediately bent her knees again, started to force herself to sit back down. But how often had she ever given in to that voice? Hadn't she always scolded it for wanting another brownie—or the red coat that matched nothing else she owned—or maybe even to see Thomas just once more? Wasn't she due for a purely selfish indulgence? Wasn't it time?

She grabbed the phone and dialed, crossing her fingers and hoping she hadn't already forgotten the number that had flashed across her TV screen.

"Granite Ridge hotline," the voice answered. It was so late, though, that the voice was recorded. Of course it was.

"I'd like to inquire about renting a room," Mildred answered. "No—I don't want to inquire. I want the room." She left her contact information at the end of her message and she grabbed a black plastic trash bag from the kitchen.

She stomped into her bedroom, where she threw open her closet door. And stared at the clothes neatly arranged by type and color and season.

"Move it, lady," she scolded herself, lunged forward, and grabbed one of her old teaching blouses— the burgundy silk with the high collar and the ruffled cuffs and the tie that draped down the front like a designer scarf.

Her breath grew raspy; her hand began to sweat against the hard curve of the hanger. "I'm not going to miss you," she informed the blouse, the same way she'd heard fellow teachers speak of ex-husbands. After that, tossing the rest of the clothes was easy; blouses and slacks and even purses she would never use, not without a job to go to, tumbled into the bag. Jackets she hadn't worn in a dozen seasons followed. Wire hangers poked like snapped tree limbs through the sides of the plastic bag.

She paused only once—when she got to her mother's old winter coat, in the back of the closet. Coats had always seemed so personal to Mildred. Probably because they wrapped a person's body for such a long stretch of time—years, in the case of her mother, who'd held onto everything she owned until it crumbled into dried-out bits. For a moment, as she held that long tweed coat by the hanger, it was like she was standing face-to-face with her mother, her white hair hovering above the collar.

It's just a thing, she scolded herself. *It's just stuff.* And she wadded it up and shoved it into a bag, too.

She wiggled in an uncharacteristically celebratory dance. Mildred Sudbury had never before been a woman who *woo-hoo*ed or *yeah, baby*ed or waved triumphant fists. Mildred Sudbury was reserved, soft-spoken, with every last strand of blond hair tucked into place. Mildred Sudbury wore tasteful clothing (never a miniskirt, not once), and had never been accused of spritzing on too much perfume. She had never taken the last cinnamon roll from the faculty lounge or asked for a raise beyond her usual standard of living increase or complained about the food at a restaurant. Now, though, with each toss, she felt as though she was fighting back. Punching those dirty boys that had somehow snuck up on her, invading her space. *Take that, take that, you really think old ladies are so easy to beat?*

She squealed happily, grabbing up a cardboard box from the garage when she was done stripping her closet. As she rushed through the house, tossing items along the way, her robe flowed out behind her in the kind of billowing waves that allowed her to imagine she was the heroine in one of the classic novels she'd once taught in English II. Only, it wasn't a tragic story. No, this one would have a happier ending, just like *Jane Eyre*.

"Reader," she announced out loud, "I conquered those filthy boys."

In the attic, Mildred creaked open the top of the nearest trunk, finding it crammed full of tintypes.

Faces she didn't recognize. Her mother would have known who they all were. But without her, the images were detached from their stories. The pictures were meaningless to Mildred. Unlike her old clothes, though, the tintypes had value. So did the rest of the items in the attic.

Less than a week after one of those boys had knocked on her bedroom window, Mildred Sudbury stood in the shade of her front yard pin oak, watching the garage sale aficionados arrive en masse—parking crazily in the street and racing up her drive to get their hands on the best deals. Mildred nodded when offers were made, and she accepted crinkled tens and twenties and dropped them into the same old cigar box her mother had once used to store her sewing embellishments: rickrack and snaps and safety pins.

A man with graying hair and the kind of cash-bulge in his jeans that said he was surely an antique dealer pointed to one of her mother's old sewing machine tables. This one had a cast iron base, though the Singer machine that had once been attached was long gone. "Fifty," he offered.

He was the first person to bid on anything sewing-related. Mildred paused, waiting for a pang—of remorse, of warning—to find her. Waited for the schoolteacher's voice to command, *Don't do it, Mildred! It's yours—your history, your heirloom; don't let him walk off with it. It won't mean anything to him—just like those pictures in the attic didn't mean anything to you. You're the one who knows the story of those sewing machines. When those machines and tables are with you, they have meaning. They're important. When they leave, they have no significance anymore. They're just stuff.*

Mildred glanced behind her, up at the three-story house, remembering the clatter of the sewing machines her mother'd used to complete the seamstress jobs that had put food on their table. The *rat-a-tat-a-tat* of machines had filled Mildred's childhood—so much so, even the similar rattle of boys' baseball cards in spokes had once made Mildred think of her mother, bent over in concentration, feeding pieces of material beneath a hammering needle.

It had been a comfortable life, Mildred thought with sudden appreciation. Even though it could have been so incredibly sad, her father having died in a construction accident when she was still a baby. But, no—it had been remarkably ordinary. No wild story of poverty or starvation, nothing like the somewhat melodramatic Victorian works she had once tried to convince her students they loved. Her mother had simply cashed in her father's small insurance policy, bought a house to raise Mildred in, and paid for their living expenses by doing alterations for several department stores and tailor shops, the machines knocking like woodpeckers well into the night.

The two of them had celebrated birthdays and Christmases with plenty of packages wrapped in white tissue and sealed with various colors of ribbon. Always, there was a new dress for every special occasion. Each first day of school, Mildred was sure to wear something that would snag plenty of compliments and attention from the other little girls and even her teacher. Mildred couldn't recall a first day dress that had not opened a door with another girl—every single year, there was one who started talking to Mildred about the pretty thing that she was wearing, and suddenly, they weren't just talking about the violets on the fabric anymore, but having a full-blown conversation at lunch or swinging side-by-side, and Mildred would know, right then, that she had her best girlfriend lined up for the whole school year.

It *had* been a happy life, Mildred suddenly knew with assurance, the kind of life that it seemed to her the boys in the neighborhood could still have, if they would only allow themselves the pleasure. With the possibility of the simple, good life stretched out in front of them, why chose the nasty way instead? The hard way, the way of sneaking, of hiding, of always assuming anyone who stared at them too long was about to turn them in?

A drug house. In the neighborhood where Mildred's mother had pinned together the scraps left after the tragic loss of her husband, and stitched together a sweet existence for herself and her child. Imagine.

"Ma'am?" the antique dealer pressed. "Ma'am? Fifty for the table?"

The neighborhood has changed. The world has changed. Time for me to change, too, Mildred told herself. "Fifty's fine."

She dropped his cash into her cigar box, and turned to the next people in line. She took a hundred forty-five for her entire Hummel collection, and two hundred for her butcher block kitchen table and chairs. Money changed hands, and people carried away the pieces of Mildred's life like ants carting off crumbs at a picnic. Through it all, her eyes kept roving toward the front edge of her lawn, where the "For Sale" sign leaned into the soft ground like one of those troublemaker boys against the fence at the pool. Who would want to live surrounded by houses on the five-o'clock news? Who wanted their kids to grow up around yellow crime scene tape? What if she sold all her belongings only to find she couldn't get rid of the biggest item of all—her house?

"What about the pen?" a man called out to her.

Mildred turned his way; the antique dealer was staring at her expectantly, pointing toward one of the wooden drawers in the side of the old sewing machine table. She took a few steps toward him, pausing to look at the fountain pen desk set that lay inside.

"Good thing I saw that," the dealer said, leaning toward Mildred. "It's a nice one. I'll buy it, too, if you want to sell it."

But Mildred's throat suddenly felt too dry to talk.

"Marble base," he added, pointing at the forgotten set that also held an inkwell. He slipped the pen out; the tip shone like a dagger in the sunlight.

For the first time since she'd begun to clean out her mother's house, Mildred finally got a pang. A slice right into her heart.

Thomas had given her the pen.

She could still see him. Or the way he had looked in 1975, anyway. On a late summer afternoon in the park beside their school. She could see his blue seersucker suit jacket (*Suit jacket*! Mildred caught herself thinking. *A suit jacket while picnicking*!) folded neatly in the grass beside them, his shirt sleeves rolled, tie loosened. And Mildred, there in her silk stockings and her matching daisy earrings and pin and her perfect French roll. It had all felt so grown-up to her, the suit and the heels, the fact that they'd both just been at school to receive the piles of textbooks they would use that school year, the books they would hand out to their students on day one. And love—the love made her feel the most grown-up of all. Her first real love. Even the hiding, the sneaking around felt grown-up, too. Because they weren't doing anything wrong, only protecting their jobs, especially Mildred's—her first teaching job, the one she would officially start come fall. After Labor Day, they would both be teachers at the same high school.

They'd met earlier in the summer, at an informal

luncheon for old and new faculty members, a get-to-know-you gathering that hadn't ended for Thomas and Mildred with the Home Economics teacher's orange JELL-O mold. Following an afternoon of stealing glances at each other, she had gladly accepted his gentlemanly offer of a ride home. They'd wound up taking the long way to her house, which had turned into a drive—just to keep talking—which had meant they'd wound up a full forty miles away, having drinks and stealing touches by then, not just glances, and making plans to meet again the next day...and the next.

In the park, though, there they were, barely a month later, unable to let anyone know they were together, a real couple, because the principal would frown on such behavior—faculty dating—*what a scandal!* That's what Thomas said for about the fiftieth time, laying his head in her lap beneath the isolating clump of trees. They would both lose their jobs. Thomas should know about that; he'd worked at the high school for a good five years at that point—and then where would either of them be?

But they would have to let the word out soon enough, Mildred was sure. Because this was *It*, capital "I." It was love; it was the dance the blue jays did in her yard each spring, two hands linked, butterflies dancing through the stomach. Their principal would find out, Mildred knew, once there was a ring. Oh, that was a fast way of thinking, skipping straight to the ring—it was like reading the first chapter of a novel and flipping ahead to the last paragraph. *Don't rush through your life*, that's what her mother would have told her. But Mildred knew—it was okay to skip to the ring, because they had already skipped over all the unnecessary polite courtship rules; they had already moved so fast, behaving, already, like husband and wife.

Yes, Mildred and Thomas had already

bypassed polite chitchat and lunged straight into the conversation only lovers had. They would talk that way again, Mildred knew—judging by the way Thomas was looking at her, judging by the way he was letting his fingers trace the inside of her elbow, the way he kept nodding his head, slightly, in her lap, so that his forehead traced the bottom curve of her breast.

Standing in her driveway, Mildred remembered him with a sense of longing that had never died, not in all these years. And her heart broke all over again as she stared at the pen. Yes, Thomas Clyde had given her a pen, not a ring, as though to warn her that she needed to put a giant red check mark next to the two of them. WRONG ANSWER. Not that he ever would have said something so honest straight out. "To grade your essays on," *that* was what he'd actually said the day he'd given it to her. He'd seemed distant, though, only days before the fall semester. Mildred was setting up her classroom, and he'd stopped by with his present. But he hadn't tried to touch her hand. Not once.

Confused, Mildred had replayed his words from the park—"we'll lose our jobs, darling"—hadn't he called her that? Hadn't he said "darling"? And she'd clung to them.

Later, the click of shoes outside her classroom drew her attention. Mildred had smiled, thinking, *This is it; it's him.* Of course it would have to be him. It was Friday, after all, and in a few hours, they would be standing in the midst of a long three-day holiday weekend. They would make plans for a getaway, a playful end to their beautiful summer. When school started on Tuesday, they would be back to sneaking. She wondered how they would hide when it got cold and the park was no longer an option. Oh, but that wasn't the right way to think, either. Because there would be a ring by then.

Mildred's eager smile collapsed as the sophomore-year English instructor stepped into her room. Mrs. Eggers, that was the woman's name. An old pudgy thing, in a dress that had grown too small for her figure and was out of fashion, to boot—a brown shapeless shirtdress with large front pockets that just looked dowdy and past its prime, more like a housedress than a dress a woman should be teaching in. Mildred herself was wearing a bright yellow A-line dress with a headband made from the same material; sandwiched between her bangs and her curls, the headband drew attention to her pretty summer-streaked locks. Her dress was sleeveless, allowing her to stay cool as she whipped her classroom into the perfect order to make a good first impression with her first group of students, and it had a bright floral short-sleeved jacket should she need to venture into the hallway or speak to the principal. Yes, Mildred Sudbury was so utterly professional—in behavior and ability and manner of dress—their principal would be more than willing to accept her relationship with Thomas, when the time came to make that announcement. He would be happy for them, Mildred knew. How could he not?

Mrs. Eggers kept babbling on, her nerves over the impending school year getting the best of her, it seemed that day. "Have you picked up your roster yet?" she was asking, and, "I've decided to start the year with Shakespeare, a good dose of iambic pentameter, the rhythm of life, and by the way, have you met Thomas Clyde, the history teacher, he's here, just a few doors down from you, he loves to use Shakespeare, too, *Julius Caesar*, and maybe I might start with that play, because I could get the history teachers in on it."

Mildred nodded. "Oh, yes, Mr. Clyde. I met him briefly," she'd said. She couldn't tell Mrs. Eggers that *Clyde* was going to be her very own last name—and that they had read poetry to each other—no, whispered it, the rhythm of their bodies beating in time to one another there in the park, in the sweet green grass.

"You know," that old teacher went on, "his wife is the dramatics teacher, and *she* might even get in on it. With a reading of the work. Start the year out with a bang. She's been gone all summer, caring for her mother, but now she's back and so anxious for a new year..."

Mildred's head spiraled. Her pulse exploded in her ears like cars crashing in a giant pileup on the highway. She asked the old teacher to repeat herself. Repeat it again. Again.

"You look pale, dear," the old teacher had said.

"I guess it's all becoming real," Mildred had muttered, sinking deep into her chair and rubbing her forehead. The room was spinning—spinning—and she was trying to grasp onto something that was real, that was true, maybe even Thomas's words, but they crumbled in her hand. Thomas had once been real, and now he wasn't, and that made everything feel mushy to her. "My first class," she lied.

"It *is* such a responsibility," Mrs. Eggers had said, rubbing Mildred's shoulders.

Mildred felt the pain all over again as the scene played itself out in her mind. And she wondered, as she often had over the years, how the poets could have stood to endure this kind of thing over and over—how they could have been hurt like this and simply turned on their heel, pointed at the next could-be love, and opened themselves to them, too. How could Tennyson have truly meant it, that bit about being happy to have loved and lost? How could anyone ever be happy to feel this way?

Perhaps other girls were not as innocent as she'd been back then. Those girls in the footage of

Woodstock, dancing nude in the mud a full six years before she'd met Thomas, stoned and full of notions of free love, surely they would have been worldly enough to have seen through Thomas Clyde. Maybe they would have been the kind to have laughed at his lies. But Mildred had believed him. She'd given herself to him. And even now, forty years later, he had been it, the only one. The first and last time. Because no one ever got hurt quite as deeply as a child. Children did not know how to put up defenses, after all. They came at the world with their arms open, assuming that everyone around them was just as innocent, assuming they were all sweet characters on TV; yes, poor young Mildred had been Mary Ellen Rogers, and Thomas, in her mind, had been Wally Cleaver.

She'd taken a job in a school library across town the next year, Mildred remembered. To get away from Thomas and his wife. A school library, stamping due dates onto the cards in the backs of books. And aching because she wanted to *talk* to the kids about what was in those books. She felt, somehow, it was her due punishment that first year, hiding in the library shelves, hoping the words from her much-loved classic literature would pour over her, mend her gaping wounds.

The next year, she'd started a reading group in the library—only to find, at the first scheduled meeting, that no one had signed up. So she'd begged. She'd left letters on the desks of English teachers, asking them to send her anyone. Which meant she spent a semester tutoring two near-failing students in basic reading skills, rather than discussing the beautiful works she'd loved so much. That had gone so well, though, that the next semester, she'd gotten ten students. The spring of the following year, she tutored four different groups: Remedial Reading, Classics, College Preparatory

Writing, Research Skills.

The year after that, she was out of the library, teaching again, at the same school where she had sought refuge from Thomas Clyde.

Mildred had retired from that school—Central High, Home of the Bulldogs.

And now, here she was, standing in a driveway that would soon not belong to her anymore. And the longer she stared at the fountain pen, the hotter her embarrassment grew, until it felt like it was charring her insides.

"Deal's already done," she told the antique dealer, pulling the pen and display base from his hands. She dropped them into the drawer and shut it. "Pen's yours."

Even as the dealer carted it off, that pen was still nagging at her. As was the memory of Thomas Clyde.

"You didn't tell me," a man's voice cut into her thoughts. And because she'd just had Thomas on her mind, she really did expect to swivel and see him, in a suit, even to that day looking like Rock Hudson and Cary Grant and James Garner all rolled into one.

"*You* should have," she muttered sadly. "You should have told me." *How was I supposed to know, supposed to suspect? You didn't wear a wedding ring, not ever. I suppose that was common then—far more common than it is now. But why would I not have believed you? A teacher at my own school? A teacher just like me? My specialty was listening to boys; I listened to you. I trusted what you told me. Why would doubt ever enter my mind? Why did you do that to me?*

"What was that?" the voice persisted. "Ms. Sudbury? What are you talking about? Did I miss something? Did you call the station, leave a message for me?"

When Mildred turned, she found herself staring

at Chad Prescott, in his black uniform.

"No—I—sorry," she muttered. "I was thinking about something else."

"Good," Chad breathed. "You seemed mad for a minute. Guess you never do get over being afraid of your teacher getting mad at you, do you?"

They stared at each other through an awkward, wordless moment, both of them waiting for the other to speak.

"I just came out to check on you," Chad said. "See if you'd ever had another incident like the one the other night. And here you are, packing up, getting ready to leave. I didn't mean to scare you—I only wanted you to know what was happening around here. I hope I didn't make you rush into something you'll regret."

Mildred shook her head emphatically. "No," she insisted. "It was just the push I needed."

"You really are sure about all this, Ms. Sudbury?" Chad pressed. "This is an awfully quick decision."

"The only thing I'm honestly not sure about is the house. *How* to sell it, I mean. I have a place rented already. I figure a quick sale probably depends on doing something online." She shuddered as she said it—*online*—like she was thinking of having to eat a bucket of raw chicken livers. "Any advice?"

"Actually," Chad said with a smile, "I think I might be able to do you one better. If you let me take a look at the place in the daytime."

"The front door's open," Mildred offered. "Take all the time you need. I'd go with you, but—" She pointed at the stream of people crawling up and down her driveway.

After Chad slipped through the front door, Mildred turned toward the street, finding them all huddled together at the edge of her curb like a group of sharks—more nasty boys, in a cluster, shirtless, sweaty.

Boys, she thought bitterly, the taste of Thomas's memory still in her mouth.

7.

Norma paced the floor of her apartment, her insides bubbling over with a mixture of emotions that hadn't surfaced in ages: fear and anticipation and wondering if her slip was hanging out below the hem of her chiffon skirt and a general sick-to-her-stomach-ness. Was this how she'd felt when she was young? Had this been the general tone of those early years? If so, Norma didn't want to be twenty again. She would welcome the body, sure—who wouldn't? Norma was still vain enough to miss her perfectly flat stomach, the one she'd had in her bikini days, before she'd grown to the grotesque size of a prize-winning pumpkin, then forced said pumpkin out using the same kind of strength that it would have taken to lift a Winnebago with nothing more than her tongue. Sure, the pre-Winnebago (aka Elaine) stomach would be nice. But Norma didn't want to go back to the awkwardness, the queasiness, the *What-will-he-think-of me?* jitters.

That would be ridiculous. Utterly. Completely.

She knew she should call the whole thing off. In fact, she had just put her hand on the phone when a knock rattled her apartment door.

Norma gasped. She hadn't been on a date since she was eighteen years old. Was this stupid? Like trick-or-treating at forty-five with no child in tow? What was she *doing*, and how had Jim Avers snookered her into this mess?

Norma opened the door to find Jim standing in the hallway, freshly showered and smelling of aftershave. Norma took a small backward step—a shocked step, as she realized how much she'd missed the fresh smell of a man just out of the shower.

He was wearing an obviously expensive blue suit jacket, no tie, and his usual white sneakers. All of which made her feel instantly overdressed in her gauzy gray dress and matching long jacket, both trimmed in smoky gray sequin detail. She hadn't even thought about it as she'd rolled on her stockings and used the end of a stopper to dab perfume behind her ears. But she'd put herself together as she would have if she were going out with Charlie. She'd dressed to match what she knew Charlie would have chosen to wear: a full suit, with wingtips, not New Balances. Charlie's taste had improved as the years had gone by, growing in the same increments as his ability to buy clothes from higher-end stores. He'd relished his suits, his perfect Windsor knots. And they would have been the sharpest couple of all.

Now, here she was, going out instead with a guy in white sneakers. It felt bizarre—like suddenly, she'd sprouted an extra tooth, and couldn't figure out how to chew.

"Hey, Normal," Jim said, obviously intent on using her nickname from here on. "Never did have a date who lived right next door before."

Norma smoothed the front of her dress with her sweaty hands. "Have you seen our new neighbor yet?" she asked, hating that her voice cracked and her mouth was so tacky and dry, her tongue clicked against the roof of her mouth.

Jim glanced over toward Frank's old apartment, took a deep breath, and shook his head no. "Not yet. They painted it yellow, though," he added, referring to the Granite Ridge policy of painting each room the color of the new resident's choice—a pale celery green for Norma that Elaine had crinkled her nose at. (But the grass was green, Norma had wanted to protest. Did the grass ever clash with any of the buildings or cars or people who stood beside it, drove past it, or walked across it? Of course not. That meant green went with everything. Case closed.) "Yellow," Jim went on. "That's a woman's color."

Norma nodded slightly, unable to disagree.

Jim extended his right elbow; after a slight hesitation, Norma linked her arm in his, and they headed down toward the dining room and her first candlelight dinner.

Norma's head swarmed, her thoughts a buzzing cloud of gnats. This wasn't why she had come to the Ridge. Another man had not been one of her goals. The possibility of friendship? Yes. But this stage of life—widowhood—called for a woman to have complete and total self-sufficiency. Didn't it?

Norma'd had her love story—and it had been a good one. Charlie deserved credit for that. But love was messy, too—it involved dandruff and used Kleenex as much as it involved sweeping romantic overtures. Did Norma even want to go through it all over again? Wasn't it time for Norma to enjoy a few selfish pleasures? Little decisions she'd never be able to make, not with another man around and an entire house to keep up: She could sleep in until a quarter to eleven. She could let her laundry pile up until it pushed open the hamper lid. She could spend the morning in a bubble bath. It was time for the rudder to finally be in her hands.

A streak of embarrassment hit her as she recognized she could already be doing those things—and wasn't. In the past few weeks of living at the Ridge, she'd risen early and read the paper in her favorite chair while she nibbled on a bagel and sipped coffee (even though she could have been eating her favorite Denver omelets in the dining room), and she straightened her apartment (even though she had housekeeping to do that), and she puttered about, flipping through cable channels and reading books and waiting. And waiting. For her to finally find it, that thing that said *Norma Johnson*. Not Norma Johnson, wife of, mother of. *Norma Johnson*.

Yes, there, finally—it had taken nearly a month at the Ridge and a Gorilla Glue strength to finally admit it, but there it was: She wanted something for herself. For the first time in her life. All the other reasons—saving Elaine and finding adult friendship—was but a tiny distant beep on her radar now compared to this desire: She wanted something that belonged to her and no one else. Something she didn't have to share—not with Elaine or Barbara or this Jim person.

Right now, she reminded herself, rather than a *something*, she had a date. And the responsibility for how miserable or decent the night turned out to be wasn't all Jim's. Time to stop acting like a porcupine with her needles out.

The pianist was pounding away at the keys as they walked into the dining room—Anne Murray's "Could I Have This Dance." Norma spied a table of widows just like herself, swaying slightly in their chairs, their eyes misty.

Before she could really even decide what she thought of those widows' display of—What? Longing? Nostalgia? Mourning? Wish to start again?—Jim led her to a table of men. Norma felt herself relax. This would be easier, she thought, if she and Jim had company. Maybe Jim had known that all along. She let out a relieved sigh as he pulled her chair out.

"Bringing you fresh blood, boys," Jim said. "Norma Johnson, from 246."

The man to her immediate right winked beneath a mop of white wavy hair—which Norma strongly suspected was probably a toupee. "Pretty thing," he summed up, extending his hand to her. "Ted Masters. Ex-lawyer."

"Patrick Dane," the man on the opposite side of the table—completely bald and as round as a donut—piped up as he scooted his own chair closer. "You wouldn't have any experience sitting for an artist, now, would you?"

"That's a line, Normal," Jim warned, sitting down beside her.

"No it isn't," Patrick protested. "I'm an artist!"

"Of bad trees," Jim finished. "Only let him paint you if you want to come out looking like something your granddaughter might make with her finger paints."

"Finger paints!" Patrick exclaimed. "That could be interesting." He wiggled his eyebrows at Norma.

"Watch out," Jim said, "He's trying to get you out of your pantaloons, Normal."

"Oh, posh," Patrick said, leaning away from Jim. "You always have to ruin a guy's fun."

"Just remember who she came with, boys," Jim said sternly, like he was getting after a room of third graders.

"Did you make the wind chimes?" Norma asked.

"The metal ones on one of the balconies facing the courtyard?"

"*She* likes my stuff," Patrick told Jim.

"Bad trees, Norma. I'm telling you, he paints bad trees," Jim grumbled.

"Bet there's a pretty daughter walking around somewhere. Has to be with a face like that." A wiry man in suspenders and a full gray beard extended his hand to Norma. "Larry the used-to-be pediatrician," he said. "I specialize in predicting how cute a girl will turn out when she grows up. Yours, I would say, is a looker."

Norma's first instinct was to roll her eyes behind her auburn bangs. But she settled deeper into her chair as the men stared at her, all of them—Jim and Larry and Patrick and Ted—and she decided, at that moment, to go with it. To drink in their attention. Right then, she felt like Scarlett O'Hara in the opening scene of *Gone With the Wind*. The star of the show, *fiddle-dee-dee*, underneath the Ridge's tacky ornate chandelier, against an off-key piano rendition of "The Wind Beneath My Wings." She wished for a fan and a hoop skirt so that she could make a regular spectacle of herself, parading across the floor of the dining room while everyone stared. It was *fun* to be gawked at. Wasn't that the point of life, too, to get a little fun out of the bargain?

"A daughter?" Norma finally said. "Not tonight. Mama's out on her own." She offered a sly grin as she snapped her cloth napkin into her lap, then reached behind her to snatch a glass of white wine from the tray in a waitress's hands.

"Oooops!" Hannah exclaimed, fighting to regain balance of her tray. Her face flamed. "I'm just—I—they never let me serve *alcohol* before." She whispered it— *alcohol*—as if she suspected the idea of it would offend most Granite Ridge residents. Which seemed utterly ridiculous to Norma. The white hairs in that dining room had been young during free love and rock and roll. They'd grown their hair and smoked dope and followed the Grateful Dead. And Hannah thought they'd be offended by Chardonnay? Could the girl not do math, realize what age so many of them had been during the Summer of Love?

Hannah continued to teeter, but Norma refused to help steady her or offer so much as a sympathetic smile. *You're all on your own tonight*, she thought. And for the first time since she was—nineteen, maybe—Norma meant it. Everyone else—Barbara and Elaine and Hannah and Jim—they were all on their own. Norma was going to do what *Norma* wanted, no obligations. Finally.

The piano trickled on behind her shoulder, and the smell of grilled rib eye and steamed fish slipped out from the kitchen. Jim ordered the steak and received what Norma swore was the stink eye from Larry. It was the red meat, she figured—surely the red meat had gotten the old doctor's hackles up. She remembered the way her own cooking had changed, those last years with Charlie. But she'd thought of it as something good for both of them—less salt, more steamed vegetables. It had been easy to forget Charlie'd had heart failure. Mostly because the heart Charlie had shown her had been good always. Up until the very last beat. When Norma placed the same order for the steak, though, she didn't get the same look from Larry.

She might have wondered why if Jim hadn't instantly interrupted her thoughts by reaching in front of her to slide a handful of stuffed shiitakes from the hors d'oeuvre tray.

"So where's yours?" Norma asked, watching him fork a mushroom into his mouth.

"My what?"

78

"Your kids—or kid. The way you talked to Elaine the other day, it sounded like you have some around somewhere."

"Oh—I—have one," Jim admitted. "A son."

"What's he like?"

"Computer guy. Programmer."

"No—not what does he do. What is he *like*?" Norma persisted.

"Carl," Jim barked. "His name is Carl."

Norma squinted at him, drinking in his sudden and complete discomfort. "Well," she said. "Maybe Carl and Elaine should get together sometime."

Jim chuckled as he reached for her hand and pulled her to her feet. Norma was suddenly all nervous and sweaty again, just as she'd been in her room before Jim had picked her up. Could it even really be called that? Did you really pick up a person who lived in the same building? There she went, thinking it all over again—thinking that maybe this whole thing was stupid. Maybe the way she'd been feeling a moment ago was stupid, too. *Scarlett O'Hara! Really!*

But Jim was pulling her onto the dance floor, and Norma was traveling back through decades of memories—all the way back to the country club of her youth.

Yes, here it was, coming back to her again, that first night she'd invited Charlie to the club, the night he'd met her parents. All of it was still so clear— Charlie's hand in hers as he led her across the dance floor, his suit too large and out of fashion, the jacket long and sloppy and double-breasted and generally looking like something that a fifty-year-old man would be wearing to his office, not like one of the slimmer-fitting suits with the solid color slender ties that the rest of the young boys their own age were wearing.

Norma had worn white, causing her father to

visibly cringe. Hadn't her mother often told her that she'd gotten to the age that her father saw a wedding dress every time Norma wore white? Yes, there Norma had been, in wedding white, hair in a bubble flip, with the first boy she'd ever brought to meet her family. Charles Johnson.

By the time Charlie'd led her toward the dance floor, they'd already eaten their Chicken à la King and Norma's mother had spent an hour smiling nervously at Charlie while her father had downed an unusual number of whiskey sours. The whiskey'd made him brave, and instead of letting Norma just have that one dance, he kept sticking his hand under her armpit, hauling her toward boys dining with their own country club families. Introduction after introduction, the hellos getting increasingly more awkward as her father got drunker and his hair fell farther down over his eyes. Those poor boys tried to nod back politely, as if they had not known Norma for as long as their families had all been members. As if they did not themselves already have girls at their sides. As if they were not fully aware that Dr. Fletcher would have paid for their college education if it meant his daughter would forget about Charles Johnson.

With each mortifying introduction, Norma nodded politely, and shrank away, back to her Charlie. Maybe those boys had better labels in their jackets. But they didn't have eyes as bright and wide as movie screens—not like Charlie did. None of them sparkled with the same excitement, told the same grand stories of the way life would be. Had the same grand plans. Life, for those boys, was a couch cushion to sink into. Not an adventure to be roped like some wild creature bucking in a rodeo ring.

"For God's sake, Norma," her father grumbled as he snatched her by the elbow for what had to be the twentieth time. "Charles Johnson."

Norma glanced across the room; Charlie was not going to college. He was not going to be a lawyer or doctor. He was not the third generation in his family to be a member of the country club. His father didn't play golf. Charlie had gotten mediocre grades. He had been the star of nothing, all the way through high school.

But Charlie had dreams. Where were you in life if you didn't have dreams—especially when you were seventeen years old?

Norma wrenched herself away. "Don't you think it's about time you had some dessert and *coffee*?" she asked pointedly. Her father's face drooped, aging fifty years beneath the black waves that had worked their way loose from his pomade—as though even his hair was frustrated, fighting for this not to be true. Fighting for his Norma, his only child, not to be drifting down a path that he did not approve of. The other years had been so easy—*wear this dress, go to school, take algebra, come to church.* Or, at least, she had made them seem easy, the way she had done everything he'd asked. Now he looked at her as though she had duped him. *You'd made me believe it would always be so easy,* his wounded face accused her, as she gathered her dress up in her fists and hurried back to her Charlie.

They'd grabbed hold of each other right then in a giant bear hug. And it didn't matter, as Charlie fumbled for her right hand, that he was humming off-key. It didn't matter that she was stepping on his feet.

"Don't worry, Norma," he'd said, that excited twinkle flashing in his eyes. "We're going to figure this thing out together."

Norma'd believed him then. Wholly, completely. As the music swirled and her father fumed and her mother tried to comfort him; as the boys looked on, shaking their heads at Norma and the foolish choice they all knew she was about to make, Norma had known that this dance would become their life. They would fumble, but they would laugh as they just kept going.

And it *had*. It had been just that way. Norma had started out playing house in a crummy apartment with leaky windows and little more than a hot plate to cook supper on; Charlie had started out selling typewriters and mimeograph machines. But the business had grown, first from one hole in the wall to a slightly larger hole in the wall, then to warehouses, chains, computers, networks—the office tech king of the Midwest. Maybe that wasn't glamorous, but it was Charlie's; he'd built it from scratch. And, sure, there were setbacks along the way. Business wasn't always up; there were dips. But they still moved from their crummy apartment to a small cottage to a ranch house to that tri-level with a pool that Norma had meticulously decorated with her antiques, whipping it into a regular spread in *House Beautiful*. And really, who cared about a few stepped-on toes if you didn't quit, you just kept dancing? Didn't it always look like you were out there having the time of your life? And for the most part, didn't that make you believe that you *were* having the time of your life?

Only, Norma told herself, her thoughts spiraling forward through time, it was Charlie's life. He'd built it, and Norma had maintained it. And that wasn't what she wanted anymore. She wanted her own life, built by Norma—even if the foundation was crooked and it leaned. So what? It would be Norma's; it would belong to her alone.

What was she doing on another dance floor with another man? Wasn't this how it had started with Charlie, too? Hadn't she already done this? She grew dizzy and pulled her hands away from Jim.

"You okay, there, Normal?" he asked, his face

reflecting genuine concern.

"Too much wine, not enough steak," she said, turning back toward their table.

She settled herself into her seat, accepting the mushrooms and the dinner salad and the bowl of soup that Larry the pediatrician insisted she eat. And she listened as Patrick the painter told her that her cheeks had just flushed a lovely shade of peony pink—nothing to be embarrassed about at all—and she smiled as Ted the lawyer claimed that he would have her back if she were to get dizzy enough to fall and hit her head on anything. "Get you a cool ten million for sure, Norma. You could retire in Jamaica."

She drank in their attention along with a glass of sweet tea, and she allowed them to refill any plate she emptied.

"Ooooh, Jim," Patrick said, as Hannah approached their table with their entrées. "Whoa. Really. Whoa—oaaah." His own round face was flushing a shade closer to magenta.

"Are you having a brain aneurysm?" Jim asked. "Larry, help the poor man out."

"No," Patrick said, his tone turning serious. "Look. Over there at what just came through the door. Is *that* your new neighbor?"

Jim raised his head as the rest of the table turned toward the doorway. The newest Ridge resident stood nearly six feet tall. Tonight, her platinum blond hair was twisted into a French roll. She wore a glittering beaded gown with long sleeves and a sheer top that cinched at the waist. And she was gorgeous. With a figure far better than Hannah's, who was forty years younger. A regular 36-24-36.

"Marilyn Monroe," Jim sighed, staring.

The heat of anger began to rise inside Norma. She could feel the men begin to push her away like an unwanted broccoli garnish on their plates.

As she fumed, she also began to wonder: *What would Scarlett O'Hara do?*

8.

Mildred paused in the doorway of the dining room wearing a Halloween costume. That's what it was: a costume. Because Mildred Sudbury most certainly was not long red beaded dresses, no more than seven-year-old girls were the homicidal ax-wielding cyclops maniacs they'd dressed up as before ringing Mildred's bell last October.

Why had she even *bought* a red beaded dress? She knew the answer, even before she'd finished asking herself: because the welcome brochures Granite Ridge had sent her promised dances and vacations. And because she believed the photos inside those brochures, the ones depicting senior residents who were all happy, smiling, and formally dressed (in tuxes and sequins!), just like she had once believed Thomas. Was she still just as naive as ever? Overly trusting? Why had it never crossed her mind that the pictures were probably just stock images?

Mildred's face flamed as she scanned the crowd one more time. She looked like she was going to the Oscars, and everyone else looked more like they were showing up for the company party. She tried to take a step backward, before anyone could notice her standing there. But, no—one of the men stood, waving her over toward his table. A full table from the looks of it, with three other men and a woman.

Drat. Mildred smiled and waved back before approaching them, holding her arms over her front in a giant "X"—as though trying to hide a nude body.

The men all jumped to their feet, vying to be the one to pull her chair back.

Which made Mildred's face flame all over again. There would be wisecracks. She knew boys, after all, and she knew that they would tease her about her dress.

Slowly, though, she began to realize they were looking her straight in the eye. They were asking for her name and wanting to know if she was completely moved in. If she needed their help—or their sons'. If she was in a single or double room. They wanted to know if she'd had a chance to check out the entire building yet. What she'd done for a living. A library, one of them told her. Granite Ridge had a spectacular library that she was bound to love.

There would be no mocking, Mildred thought with amazement. As she stared into their interested, pink faces, she slowly stopped seeing white hair and crinkles in the corners of their eyes. She saw instead letter sweaters and thick horn-rimmed Buddy Holly-style glasses. These were the boys that Mildred had known during her first year of teaching—a mere four years younger than she was then. These were the blushing boys, the sweet boys.

They didn't see a crazily-dressed old woman. They saw *her*, Mildred, a pretty creature in an eye-catching outfit. They looked at her the same way the boys had forty years ago when she'd strutted into her classroom in a one-of-a-kind dress sewn by her mother, her blond hair bouncing against her shoulders. Here they were, the boys who'd once called her "ma'am" and dreamed of her in a not-so-teacherly way when they were curled up in bed, sliding toward sleep.

Suddenly, the dining room began to sparkle—almost as though they were all living inside a disco ball.

Mildred danced with every man at the table. And then with every man in the dining room. She danced until her feet swelled in her heels. She danced, going from man to man, introduction to introduction, until she realized she'd forgotten to eat. But she was so excited, so worked up, she merely nibbled at her rib eye. One bite of roasted rutabaga. Three bites of her dinner salad.

"Marilyn Monroe." If she heard it once, she heard it fifty times. It wasn't until she also heard, "Trade you rooms, Jim? I'd kill to have her for a neighbor," that she realized they were talking about her. That was her new nickname; "Mildred" didn't fit, not for a woman of her caliber; she'd become a star.

Yes, Mildred Sudbury—fashionable but modest Mildred Sudbury, bookish Mildred Sudbury, and the same Mildred Sudbury who had been without a male admirer of her own age for four decades—was now Marilyn Monroe. She was admired by all of them. Well. All of the men. The women started out by sneaking judgmental looks her way, but all it really took was a shrug and the roll of the eyes, a bewildered, wordless *Can you believe all this attention?* from Mildred to make their mouths widen into understanding smiles. They were comrades, too, then. *Oh, yes, we've all been there, so many men, so little time.* The only exception had been the woman at Mildred's own table—Norma.

She didn't seem to belong to the Mildred Sudbury fan club. Not that Mildred cared. Not then. Not when another song was kicking into gear, another opening chord, a waltz this time.

Mildred danced until the pianist finally slammed the lid down over the keyboard with a thud. Glancing around, Mildred realized the dining room had all but emptied. The only ones left were the four men and one woman at her own table. And a waitress. The young nervous one, leaning now against the salad bar in an exhausted slump, waiting for Mildred and her new friends to finally leave so she could clear their table.

"Walk you to your room?" one of men—the one with the white sneakers—asked her. What was his name again? Hard to remember when so many new names had been tossed at her, along with so much attention, so much unexpected delightful goodness. Her chest heaved as she panted. Her red beaded dress was full of sweat.

Norma let out a "Humph," tossed her napkin onto her dinner plate, and stomped away.

"No," Mildred said. "You go on, Jim." Yes. That was his name. But it shouldn't surprise her that it had come to her, even in the midst of the blur the night had become. She'd always been good with names. By the end of the first week of school, she'd had them down pat. Five classes' worth.

And besides, Norma's angry exit had just put a wound on Jim's face. He needed to catch up to Norma, not dig himself deeper walking her to her door.

"Thanks," Jim told Mildred, and raced off, leaving three other men behind who wanted to escort her home.

But Mildred was in the mood to celebrate a little on her own. She waved them goodbye, and she shimmied right out of the dining room, hands flying out from her sides. She Charlestoned up the stairs and did the camel walk down the second-floor hallway, humming under her breath. She unlocked her door, stepped inside, and kicked off her heels. And just kept right on dancing into the bedroom, her pantyhose making her feet slip across the carpet. But even sliding around was fun—made her strike a few goofy dance poses. And then giggle at herself.

"Woooooaaweeee," she squealed, falling onto her bed. She dissolved into a hearty belly laugh.

"Whew," she added as her laughter wound down and hunger finally found her. "I need a pizza," she announced.

The phone rang. She was still on such a high that she simply rolled onto her side and laughed into the receiver.

"Ms. Sudbury?" the voice asked.

"Yes," she said. Really, though, it was the only word she could use to describe the whole evening: yes, yes, *yes*. Hadn't she hit a gold mine when she decided to move in? Wasn't this the most perfect night ever? Wasn't life utterly, incredibly beautiful?

"Ms. Sudbury!" he exclaimed. "You are one hard woman to track down."

"I moved," she giggled. For the first time in sixty-two years! Maybe this was Chad Prescott calling to thank her again for selling the house to him. Wasn't that just the greatest revenge of all on those boys? They'd wanted to chase off the old schoolteacher, who was surely obsessed with rules, who would have snitched, and she'd left them with a police officer. Ha! Maybe it was even one of those nasty boys, calling to plead with her to come back. Because that was just how funny the world seemed to her right then. It seemed like a place where that could actually happen.

"Right," the voice on the other end said. "I got

that. Ms. Sudbury, I'm an estate attorney with Gurtler and Associates. I've been trying to contact you regarding the will of Mr. Clyde."

Mildred coughed, suddenly feeling like an ice cube was lodged in her throat. "A will? What? Who?" Her mind swirled, like she had somehow found herself on a ride going too fast at an amusement park, and she couldn't figure out how to raise her arm to get the attendant's attention, tell him to stop the crazy contraption so she could get off.

"Yes. I represent the estate of Mr. Thomas Clyde. Ms. Sudbury, he left everything he owned to you."

Mildred's stomach bottomed out. She bolted upright. "Thomas? Thomas Clyde?"

"Yes."

"Left—?"

"Yes. Left you his entire estate."

Mildred flinched. She bolted from the bed, snatched up the phone from her bedside, and hugged it to her chest. She was spinning and falling all at the same time. "No—I'm sorry," the polite Mildred Sudbury said, even as her mind spun still faster and her blood pooled in her ankles. "You're mistaken. He wouldn't do that."

"He absolutely did, Ms. Sudbury."

After forty years? Why? Out of nowhere, he was back? For what? Why would he do this to her? She didn't want anything belonging to Thomas Clyde, anything that would remind her of the awful thing she'd done with him.

"There's been a mistake," she asserted. "Do whatever you need to dispose of the matter." And she hung up the phone.

9.

Jim went down to the garage after knocking at Norma's door and receiving no answer—not even an angry, "Go away!" He wasn't entirely sure why. It wasn't Sunday. He wasn't going to drive the car around the lot. Maybe he felt like he had some things to explain to Sarah. Was he feeling guilty about having just taken Norma to the candlelight dinner—and caring so much that she was apparently upset about his reaction to their new neighbor?

He flicked on the overhead light in his garage unit and stared at her, the car of his youth. Somehow, it was easier to stare at the car right then—easier than it would have been to look at the picture in the rearview. His eyes rolled across the Mustang, the inanimate object that never made a choice on its own, only reacted to the turn of the key, the swivel of the steering wheel, the pressure of the gas pedal.

Standing there in a stream of moonlight, Jim

found himself sympathizing. Of all things. Sympathizing with a collection of steel and chrome. Because every bit as much as he'd made his own decisions, decisions had been made for him, too. Of course they had been.

Didn't the military make every decision for the eighteen-year-old Jim, during his own teenage four-year stint? Didn't being married make decisions for him, too—especially when Sarah wanted to remain close to her parents, keeping him from applying for any out-of-state jobs? Didn't his son make them when he was all sticky fingers and bad ideas, causing Jim to devote his weekends to being a giant watchful eye (like that old Jimi Hendrix flying eyeball poster, he'd often caught himself thinking, standing at the kitchen window as he waited for the next "Don't" or "Watch out" to bubble out from the back of his throat)?

Didn't his job make decisions for him as it sent him out on the road, or his parents as they guided him toward college after his military stint, or his English teachers when they told him they thought he had admirable skills of persuasion, or the damned cable guy just by telling him that he'd be at the house anywhere from eight a.m. to a quarter till never on one of Jim's rare days off, and there he was, a hostage in his own living room? Didn't every single one of them have a hand in directing his life?

Those two women upstairs—Norma and Mildred—weren't they directing his life now? Even though he barely even knew them. He couldn't quite figure out how or why, but it seemed that they were. At the very least, they'd invaded his emotions—especially that Norma.

Who's in the driver's seat now? he caught himself thinking as he stared at the Mustang.

It seemed to him at that moment that every single person on the planet was nothing more than a car, gas in the tank, waiting for someone to climb behind the wheel, pop the clutch, and hit the accelerator.

10.

Mildred's phone screeched. She jumped, knocking the ceramic drip pan for her African violets onto the floor and breaking it in two. The phone screeched again, sounding closer this time—almost like the thing had feet and was chasing her. This was the fifth time Gurtler had called her today—already, before Mildred had even gone downstairs for breakfast. Of course it was him. She swore she could recognize a difference in the tone of the ring.

"Don't you have any other—living—clients?" Mildred hissed at the still-ringing phone.

She placed a hand to her chest and tried to convince herself that breathing really was as easy as it had ever been. *Get a grip, Mildred*, she scolded herself and leaned her violets closer to the water running in the sink.

Still, though—the phone continued to scream at her. Between the bloodcurdling cries, Mildred caught herself thinking that the splash of water in her sink was rhythmic—like rain. And suddenly, Mildred's memory was dragging her all the way back to the fall of 1978, the afternoon she'd stood on the covered walkway outside of Central High School, staring out at the drenched parking lot. Wondering how she would make it to her six-year-old Pinto without letting the downpour completely destroy the hair she had professionally styled three times a week.

She'd left her umbrella in the car—of course she had. And she'd been so absorbed in finalizing her first quarter grades, she hadn't realized how late it had grown or how hard the rain had started to fall until that very moment.

She growled in frustration, then took a deep breath, finding that the autumn leaves gave the air a lovely musky smell—homey and cozy, like a fireplace in a living room. And besides, she was just so incredibly *happy*. Here she was, out of the library and back to teaching again, the first full quarter officially completed. She was in such a good mood, in fact, that it seemed to her the rain had popped up out of nowhere, surprising her like a good-natured joke from a best friend. She couldn't be mad at a *friend*. Slowly, the rain stopped being something to resent. So what if she'd had her hair done the day before?

No one was watching. The school was empty. Mildred chuckled softly. *When we're alone*, she thought as she stared at the blacktop, *aren't we any age we decide to be?* Mildred decided she would be, for the briefest of moments, even younger than her ninth-grade students—twelve, she thought. With a twelve-year-old's utter freedom. And no twelve-year-olds cared about hairdos. Or umbrellas.

She raced into the lot, skipping straight through the puddles instead of around them, her laughter pinging against the school's bricks like a wand against a triangle. Right then, everything felt so joyful that it didn't seem impossible for Gene Kelly himself to be there on the opposite side of the Pinto, ready to put his arm around her waist and lead her in a smashing song and dance routine.

She hummed as she piled into the car and started for home—until the headlights appeared. Two bright shining eyes in her rearview mirror, watching her. Turning two corners with her. Mildred's smile melted. Suddenly, the droopy hair plastered to her forehead and the damp cling of both her pantyhose and her polyester dress didn't feel funny to her at all. Mildred felt instead like she was in a stranglehold.

Her heart wasn't beating so much as it was slamming like an angry door, over and over. She bit her lip, taking a turn that was out of the way just to test what would happen. The headlights came with her.

She whimpered, both hands gripping the steering wheel. Her foot nudged the gas pedal and her eyes swiveled between the two rearview mirrors, the one stuck to the windshield and the one on the side of the car. She forgot about the rain just long enough for her tires to drift into a pool of water, throwing a tidal wave over the fender. Mildred's face twisted and she let out a scream of utter terror as the balding Goodyears lost their grip and slipped off the pavement completely. Mildred slammed her foot against the brake, yelping when the front bumper slammed against the ditch.

Panting, whining, Mildred squeezed her eyes shut. The rain tapped on the roof above her. The engine of the other car grew closer. And pulled to a stop beside her.

"Go away," Mildred whispered as the strange car idled. She had nothing. No protection—other than her umbrella and the prayers pouring out of her mouth.

"Please, please, please. Go away."

But the strange car kept snarling at her like an angry dragon. Or purring, maybe. Yes, that car sounded like some awful creature purring happily at the idea of swallowing her whole.

Mildred swiveled to smack the lock down on her door. She grew brave enough to glance through the window and the rain, toward the other car. The figure in the driver's seat—mostly obscured by the darkness and the deluge—stared back. The silhouette leaned to the side; the door popped open.

Mildred screamed. She screamed like a woman in a horror movie. She screamed like a kid being kidnapped and thrown in the back of a van. She screamed like she believed every police and fire department in the Midwest would be able to hear her and race to her rescue.

The hazy figure in the other car paused, the driver's door still only half-open. After a moment, the door shut again, and the car pulled away—almost apologetically, Mildred caught herself thinking. The red tail lights inched forward, turning into two dots, then disappeared completely into the white sheet of water.

Mildred placed her forehead on the wheel, whispering, "Thank you. Thank you. Thank you." She didn't even care that she was stuck in the ditch with no way out until daybreak. She didn't care that she might actually have to sleep right there, in the front seat. She didn't care that she was going to worry her sweet mother into her grave when she didn't show up at home. She was not going to wind up hacked into bits of cubed steak. Nothing else mattered. She shuddered as the fear continued to leak out of her.

"Ma'am?" a man called as he knocked on her window.

She jerked her head up, staring straight into the silver badge on the front of a police officer's hat. The man beneath it moved his hand in a circle, asking her to roll her window down.

"We got a call," he said. "Anonymous tip saying you were out here in need of help."

Anonymous. The word had made her feel off-kilter then, and it made her feel off-kilter now as she relived the memory of that late night. Because after the tow truck and her mother's relieved hug and the hot tea, hadn't Mildred finally admitted to herself that the figure inside the other car had looked somehow familiar?

No—not possible. *Or was it?* Mildred thought now, with the phone screaming and the water in the sink reminding her of the sound of pouring rain, with the tight panicked feeling invading her chest all over again. The shape of that face in her rearview mirror, the way he had stared at her then driven off when she had screamed, the anonymous call. It had been him. Hadn't it? Hadn't it been Thomas? Following her from school? But why would he do that?

The answer appeared in Mildred's mind, as clear as giant block letters on a bulletin board: *Because he thought of you as his.* Her face flamed. How often had he followed her? Had he watched her all these years? Did he know she'd never married? Did he know there'd never been anyone after him?

Mildred was mortified by that thought. Mortified by the idea that maybe Thomas had thought he'd been the One, capital O. The love of her life. It infuriated her.

She turned the water off, raised the receiver and slammed it down, then took it off the hook. Mr. Gurtler was making her feel chased, too.

11.

Jim stepped into the hallway at the same moment Norma emerged. He'd timed it that way, just as he'd once timed getting up from the basement couch and racing into the kitchen before Sarah could get there, those mornings when she was still holding tight to a grudge against him.

He and Sarah had never had any serious spats, looking back on it. It was only that women were such serious, sensitive creatures. If women were tools, they'd be embroidery needles or stippling paintbrushes. Something built for fine detail work. Men were more like jackhammers and bulldozers. It was easy for a jackhammer to muck up the intricate pattern that had been painstakingly laid into a wood floor with parquetry tools. And so it was, at times, with Jim and Sarah.

He'd be in the kitchen at a quarter to six on those mornings when he was ready to make up. He'd mix up his chocolate chip pancakes and fry up some bacon and brew a fresh pot of coffee. Sarah would try to ignore it, but inevitably, the smell would be too much for her and she'd show up, her morning dose of cold cream shining on the chin she held high. She'd retie the belt on her robe, like she was telling him that she was a locked door and he was going to just keep on standing outside. She would pour herself a cup of coffee and turn the back of her shoulder and that was that, she didn't want his crummy old pancakes, but then Jim was tickling her and she was finally laughing about how ridiculous the whole thing was, and then they'd be eating and later the robe would fall and everything was fine, just fine.

He'd sat on his couch listening to Norma rustling around inside her apartment and trying to imagine the movement attached to each sound: a spoon in a coffee cup, hairbrush clattering against a sink. The moment he'd heard her door swing open, he'd lunged into the hallway. But he was suddenly at a loss, standing there in front of her.

I'm trying, here, Jim's breakfasts had once told Sarah. *I'm sorry. I'm a dope.* He wanted to say the same thing to Norma, but how could a man make up to a woman when he didn't really even know her? When tugging on the belt of a robe was out of the question? When the woman standing in front of him wasn't even *wearing* a robe?

Jim couldn't think of a time when he'd ever had a spat with a still-relative-stranger—and he had to admit, he liked that. It made his heart do a tap-dance routine. He preferred a sparring partner to a yes-man. He liked that Norma was tough and obviously wouldn't put up with crap—and he loved all the exciting scuffling that her attitude promised. But how did you say all that to someone when you hadn't yet done anything to erase the polite distance between the two of you? Could simply saying what was floating around in his mind erase the distance? Or would it embarrass her? He didn't know her well enough to know how she would take it.

Norma clenched her jaw tighter, staring. She was waiting, Jim knew. She was open to—what? Being neighbors? Pushing bits of small talk around between them like Scrabble tiles on a game board?

Jim hated small talk. It dug into his skin like a paring knife. He ached for another person in this world who knew him as Sarah had known him. He ached for someone to smell bacon and know it was an apology.

He opened his mouth. He was going to do it. He was going to tell her, "Look. I like you. You, not the other woman. I know that's what you think. But really, that girl had sequins on her dress, and it just kept catching the light. She looked like a neon sign. You can't help but look at neon signs, right? Then you move on, heading down the same street, putting the neon sign behind you. That's what I was doing—I just glanced up, and when I brought my head back down, you were gone."

Behind Jim, a door opened. He glanced behind his shoulder as Mildred stepped into the hallway. While his head was still turned, he could hear Norma letting out a grunt of utter frustration. Her door slammed shut.

"Normal?" Jim asked, whipping his face toward her room number. He took a few steps forward and knocked gently. "Normal?" No response. There really was a locked door between them this time—not just the belt of a robe.

Behind him, Mildred sighed forcefully. "I think I made a bit of a ripple last night. First time in the history of the world that a spinster schoolteacher ever did."

"Don't quite look like a spinster schoolteacher," he said with a chuckle.

"No. I really am. In the most stereotypical way.

The Sudbury residence has never had a Saturday night wilder than a good book and a hot bath." She sucked in a deep breath; her face was looking nearly as white as her platinum hair as she shoved her hands deep into the pockets of her slacks. "Attention is a drug. Especially when you've never really been the recipient of it before. It felt good, and I couldn't stop myself—I wound up gulping down far too many glasses of it. I think I became the girl with the lampshade on her head."

Jim nodded. "Fair enough."

"I can't say, though, that the dining room seems especially inviting this morning."

"Like going back to work after you got drunk and made out with three different people at the Christmas office party."

"Everyone got the wrong impression," she said, forcing a smile. "I know they'll have the wrong impression until I give them the right one, but I just—I guess I'm not feeling especially brave right now. I'd invite you in for a delicious bowl of cold cereal and a banana, but I'm afraid, at this point, that also might be quite scandalous."

Jim glanced once more at Norma's door. As he stared, he swore that he saw it cinch itself tighter, just as Sarah had once cinched her robe tighter in order to insist, wordlessly, that she had every right to be angry and to warn him that her anger just might go on at a length to rival the Hundred Years' War.

He sighed. "Let's throw caution to the wind," he said, stepping toward Mildred's room.

The new Sudbury residence offered all the proof that anyone would ever need that she was no racy number. Shelves were neatly organized with classics—books and records both. And the rest of the décor—it all looked like the things a woman gravitated toward when she never had to get used to a man's taste. It was floral. Dusty rose. Mildred poured his coffee into a delicate china teacup. The bowls she tugged from the cabinet were pink ceramic.

Jim wondered what Sarah would have chosen for herself had she never had to think about him. He pictured her in a department store, sighing in admiration at a floral comforter and then letting her face droop in disappointment as she tugged a plain blue king-sized cord bedspread off a shelf.

"Place really does smell like a department store." Jim didn't realize he'd actually said it out loud until Mildred laughed—a tight little nervous laugh.

"Everything's new," she acknowledged. "Every last little thing. I sold everything I had at the house and started over. Some of it was out of necessity—I had to have a smaller couch for the smaller living room space, a twin bed for the apartment-sized bedroom. But some of it was simply that I had a desire to start a completely new chapter."

The phone rang. Mildred jumped, so startled that she nearly dropped her own cereal bowl on the kitchenette's tile floor. She stood hugging the bowl to her chest and staring at the kitchen phone as though it had cornered her and was slinging threats.

"You on the lam?" Jim asked.

"What?" When Mildred faced him, her eyes were wild and her forehead covered in tiny beads of sweat.

"You going to answer?" he asked quietly, nodding once at the phone.

"Oh." She raised the receiver and slammed it back down, ending the call without ever speaking. When it instantly started to ring again, she repeated the action, raising and slamming the receiver. This time, she took the phone off the hook, letting the receiver dangle toward the floor on the curly cord.

"You *are* on the lam," Jim said.

He meant it as a joke, but it made Mildred whack the bowl onto the counter and start to wring her hands nervously.

Jim figured if this were Norma, he'd find it all intriguing. It'd be a mystery he'd be scrambling to get to the bottom of. This was Mildred, though—and that meant he was instead jumping at the chance to use this to his advantage. Mildred wanted to get as far away from that phone as possible. And he wished he was sitting in another apartment himself. So...

"Come on," Jim said, grabbing a bunch of bananas off the counter. "Get the cereal. Let's go have breakfast at Norma's place."

Mildred eagerly nodded as Jim raced toward the door. This was going to be perfect. He could prove he was into Norma by showing up with Mildred and paying attention to Norma instead. But—no—something was missing. He needed...a distraction. Norma was pissed, and he needed something that would take her attention completely away from her anger. Honey Nut Cheerios, while tasty, were not going to manage that all on their own.

"Bring your flute," Jim said, pointing at the instrument case.

"Why?" Mildred asked.

"Gal, it's your own flute. No need to be horrified."

"It just sounded like you were telling me to prepare for something awful." When she glanced at Jim's utterly confused expression, she explained, "The last time I had it out, I was going to use it as a club to beat someone's head in."

"See, now, that makes me think of that on-the-lam thing in a far more serious light. I probably should ask for a few more details."

"Please don't," Mildred said, reaching for the

flute case.

Together, they stepped into the hallway and knocked on Norma's door. Jim felt it bubbling up from his stomach: those hopeful nerves that had attacked him when he'd first decided to park his Mustang at Sarah's curb, walk up her parents' front yard, and knock on the door.

"We come bearing gifts," Jim said when the door flew open, pointing at the bananas and the box of cereal.

Norma crossed her arms over her chest. "The way my luck is going, you're Greek."

Norma's quip instantly brightened Mildred. She burst out into laughter. "Beware," she told Jim, nudging him with the cereal box. "Beware of Greeks bearing..."

"Yeah," he said. "I got it."

But Mildred was still laughing in an appreciative manner, which meant that Norma was swinging her door all the way open, and suddenly, they were inside.

Norma's apartment was every bit as feminine as Mildred's, but the items all had age. She obviously liked her antiques. Her coffee table was a hundred-plus-year-old trunk, her side chair ripped straight from a *Masterpiece Theater* set. He guessed even her sofa was a good fifty years old.

"Noticed your piano through the open doorway last night," Jim said. "So I told Mildred to bring her flute."

"For a wicked jam session," Norma observed. "Me and Jethro Tull."

Jim smiled as he peeled his banana. "Surely you have something over there," he said, gesturing toward a large pile of sheet music pushing at the sides of an ancient basket. "Something you two could play together."

Mildred clicked open her instrument case. "I'm

game," she said. "Has your piano been with you a long time?"

Norma nodded, still refusing to take a step closer to the spinet. "My grandmother bought it for me when I started taking lessons. I was never very good. Loved it—but was never great. I dragged this old thing everywhere, though," she went on, her eyes getting a faraway look. "Every single place my husband and I lived. Even when it had been years since I'd played last. Funny the things you keep, the things you hang on to. The things that wind up being important."

But she was still making no attempt at moving any closer to the piano—or at plucking the milk from her fridge—or at sitting down, for that matter. She simply stood, flat-footed, leaning neither to the right nor the left, arms folded over her chest.

In the awkward silence, Mildred shifted the cereal box from one hand to another.

"Nice of your grandmother to do that," Jim finally said. "My grandmother—what a piece of work. Grumpy old gal. Never saw my mother make her a dinner she didn't shake her head at and push away. Never saw her get a gift for Christmas when she didn't ask, 'What am I supposed to do with *that*?' Once, you know, when I was maybe eight or nine, we got a puppy. And I was telling her about it on the phone, and she said, 'Well, hopefully it'll run away before I have to come for Thanksgiving.' I used to wonder what had happened to her to make her that way."

Norma narrowed her eyes at him, staring for a moment. Finally, she uncrossed her arms in an *okay, okay, I get it* manner and slid onto her piano bench.

She opened a piece of sheet music. "Some Enchanted Evening." And she began to play the chords, allowing Mildred to pick up the melody line.

Jim took a bite of his banana as he watched

the two women—but his gaze quickly narrowed, like a camera zooming in, to include Norma alone.

Ah, Norma. What a delicious, lovely project. She was a fresh box of crayons, a notebook at the beginning of a school year, a tie intended to be worn at an interview, a sunrise, a "Once upon a time." More of a project, even, than Sarah had been when they'd met. Because Sarah had been sweet. Oh, sure, there was a feisty streak in Sarah. But Norma—this wasn't mere feistiness, this was full-on attitude. She reminded Jim of a pocketknife. The kind of thing that gleamed beautifully and dangerously in the sun and just might wind up saving your life, given the right situation.

He flat-out wanted Norma. That much as was as clear as the notes bouncing between her apartment walls. He wanted her because she was—what had his father called it?—a tough nut to crack. He wanted her because he just knew there was also a softness inside. He wanted her because she was funny and she had her own mind. He began to imagine it—sparring with Norma, who clearly was not afraid to fight back. He told himself that the closeness they'd form would not simply be a repeat of what he'd had before, but a new beginning that would be challenging and stimulating and never before navigated. Imagine—here, at this point in his life. Something brand new.

He felt a goofy grin etching itself into his face.

When Norma glanced up, she flinched at his crooked smile.

"Show's over," she grumbled. And slammed the cover down over the keys.

12.

Norma didn't know what Jim was up to with that Mildred business. She didn't need someone making play dates for her. At this point, hadn't she also earned the right to dislike someone? What did Jim care if she didn't like Mildred? And what was with that goofy look on his face when she was playing her piano? He was persistent, though. Whatever the goal was, he wasn't letting it go. And it flattered her to be pursued.

As the days went by, he asked her to go on walks. She agreed, simply because she had nothing better to do—or so she told herself. On one such walk, he stopped to buy them both ice cream cones from a food truck in a grocery store parking lot. And with the June sun shining on her, and her feet throbbing in her shoes, and the taste of ice cream on her tongue, Norma felt so young that she almost thought she could smell it, wafting in the air—the kid side of the world. Glancing down at the sidewalk, she blurted, in the same straightforward, borderline rude manner that all children had, "What's up with those white sneakers, anyway?"

Jim laughed, unoffended. "I wore dress shoes every single day when I was working. Awful dress shoes. Pinched. Gave me blisters. Had Band-Aids from my ankles to my big toes. Swore when I retired I'd never wear another dress shoe again."

At that moment, Norma wondered if she'd found the one person in the world who felt the same way she did. Who remembered the sidewalks of youth—who was wearing the kind of footwear that announced he intended to travel them once again. Norma pointed Jim in the direction of the park, and they each claimed a swing. The black rubber seats were tighter than Norma remembered, but she tugged against the chains with both hands and pumped her feet and suddenly she was soaring. And when two kids—a boy and girl, both of them about Barbara's age—showed up, their jaws dropping at the sight of a couple of grandparents on their playground equipment, Norma laughed harder than she had in years.

Yes, there it was: Norma liked Jim, despite her best intentions not to. She liked him, even though the voice yammering in the back of her head contended that she would never be as happy latching on to someone else as she would be finally claiming a life all her own. Still, though—she liked him.

So much so that the next time they all piled into the Granite Ridge van, all of them heading downtown to the bistro market to pick up their cupboard goodies— milk and bread and their favorite cheeses or wine or the gourmet cookies with the dark chocolate chips— Norma took his hand and dragged him down the street, away from the group. She scoured the shelves of a flea market, all while Jim chuckled, telling her, "We *are* a couple of antiques, Normal. No need to buy any more."

But she ignored him as her eyes bounced through the shelves. He wasn't a fisherman. He didn't bowl. He certainly didn't seem the type for either stuffy-looking silver pitchers or cheap collectible remembrances of pop culture past. She gasped when she finally saw it, snatching it from the wall—a clock made out of an old Thunderbird hubcap.

"It's not a Mustang," she told Jim as the cashier ran her credit card, "but I think it'll look great on your wall. Add a little something different."

Jim looked touched as she handed it over. "That's nice of you, Norma," he said quietly, running his fingers along the rim. "I can't wait to get it home."

It crossed her mind that maybe she was the first woman to buy him a gift since his wife had died. The thought warmed her instantly, like a swallow of sherry.

Two weeks later, when the knock came to her door, she knew it was Jim. It didn't exactly take much to whittle her way through the possibilities. Norma could easily screen the knocks, just as Elaine screened her phone calls: soft and polite—housekeeping. Louder, followed by a, "Mother?"—Elaine. Persistent three knocks, followed by another three knocks, followed by an unending stream of knocks, one right after the other, that only let up when Norma finally twisted the knob of her door?

Jim.

So when the knock persisted after two rounds of threes, she put on her greeting-Jim face: a mix of raised eyebrow, arms crossed over her chest, and a half smile, despite herself.

"I have gotten to the bottom of it," Jim announced, stepping into her apartment and slamming the door with a flourish.

"I wasn't sure there was a bottom you were

interested in getting to," Norma quipped, arms still crossed over her chest. "Seeing as how you've never once gotten out your red thing."

Jim wagged his finger. "Now, now, Normal—" he started, his eyes twinkling. The way he was taking a deep breath and twisting his mouth said he was about to get her with a juicy comeback of his own. But, no— he stopped himself, cleared his throat, and announced, "I've discovered it—the real reason why Patrick paints such bad trees."

"And why is that?"

"Cataracts. Perfectly elementary, dear Normal."

"Uggh," Norma grimaced. They were still standing in the center of her living room, neither one of them making a move toward the small sofa or any of the chairs. They had the appearance of two people who'd recognized each other in a hallway, and had only barely paused to nod before moving hastily on in their own directions. "Has it really come to this?" Norma moaned. "To talking about physical ailments? Here we are, a bunch of old people, griping about our aches and pains."

"Oh, Normal," Jim protested, shrugging in a way that made him look a little squashed. "We always talk about body ailments. Our whole lives through. It's just that when we're thirteen, it's zits and farts. This time in our lives, hemorrhoids and cataracts."

"How, exactly, did you arrive at this conclusion about Patrick?" Norma asked.

"Well, it was either my powers of deduction, or the fact that Patrick asked me two days ago to pick him up from the clinic following his surgery."

"I see."

"So should Patrick, now." Jim winked. "Come on, Normal. I've got the driver downstairs with the car revved. You're not going to let me down, now, are you?"

Norma cocked her head to the side. "You say this as though I already agreed to come with you."

Jim grinned.

Norma sighed and slipped into her bedroom in search of a pair of shoes.

She had become oddly fixated with shoes in the last couple of weeks. She had thrown away her pumps, every last pair. Even the flocked red pair of platforms she'd purchased on a whim in the late '60s and then taken such pains to hide from Elaine, to protect them from the mud and the awful nasty club floors and the spilled beers that would have surely befallen them during her college years. All of that fighting to hold on to them, and now, they went straight into the Dumpster out back. Norma replaced them with flats—dress flats and loafers and brightly colored canvas Keds, every shade in the rainbow.

In part, she'd been inspired by Jim. Also, at that awful candlelight dinner, Norma had decided pumps felt wobbly and unsure. She wanted solid ground beneath her. She wanted to look like the Gorilla Glue woman she felt she was, and she could not do that if she couldn't stand on her own two feet. Besides, weren't pumps a way to fulfill a man's fantasy, even in the business world? Women of her generation had scratched and clawed and fought to get in the office, and once they'd finally gotten a seat beneath the glass ceiling, they'd still been stuck with Frederick's of Hollywood on their feet.

Norma wiggled her toes into a pair of blue Keds (just a shade lighter than the blue stripes in her blouse) and nodded to Jim in the living room. "Well?" she said, and powered on ahead of him, like she was tired of having to wait on him to comb his pretty hair. She'd done that, too, hadn't she? She'd waited on Charlie to get pretty. Norma had herself always been the fastest makeup job in the Midwest, able to apply liquid eyeliner in a single perfect stroke. She could have watched an entire episode of *Knots Landing* in the time it took Charlie to get himself gussied up to go to dinner. Once, she actually did.

Norma was ready for a little outdoor air. Ready to put her flat-soled shoes to use.

She'd started to head for the line of garage doors when Jim grabbed hold of her arm and pointed toward the car with the Granite Ridge logo on the door. The driver—a man surely nearing his own retirement, with silver hair and a long slender body—waved. "Was beginning to think you were going to stand me up," he said.

"Still no red thing," Norma said, eyeing Jim.

Instead of answering, he ushered her closer to the Granite Ridge private car.

Just plain weird, Norma thought. The driver was their age. And Jim had a car. What did they need a driver for, anyway? She was about to speak up against the whole ridiculous thing when Jim announced, "Don't forget, it's to the store first, Jeeves."

"Hey, that's Richard to you," the driver grumbled. "Or *Mister* Jeeves."

"The store first, not the hospital? What does Patrick expect—jewelry, wine, flowers?" Norma challenged.

"Listen," Richard said as he settled into the front seat. "I used to drive a school bus. Don't think I don't know how to get between you two."

Norma liked this—the back and forth, the elbows nudging each other in the ribs. This hadn't been in her life for so long—this teasing, this fun. Maybe not even since her playground days. Since saddle shoes. Since playing tag in the middle of the quiet intersection, back when no one ever had to worry about oncoming traffic.

Something was happening; she knew it as she settled deep into the backseat next to Jim. She wasn't quite sure what it was yet—she only knew that every time she was with him, she felt lighter, like her chest had more space. So when the voice in her head popped to life yet again: *Are you really going to do this, just let another man steer you, decide for you where you're going to go when you went to all that trouble to plant your feet flat on the ground?* she rolled her eyes and tossed the thought right out the rolled-down window.

She felt good. Why was there a need to second-guess anything?

The Granite Ridge car wound along the edge of town, past the striped firecracker tents beginning to pop up in time for Independence Day, and pulled to a stop in front of a Five and Dime store—with two giant gray coins plastered on the sign above the door. Buckets of plastic pinwheels and flip-flops and horrifically fake flowers stood in crooked arrangements beneath the cloth front awning.

"What?" Norma asked. It was all she could think of. She didn't know this building even existed before now. What were they doing here? What was the goal?

Jim winked, popped the door, and headed straight for the entrance.

Head spinning, Norma stepped out of the car and followed him.

The Five and Dime smelled like cheap plastic and was arranged like Elaine's closet when she was eleven: shelves looked picked-through and haphazard; round racks had been crammed with clothes, the plastic hangers pointing at odd angles; already-played-with toys lay scattered across the tile floor.

"Ah-ha!" Jim shouted, racing to a wooden barrel and pulling out...a clown horn. As Norma watched, shocked, Jim announced, "Just what I was looking for," and squeaked it twice.

Norma smiled, catching on. She grabbed a pair of fake glasses with eyes hanging down by springs. "Aren't these recommended for post-operative cataract recuperation?"

"Why, yes, I believe it was in the pamphlet," Jim agreed. He lunged toward a metal rack and grabbed large elf ears, while Norma picked up a fake mustache and a rainbow-striped clown wig. Jim put a red squishy nose on over his own.

The two of them raced through the parking lot, jumped into the car, and twittered with anticipation all the way to the hospital.

"He told me he'd meet us in the cafeteria," Jim said, pointing.

Eyes swelled above every white coat they passed as they hurried through the building. Norma tried to remain serious, but an enormous smile betrayed her, spreading across her face. Glancing at herself in a door's glass panel, she could have sworn it was just the kind of wacky grin that had once been decorated with gaps left by the teeth the Tooth Fairy had whisked away.

They found Patrick's round-as-a-donut body plunked down at a table in the center of the cafeteria. The top of his bald head shimmered in the overhead light as he stared sadly into a plate of biscuits and gravy.

Jim knocked on the edge of the table.

"Who goes there?" Patrick thundered, raising his head to reveal he was wearing a patch over one eye. He forced a partial smile in the attempt to look like he was only pretending to be grumpy, but Norma had a sneaking suspicion that there wasn't much pretending about it. Patrick had a sick look plastered on his face. The anesthesia had done a number on him, turned his stomach.

Jim squeezed his horn, drawing the attention of

everyone in the cafeteria.

Patrick began to wheeze out a chuckle. "Don't make me laugh, you fools. Can't you see I'm in a coma here?"

Norma wiggled her lips beneath her fake mustache.

Jim turned his back for just a moment, then swiveled again to face Norma and Patrick wielding a fake cigar butt with a thermometer coming out the end.

"Doctor," Jim said, tugging the cigar from his mouth, "What can you tell me about our patient here?"

Norma pulled a chair back. "I never talk about people," she announced. "My mother taught me better than that."

"Doctor, will he live?" Jim asked.

"Not if he keeps eating this garbage."

"Are you sure we got it all?" Jim asked.

"Got all of what?"

"The cataract."

"Well," Norma said, "your guess is as good as mine. Lights went out in the OR at seven a.m. and he was still on the table."

Patrick laughed until he cried out of his good eye.

Was it ridiculous? Utterly. And Norma loved it; she drank it down in giant gulps. She relished the stupidity of it all. Her laughter was fruitful and multiplied, over and over again, until there was a giant cloud of giggles all around her, so thick she could barely see the table in front of her.

But she could feel a hand, warm, on her own. When she glanced up, swiping the tears out of the corners of her eyes, Jim was smiling at her. In a way that said this whole scene had been for her as much as it had been for Patrick. Norma'd needed this. Jim had known that. He'd known it when they'd eaten ice cream

116

and raced for the swings.

How long had it been since laughter was all someone wanted from her? Not her money, not her house, not her rescue. Just a sign that Norma was happy? When was it that she had stopped laughing like this? And why? Maybe some of Norma's edges had gotten a little hard over the past few years. Like dried-out stale bread crusts. And here Jim was, cutting those crusts away.

Jim was captivating. Right then, he could have been covered in warts and werewolf hair and had the head of an ox—literally—and he would have been the one for her.

She felt her hand slowly swiveling, so that her palm turned upward and her fingers wove between Jim's.

"Don't think I'm too blind to see that," Patrick said.

13.

The phone rang yet again. Two weeks, and Gurtler still hadn't given up.

Mildred hung up on him—without speaking, as usual—and stomped toward her bookcase, searching for something that would calm her out-of-control jitters. Because Gurtler really was making her nervous. More so with every single unwanted phone call. If this kept on much longer, she'd wind up with earplugs or a new unlisted number or another move—this time to Mars.

For now, though—Shakespeare's collected plays. That would do.

She carried the book down to the courtyard, which smelled sweet, courtesy of the roses artistically arranged around the gurgling fountain. The music of the water, the perfume, the cool air—it all helped push the nerve endings away from the top layer of her skin.

The wrought iron legs of two patio chairs

screeched against the brick floor as she dragged them into place. She sat in one, propped her feet into the other. Her volume fell open to *The Tempest*, and Mildred laughed. What was Prospero when he broke his staff, other than a retiree? She sank deeper into her seat, and had just settled in to read when she glanced over the edge of her book and found a woman with white curly hair staring out at her from the door of the dining room.

Mildred smiled and waved, not minding at all that someone would maybe pull her attention away from old Prospero's tale. After all, Granite Ridge was a kind of island, too, wasn't it? Filled with a bunch of people who had all found themselves shipwrecked? And here they all were, each one of them marooned, and what was there to do other than share their own unique stories? After two weeks of relative solitude, she was ready to dive into the story of one of her neighbors. That would certainly help take her mind away from Gurtler—every bit as much as The Bard. Maybe, if she sat quietly and listened long enough, they would move beyond the mundane details, into something juicy. But instead of returning her wave, the woman darted back inside.

Mildred frowned. "Perhaps my reputation has preceded me," she grumbled, remembering her first night at the Ridge.

But that didn't really seem like reason enough for the googly eyes to have persisted. After all, Mildred had long been back to wearing her flattering but far from flashy slacks and her short-sleeved blouses. She had not once worn red lipstick. And she was always seen in flats. Besides, weren't they all old enough to know that first impressions weren't exactly spot-on? Couldn't they all see she was no real life Marilyn Monroe?

"Weird," she mumbled, but she wasn't sure,

right then, if she meant the way that sequined dress had given everyone at the Ridge such a lasting wrong impression, or if she meant the back-of-the-neck tickle that she'd just gotten—the awful suspicion someone else was watching her. She turned, spotted a figure on one of the second story balconies. Again, she raised a hand to wave.

Again, the stranger watching her skittered away.

"What is the *deal*?" she wondered aloud. The cool quiet of her courtyard now felt prickly.

She shook her head, stood, and made her way back inside, down the main hallway, toward the library. Sure, she already had a book in her hand, but that was no matter. Mildred was only thinking of the way libraries had always felt like comfort. Like a permanent welcome. How sitting in a library had always made anything seem fixable—even the mistake she'd made with Thomas.

Approaching the door, she heard it: A sniffle.

She slowed, wondering if maybe someone inside was reading something especially sad. But, no, the girl inside was holding her head, rather than a book. And she was crying so hard, her black pants, white blouse, and apron were all trembling. The clothes, Mildred thought as she stared, all revealed that the girl was a Granite Ridge waitress. The ponytail, the build— Mildred recognized her, even without looking at her face. It was the young one, she thought.

Hannah glanced up; Mildred flinched and lurched out of the doorway. She was about to race up to her room, but stopped when she considered that the same thing just happened to her. Wouldn't she have welcomed an interruption from her reading? Hadn't she wished for it? And wasn't that maybe what Hannah was doing—crying in public in the hopes that someone would see her and offer some sort of life preserver?

After all, if the girl wanted to be completely, totally alone as she cried, wasn't the bathroom the better choice—preferably in a stall with the door closed? Better yet—how about her car, out in the parking lot?

Mildred took a step forward, knocked on the doorjamb.

Hannah sniffed, wiped her cheeks. "Sorry," she said, her voice low and thick—indicating she had probably been crying for some time. Each breath was punctuated by either a shudder or a hiccup.

"Anything I might be able to help with?"

Hannah let out a quick, shallow chuckle. "Only if you're a magician."

Mildred sighed, taking a few steps deeper into the library. Hannah was so familiar, in a shirt covered with splatters of red sauce and snot running down her face. Mildred half-expected her to swipe her nose with the back of her hand just like a little girl. Oh, how many scared little mice like Hannah had Mildred seen in her own classrooms? Shy things, clumsy things, awkward things. Faces covered in pimples, hidden by crooked bangs, decorated with unflattering colors of eye shadow. Hannah was a child, Mildred told herself. Just like the children in her English I courses. It was hard to believe that at her young age she had any problem that was completely unsolvable.

Mildred smiled warmly, taking another few steps closer. But the smile faded as she reminded herself of the way the children in her classroom had changed over the decades. How their problems had gotten increasingly darker, more serious. Her eyes trolled over Hannah's figure, lingering on her midsection. What if she had a problem outside of Mildred's own life experiences? What if the girl was pregnant? What did Mildred know of morning sickness or swollen ankles?

"Boys?" Mildred asked tentatively.

Hannah spat out a sarcastic, "Ha!"

Mildred relaxed, settling into the wingback chair beside Hannah's. "Money?"

"Kind of. I may have wasted about fifty thousand dollars."

"That's quite a feat," Mildred said, her tone laced with a mix of disbelief and slight bewilderment. "I once bought a pair of shoes that pinched—cute, but pinched—and they sat in my closet for a couple of years, until the leather cracked. Never wore them. Not once. Thirty-five dollars down the drain. Wasting fifty thousand, now that's a different story. How'd you manage that, exactly?"

Hannah offered a wilted smile. "It's not hard," she confessed. "Not when I'm involved." After a hard swallow, she continued, "I don't think I'm going to graduate," in a tone that was both serious and final. "Four years, fifty thousand dollars. And now, one class. One stupid class is standing between me and a diploma. I took it last spring, and the professor gave me one last chance at the term paper. Had to finish it this summer. So I agreed. But—it's not making any more sense this summer than it made last spring, and that means I'm going to flunk all over again, and if I flunk, then I won't graduate, and I'll have wasted fifty thousand dollars."

She reached for a Kleenex in a nearby box, her nose growing a far deeper shade of red. "The worst part," she added, "is that nobody's even surprised. My family, I mean. It's like this is what they expected all along."

Mildred's heart instantly went out to the girl in such a strong lurch, she placed a hand over her ribs to keep it from flying right out of her chest. "I don't think it's as dire as you're making it out to be. And I think you're misinterpreting your family's reaction. Is this a course you have to have for your major?"

"No," Hannah moaned. "Maybe that's the worst part. It's something I never needed to get involved in at all."

"So your major is—"

"Hospitality management," she grumbled. "Can't you tell?" She shook her head at herself. "I'm kind of screwing that up, too, I think."

"How so?" Mildred asked, falling back on her trusty old Socratic method.

"I came here because I kind of thought people would be easier on me. More forgiving, maybe. Kind of—" Her face twisted as she fought to come up with an adjective that wouldn't offend Mildred.

"Grandmotherly," Mildred offered.

"Well—yeah. I've never been good at interacting with a bunch of strangers. More introverted than most, I guess. But this place is just so *fancy*. I didn't expect chandeliers and linen napkins. I feel like I'm going to a four-star restaurant every day."

Now, when Mildred stared at Hannah, she didn't see one of her students. She saw herself. Maybe it was that word—*introverted*—that had pinged inside her in a familiar way. Hadn't Mildred always feared first days and unfamiliar settings? Hadn't it always been hard for her? Hadn't she always needed someone else to break the ice?

"Is this a speech class you're having trouble with?"

Hannah shook her head no.

"And you've talked to your professor?"

Again, she shook her head; some strange throaty gurgles bubbled up, warning she was about to unleash another round of sobbing.

"Your adviser?"

Hannah shrugged. "I told you, I'm not good with people. I choke up."

"You're not choking now."

"It's different."

"Why?"

"You're not making any judgments."

Mildred let out the exasperated sigh she'd once reserved for students she believed to be far smarter than they were letting on. "I still don't think it's this tragic. Your family probably just assumes you'll work it out—get your professor to agree to an incomplete, perhaps, and register for another class that meets the requirement. Graduate at the end of the fall semester."

"Incomplete." Hannah put her head back in her hands. "What an awful word."

"Tell me," Mildred insisted. "The suspense is killing me. What is this class that's giving you such fits?" And waited for Hannah to say something truly horrendous, like physics or calculus.

Instead, Hannah moaned, "British literature."

Mildred burst into laughter. "What author?"

"Shakespeare."

Mildred's laughter exploded again. "Hannah, you don't have a problem."

When she started to protest, Mildred smiled and raised her book to show Hannah the cover.

"Who reads Shakespeare for fun?" Hannah challenged.

"In his day, Shakespeare's latest work was actually the summer blockbuster."

A gentle knock on the door raised both of their eyes. "Hey, Bryan," Hannah said softly.

This Bryan person—dressed in Converse high tops and a polyester shirt with a wide collar—eyed Mildred suspiciously. Squinted at her as though he suspected Mildred wasn't trying to offer Hannah solace, but actually the reason she'd started crying in the first place. "You okay?" he asked Hannah.

She nodded, quickly tucking her tear-stained face behind her hand.

"Are you sure?" he asked, again turning his accusatory eyes toward Mildred, who in turn glared a teacherly warning at him.

Hannah waved him away with one hand and quickly slapped it back against her cheek.

Bryan let out a reluctant "Okay," before tapping the door frame a couple of times and dipping back out of the library.

Mildred frowned, slipping Bryan's reaction into the same mental file folder where she'd shelved the two residents who'd refused to wave to her in the courtyard just before darting out of her line of vision. And now that she was thinking about it, she ought to put Norma in that file, too. That neighbor of hers still remained as standoffish as ever. No matter how many times Mildred tried to wave at her or say hello or act generally neighborly and nice. And why was it that conversation had a habit of trickling to a stop when she sat at a table at dinner—any table? The only person who seemed to talk to her eagerly was Jim. But even that tapered off after a few glares from Norma, who seemed to be his regular companion. Actually, Mildred had wondered—more than once—if Jim and Norma were a couple. A new couple, judging by how much they had to say during mealtimes (those who'd been married for decades tended to slurp their soup quietly). A couple who had much to learn about each other. It had kept Mildred choosing a table alone, on the opposite side of the dining room; she would have felt rotten interrupting their evenings together.

Hannah moaned, "He'll find out I'm screwing up, too."

"Who?"

"Bryan, that's who. We go to the same university.

He's majoring in gerontology. We've had a few gen-ed classes together," she added, trying on a casual shrug. But her face was red and her shoulders were tight.

"So it is about a boy," Mildred said. "At least in part."

Hannah's eyes swelled as she raised her head. "I don't—I—"

"A crush," Mildred said.

Hannah's lips flapped together as she let out a sigh. "Yeah," she whispered.

"He seems nice." Maybe, Mildred thought, this was the reason for the dirty look he'd tossed her. He was already protective of Hannah.

"And smart," Hannah agreed. "He's here to find a subject for his final paper. He's graduating at the end of the summer—he just had one more class he had to take. I tried to pretend I just had one more class, too. A new class to take, I mean—not one to redo. I didn't want him to think I was a screwup. He's been really nice to me—he's the one who suggested this place to work." She closed her eyes and started to rub her temples, muttering, "I don't know why I care so much. I'm sure he's not interested."

Mildred shook her head. The mere look on Bryan's face when he'd stood in the library doorway showed he had far more than just a passing interest. He was invested. But Hannah, at this point in her life, was not just bad at interpreting words on a page. She was bad at reading the cues life was giving her.

And what have you misread, Mildred? The words popped into her face, shocking her. The same way Gurtler's call had initially shocked her. But she immediately pushed the thought down again.

"So this paper," Mildred said. She'd waded deep enough into the problems-with-boys area of Hannah's life. Mildred had no practical advice to provide on the subject. Not like she could offer with Hannah's schoolwork.

"What's in it for you?" Hannah finally asked Mildred. "If you help me, I mean."

"What's in it for me? What have you been doing, binge-watching mafia movies? I knew retirement would be an adjustment, but I never thought I'd feel the itch to teach as much as I do. I taught English for more than thirty years, and now—it's like trying to quit smoking cold turkey. Only, teaching isn't bad for me. So why stop?"

As Hannah considered this, Mildred added, "Besides, it's oddly lonely here, sometimes. Most of the time," she corrected herself.

"Because of the rumors, you mean. The stories are scaring some of the residents, I think."

"What rumors?"

"About—you know—your problems—legal problems."

"Legal problems?"

"Everyone's talking about it. That lawyer who keeps looking for you. He calls the front desk sometimes. I guess you take your phone off the hook. There are all kinds of stories about you. Talk about summer blockbusters! You're not *really* Mildred Sudbury—you just stole her identity and are trying to live out your retirement in peace. When you were young, you were a regular—what's her name? The bank robber."

"Oh, for Pete's sake," Mildred groaned. "Bonnie Parker."

"I didn't think it was true," Hannah protested. "I really didn't. Nothing that exciting ever is."

"It's as far from true as it gets." Mildred found herself fighting a chuckle rising up her throat. "It's so far from true, it's funny."

"So what is it, really?" Hannah whispered,

leaning forward. "The straight skinny."

"It's actually a private matter."

"No offense or anything, but actually, it's not," Hannah said. "I mean, everybody's already talking about it."

Mildred's eyes swelled. "Everyone?"

"I'm sorry, Ms. Sudbury. I didn't mean—this place is like a grapevine from hell, sometimes. So what does he want? That lawyer who keeps calling?"

Mildred took a breath. "He wants me to come get something. An inheritance."

"So why don't you?"

"I'm afraid it would mean something if I did—something I don't want it to mean."

"To who—or whom? It should be 'whom,' shouldn't it, Ms. Sudbury? Like in those letters— 'To whom it may concern.'"

"Yes. Well. I'm afraid it would mean something to the person who left it to me."

"Who's dead."

"Right."

"I'm sorry, Ms. Sudbury, but that doesn't really seem like much of a problem to me, either."

"It doesn't?"

Hannah shook her head.

"Huh," Mildred said, slumping deep into her chair.

"Your face," Hannah giggled. "You look like you've had some giant revelation."

"Maybe I have," Mildred admitted.

Mildred agreed to meet Mr. Gurtler. But not in his office. She agreed to meet him at the Handsome Diner out by M Highway.

In truth, the Handsome Diner was not handsome at all—at least, not the way Mildred had remembered it. It was decorated with wood paneling and a concrete floor and generally had the feel of either a storage unit for out-of-date restaurant furniture or a flea market. Forty years ago, it was a place to eat a perfectly cooked rib eye. A piano bar in the back had served the best martinis in town and offered pretty background music for a man's sweet nothings, murmured across a tiny table for two. Now, it was a place to eat greasy hamburgers; the back room was covered in deer antlers and served beer to men in muscle shirts and John Deere caps.

The world had gotten quite skanky, Mildred thought. And she wondered, briefly, how Chad Prescott was getting along in her old neighborhood.

She chose a booth, and she ordered a Coke to pass the time as she waited for Mr. Gurtler.

She didn't know what she would say to him. But she did know she didn't want to say it over the phone.

When he arrived, she felt herself jump with surprise. Mr. Gurtler was older than she'd anticipated. Somewhere along the way, she'd started assuming everyone else in the world was under the age of thirty.

"Sudbury?" he asked, his eyes swelling at the sight of her.

She nodded. She swore she could hear him mumble a pleasantly-surprised "Hmm" as he slid into the opposite side of her booth.

It was kind of an odd reaction. But then again, Mildred was collecting odd reactions. She was still trying to figure out what she thought of this Gurtler fellow's response when he blurted, "Thomas always said you were quite beautiful."

Mildred frowned, now knowing exactly what she thought: She didn't like it. At all. "You knew Thomas?"

"I was his lawyer for quite some time. Yes."

"What else did he tell you?" she asked. "Never mind. Don't answer that."

When the waitress arrived, Mildred pushed her Coke across the table. "Can I please have a boilermaker?"

When Gurtler eyed her with surprise, she explained, "Closest thing to a cocktail in this place."

Gurtler raised a hand and pointed two fingers skyward.

The waitress nodded and slipped away.

"Haven't had one of those since my college days. Bookplates 'n Boilermakers. That was my reading group."

Now it was Mildred's turn to eye Gurtler with surprise. "You studied literature?"

"A million years ago," he shrugged.

Mildred tightened up. She didn't know why, but she didn't like that, either. Nor did she like the fact that Mr. Gurtler had strong arms, a chiseled jaw, and perfectly combed wavy gray hair.

"Why'd you keep hanging up on me, Ms. Sudbury?"

"I don't know," she answered, somehow both flippant and honest at the same time.

The waitress appeared with two beers and two shot glasses and thunked them onto the table.

"Yes, you do," Gurtler answered.

Mildred tightened again. "You say that as though you know me."

"I feel like I do," he said softly, eyeing her like she was wearing red sequins. But this time, Mildred wasn't going to gulp down attention mindlessly. She'd learned her lesson. That's what Mildred Sudbury did—

she learned her lesson the first time around.

Mildred shook her head. "This is ridiculous," she muttered. "This whole thing. No," she corrected herself, remembering the feeling she'd gotten that night she'd been followed in the rain—the night she'd been run into a ditch and had stared through the downpour at the silhouette sitting in the strange car. "It's creepy."

"Creepy? It's romantic."

"Romantic?"

"He loved you. He remembered you. He wanted to do right by you."

"Do right? Without Thomas Clyde, my life would have been different."

"So?"

"What do you mean, 'so'?"

"Every single day makes a difference in our lives. Doesn't it? Doesn't every single day change us a bit, and suddenly, at the end of a year, or five years, a whole decade, we're different people than we were before?"

Mildred wasn't sure what to do with Gurtler's observation. His words challenged her in a way she hadn't expected. She hated the easy way that he seemed to handle the knowledge of what had happened between her and Thomas. As though it was just some childish mistake—some teenage indiscretion.

"I don't want it," she said.

"What? The drink? I think it looks a little iffy, too." Gurtler cocked his head to the side as he stared into the glasses. He pointed at a black speck inside his shot glass and asked, "Does that look like a spider to you?"

Mildred shook her head. "Thomas's estate. I don't want it."

"Why on earth not?"

"Because—look. You obviously know what

happened between the two of us. I'm mortified that you know about it. But you do. So. I'm telling you, that's not me. You know nothing about me. Don't make assumptions."

"I didn't."

"You did. You assumed I'd take his estate." Mildred shook her head, whispered, "I'd never take anything from him. I don't even know what I'm doing here." She paused to glance down at her cloudy shot glass. "I refuse it," she told Gurtler. "The estate. I refuse it."

"You can't," Gurtler announced.

"I *can't*? I'm not legally obligated to accept anything."

"But you—I have to get it in writing!" Gurtler declared. His face squirmed into a frown, as though he realized just how flimsy that sounded.

"Look, here's the thing," Gurtler told her. "You only have a month to accept. One month after being made aware of it. That was a provision in the will. Like—he didn't want you to have a chance to second-guess it. He wanted you to take it. But time's running out, Ms. Sudbury. We've already wasted—what—a couple of weeks now with all these hang-ups and—"

"The answer is no today, and I assure you, it will be no in another two weeks."

"But he never had any children," Gurtler protested. "He has no living relatives. His wife, who is also deceased, has no living relatives. They were both only children. They were frugal, too, and lived on only her salary, saved his, had some nice investments. Oh, all that *money*." He put his head of perfectly-combed gray hair in his hands. "You should have it. It'll all just go to the state. To strangers."

"Thomas and I were strangers, too, Mr. Gurtler. I did not belong to him. Do you hear me? I was not his—whatever he told you. I have no remaining ties to him. I haven't had any ties to him for forty years. I find this whole thing absolutely absurd."

"He left you a home in addition to the cash. It's a lovely home, Ms. Sudbury. Idyllic. I swear. Don't say no until you look at it. I can take you out there myself. Please? Would you let me show it to you? It's a beautiful place."

"I have absolutely no interest in seeing where Thomas and his wife spent their retirement. How utterly ludicrous," Mildred snapped. In a softer tone, she added, sincerely, "Sorry to have wasted your time."

She gathered up her purse and hurried toward the door. As she stepped outside, she swore she heard Gurtler cry out, "I'm not giving up on you, Ms. Sudbury!"

14.

"**A** *regular* Bonnie Parker," Jim told Sarah, settling a bit deeper into the Mustang's front seat. "Can you believe it? That's what they were all saying about the old schoolteacher. Quiet little bookworm. And they made her into some kind of mastermind criminal, just because a lawyer's been calling her. Oh, how you would have hated that gossip, eh, old girl?"

And still, Sarah stared back at him from the photo. That morning, she looked especially faded. Jim wondered if the overhead fluorescent light in his single-car Granite Ridge garage unit was fading the photo on triple-time. Or maybe the picture had just aged to the point that it would be fading this quickly anywhere—even tucked safely under a plastic sheet in a photo album.

Jim removed a pill from one of the vials in his

glove compartment. "Keeping up with my medication, old girl." He twisted the cap from a bottle of water and swallowed.

"Look," he told her. "I know you know about Norma." When he raised his eyes, she was still smiling, her slightly-purple hair still flying out from underneath the scarf she'd tied around her head.

"It's got nothing to do with the way I feel about you. I didn't fall out of anything with you. You hear me? That's one thing that hasn't faded. And isn't going to.

"Funny, isn't it—you turn on an old movie, and it all looks dated. The clothes, the way everybody talked. But up in your head, when you think back on your life, it never does look simplistic or out of fashion. No matter how many years old that memory is. It seems instead like something that could have happened last week. And that's how it is when I think about you. It's all right at the surface. It didn't sink down underneath some other feelings I might have. It didn't get replaced. It's all right here.

"But you're not, are you, girl?" he whispered, rubbing his chin as his eyes tingled. "You're not here. So there are different choices to be made." He chuckled in a way that said what was on his mind wasn't funny at all. "I'm not going to patronize you and say that I don't have feelings for Norma. I do. Serious feelings. But I still have them for you, too. I don't believe that junk about falling out of love. I think if it's real, it's always real. I think life gives you few options to choose from, though. Very few true forks in the road. Mostly, you're on a highway going at a breakneck pace. Focused on some distant point on the horizon. Tunnel vision."

He sighed. "I'll always wish you were someplace other than the rearview, old gal. And I'm grateful that Norma may be part of the rest of the ride from here on out. Wherever you are, I hope there's someone in your own passenger seat."

He kissed his index finger, pressed it against Sarah's image, and he climbed from the Mustang.

Jim needed some real food. Eggs and biscuits and gravy, and he wasn't going to be guilted into the fruit buffet by Larry the former pediatrician.

He had just stepped into the dining room when Linda popped her perky blond head up in his path. "Jim!" she shouted.

"Lady," Jim grumbled at the activities director, falling into his daily script, "I am never going to join your ball-throwing, jumping ridiculousness."

"No, no, not exercise today. I wanted to introduce you to Bryan."

A young, tall, and rather muscular young man stepped out from behind Linda's right shoulder, wearing an Elton John baseball-style *Goodbye Yellow Brick Road* T-shirt, and Buddy Holly-style black glasses and dirty Converse high-tops, along with a pair of dark blue jeans.

"Bryan's from the university," Linda was saying. As she spoke, Bryan's eyes danced across Hannah as she placed silverware on each table—the same way mosquitoes had once followed poor Sarah everywhere, all summer long. No matter what kind of bug spray she used. No matter how many candles or torches she tried to burn. No matter how she waved her hands in front of her face, they just buzzed back harder.

"...studying gerontology," Linda went on.

And still, Bryan's eyes followed her. Hannah wasn't exactly a blond bombshell, but even Jim had noticed the beauty she was becoming. It was just that she was so impossibly *young*. Probably no younger than Sarah had been when Jim had met her, but still—at this point, Jim looked at Hannah and saw a child. Bryan, though, was seeing something quite different—something along the lines of what Jim saw when he looked at Norma.

"...and he was wondering if he could interview you," Linda went on. "He's working on his last term paper this summer."

"Absolutely not," Jim barked, in a completely humorless manner that was out of character for him. So unlike him, in fact, Linda's head jerked backward, like he'd just slapped her. The request had annoyed Jim, completely and totally. And annoyance had gotten control of his mouth, in the same way that too many evening scotches might.

When Bryan turned his own shocked expression toward him, Jim raised his hands in surrender. "Fine," he said. "Five minutes. Grab a table."

Satisfied, Linda disappeared.

Bryan flipped open a notebook as Jim settled into a seat. A spiral notebook, not a laptop, Jim noticed.

"Hey, Hannah," Bryan croaked.

"Hey!" she answered, her voice too high and too loud. She'd been waiting for him to say something. Hoping for it. Obviously.

"Sorry," Jim told Hannah, embarrassed suddenly at the rough way he'd handled the interview request just a moment ago—sounding like every young person's picture of a grumpy old man. "I didn't realize Bryan was your boyfriend."

Bryan's and Hannah's eyes popped open and their mouths curled into "O"s and they both launched into a stuttering tirade of *Oh, no, see, we're friends, very good friends, but we're not like that—we just—it isn't—*

"Youth," Jim grumbled, like a swear word. Why were young people so afraid of everything? Were these two going to squander whatever this was between them? The way they were behaving looked to Jim like two people who both wanted to share a fresh pineapple sitting on a table between them—wanted it so much, they kept having to wipe the corners of their watering mouths. But there they were, just watching it rot and go to waste because the outer skin happened to be a little prickly, and their baby-smooth fingers were oh so sensitive.

"Sir?" Bryan asked.

Jim only waved his hand dismissively. "Your paper," he said.

"Yes!" Bryan's eyes danced over toward Hannah one last time. He smiled at Jim, his cheeks going pink. He scooted his chair closer to the table, cleared his throat, and explained, "The focus of my paper is gerontechnology, so I was wondering—"

"Geron- what?"

"Gerontechnology. I'm studying gerontology, and my paper's focus is on technology's impact on an aging population."

"Fuck," Jim snapped.

Bryan flinched. He shook his head slightly, as though telling himself he had heard wrong. "It's all about maintaining vitality and—"

"Fuck," Jim repeated.

"—independence with assistance and—"

"Uuuuuugh," Jim groaned.

"So I was wondering about whether you use Life Alert, or perhaps even—"

"Oh, my God, kid. Really. *God*," Jim said,

pounding his hand on the table.

"Sir?" Bryan asked, his voice climbing into falsetto range as he adjusted his glasses.

"Where's your computer?" Jim demanded.

"I prefer—I prefer a pen. For notes."

"What car do you drive?"

"A—Volkswagen."

"What kind of Volkswagen. What year."

"Beetle. 1970."

Jim drummed his fingers on the dining room table as he tried to decide how to handle this Bryan character.

"Sir?"

"Get up," Jim commanded. "Come with me."

Bryan's eyes swelled behind the fairly thick lenses of his glasses.

"Come. On," Jim snarled.

Reluctantly, Bryan obeyed. He followed Jim all the way up to his apartment. Jim picked up his sticks—the last Christmas present Sarah'd ever bought him, with the idea that they had years of golf still in front of them—and shoved them into Bryan's arms.

"Well?" Jim growled. "Let's go."

He stomped straight downstairs, out the back door, and toward the golf course that stretched behind the retirement community.

"You gotta squat down to get through the fence," Jim instructed, pointing at the split-rail that separated Granite Ridge from the country club.

"But—why aren't we going to the front entrance? And when are we going to finish the interview?"

"Because I don't belong to the club. And while I'm playing."

"You don't belong?"

"You ever meet anybody who belongs to a country club?" Jim asked. "What a bunch of pompous jerks."

"But you play golf."

"Right."

Bryan placed the golf bag on the lush grass, angled toward Jim in a way that required him to take hold of it. "I don't feel comfortable trespassing, sir. Why can't we just—"

"Good," Jim interrupted.

"Good?"

"Good. You make me uncomfortable, too."

"Why?"

"Because you like old stuff. Old stuff is quirky. Look at you. You've never owned an iPod, have you?"

"I like records."

"Nothing post-1979," I suppose," Jim said, shaking his head in disgust. "Bet everything in your apartment came from a flea market. You claim to be born in the wrong decade. You like *old stuff*. And that's why you're majoring in gerontology. Right?"

Bryan shifted uncomfortably.

"You're treating me like one of your flea market oddities."

"No. I—"

"Yes. You are. So we're getting away from the retirement home, which is full of *old things*. We're going to spend some time out here in the sun, and if you ask questions that aren't too terribly offensive, I'll answer."

"But I haven't—"

"You have. Gerontechnology. Life Alert. It's condescending. Do you hear me? Totally and completely condescending. You and I will have a conversation, like a couple of human beings. You can ask me questions along the way, but we will talk and you will treat me as a person. Not a tchotchke. You hear me?"

"Yes—yes, sir."

"No Life Alert. No Jitterbug phones. No AARP. That crap is off the table. Got it?"

"Yeah," Bryan said, through a half-smile. "I do."

"Fine. We're going to play nine holes."

"I don't know—I've never played before. I'd be bad. I'm afraid I'd embarrass myself."

"We can only hope," Jim said, pulling out a driver and shoving it into Bryan's hands.

15.

"**S**omething's wrong with Mildred," Hannah whispered the moment she reached Jim and Norma's table.

Norma bristled. The chandelier in the Ridge's dining room seemed to instantly dim. Her pasta dinner looked instantly congealed. All because she knew this was not a mere observation on Hannah's part. It never was, not when Norma was involved. Norma, it had always been assumed, would take care of everything. She was Elaine's room mother, grades two through six. She listened to her husband's long descriptions of bad interactions with fellow business owners (usually over the phone, while she was trying to fix dinner and bandage Elaine's bleeding kneecap and engage in a game with their cat's favorite feather-lined toy all at the same time). She was expected to come up with a way to smooth those ruffled feathers, too—not just of the business owners, but also Elaine's friends and even her own mother-in-law. It was a game with rules that benefited everyone else, and insisted it was Norma's duty to make sure that life was a giant escapade, the kind of thing that made everyone around her throw their hands into the air and squeal, "Wheee!"

Yes, she'd had to work to make it all a game—even taking care of Elaine. She'd put a dartboard up on the back of the bedroom door, where she played Charlie for who would get up for the two a.m. feeding. And, as time went on, who would pick up the dry cleaning. Who would unload the dishwasher.

She practiced while Charlie was at the store and Elaine was down for her nap. She'd gotten quite good at hitting the bullseye. She even began putting a little money down on the outcome to pad her rainy day fund.

But she didn't want to play games anymore. She didn't want to be called on to help. She wanted Mildred to be a big girl and take care of herself. Why couldn't anyone just take care of themselves? And why didn't anyone ever stop to ask Norma if *she* needed help? Hadn't she spent the first two weeks at the Ridge in her room? No one had exactly come knocking on her door, asking sheepishly, "Everything okay in there?"

Jim craned his head to look across the dining room. "Mildred does seem a little worried about something," he observed.

"She had an appointment today with that lawyer," Hannah said, worked up to the point that she was sloshing coffee from the lip of her pot onto Norma's salad. "She's been weird ever since she came back. Maybe you guys should go talk to her."

"Let's don't and say we did," Norma grumbled.

"Oh, come on, kid," Jim said, nudging her. "Take pity on poor Hannah. She needs Mildred in tip-top shape. She's helping her write her last paper. The one and only paper standing between her and graduation."

Norma glared.

"Don't you want to know what the truth is?" he whispered. "The real truth? About the lawyer and those phone calls? I bet it's juicy."

Norma felt a smile spreading. There it was again—pure fun. Norma wasn't being called upon to rescue anything. Not with Jim. She pushed her chair away and rushed toward a table in the back of the dining room, where Mildred was drinking a cup of tea and staring out into the courtyard.

"Not till February, I'm afraid," Jim said, as he and Norma sat down at the table.

"Not till February what?" Mildred murmured.

"When the Ridge residents will go on another cruise," Jim told her. "You had to be imagining something far away, what with the dreamy look on your face."

"Mmm," Mildred mumbled absently.

Jim glanced at Norma. *Your turn*, he mouthed.

"How did your meeting go?" Norma asked politely.

Mildred glanced up, her face crinkled into surprise. "You know?" She tugged her hands into her lap. "What do you know, exactly?"

"That you were with a lawyer," Norma said quietly, propping her chin on her hand.

"About?" Jim pressed.

Mildred sighed, still staring at her lap. "I inherited something. An estate. Some land and a house. I'm not sure I want it. It's got—some history attached to it."

"Something bad happened to you there?" Norma asked, her voice quickly losing its overly-courteous tone. She couldn't help herself—she was intensely curious now.

"No—I've—never been there."

"It's got history attached to it and you've never been there?" Jim asked. "I'm intrigued."

"I just—I'm supposed—to go look at it."

"Perfect! I'll take you."

Mildred laughed. "In what, the Granite Ridge van?"

"In my car!"

Norma could feel anger rising like lava inside a volcano. Before she could talk herself out of it, convince herself she wasn't even slightly perturbed, she bellowed, "You'll get your red thing out for her but not for me!"

"Oh, Norma, now, don't be jealous."

That word—*jealous*—embarrassed her and added fuel to her anger, all at once. "You're just anxious to be Marilyn Monroe's knight in shining armor."

"You can't be serious," Jim said, leaning forward as Norma crossed her arms and leaned away from him. "There's no way I'd—she's not...You're coming, too!"

"Oh, sure, like you planned it all along."

"You didn't give me a chance to ask you—"

"No. The answer is no. I'd be a third wheel!"

Hannah approached the table, wringing her hands. "Are you—is everything okay? Mildred?"

"She's taking a trip. We're all taking a trip," Jim announced.

"I can't," Mildred protested. "I've got things to do. Hannah and I have a paper to finish."

"She's coming!" Jim shouted.

"I am? I can't, can I? I mean, my schedule here... Is it far?"

"Not particularly," Mildred said. "But that's not the point, either. I don't want a fuss. It's mine to deal with and I—"

"It's not a big deal, ladies," Jim asserted as Bryan cautiously approached the table. "Mildred needs to see a property. I don't have anything pressing to do. I have the means to get her there. So why wouldn't we go?"

"They're leaving," Hannah announced.

"Who?" Bryan asked, slamming his glasses higher up on his nose.

"All of them."

"Even you, Jim?" Bryan protested. "But what about—I got my paper topic approved, and if I have to find another person to base it on, I—"

"Pack your bags, my boy," Jim said. "You're so interested in antiques, you're going to spend a day or so with three of them."

"Oh, I couldn't—"

"Hannah's going," Jim said.

"Well, I—" Hannah's cheeks turned into two cherry lollipops. "I mean—I could, I guess."

"Well, if you're going..." Bryan started.

"You two are so pathetic," Norma groaned.

Hannah and Bryan both flinched.

"It's all pathetic," Norma said.

Everyone clustered at the table threw startled looks her way. And she thought, *I refuse to smooth feathers and be cheery and make this okay for everyone, and pretend it's okay for me, too, because it's not. For the first time in my life, everyone's going to know it.*

"Uuuraaagh!" Norma screamed, threw her napkin on the table, and stomped toward the stairs.

Mile

40,603

The Trip

Begins

16.

Jim rattled the garage door open, shaking his head at himself. What had he been thinking inviting half of Granite Ridge to go on a road trip? Had he imagined his Mustang was some kind of magical clown car, able to pack thirty bodies into the front seat?

No—actually, he'd been thinking of nothing but Norma. He'd invited everyone, but he'd only pictured one person sitting beside him.

"It's not going to work, is it?" Mildred asked as she stepped into the garage unit.

"Of course it will."

Mildred rolled her eyes. "You can't lie to me. I spent my life in the classroom, and I learned a long time ago that there's a definite pitch to a lie. It has its own key."

"I don't have it all worked out in my head yet, that's all," Jim said. "Maybe tie a few of us to the trunk. Rent a U-Haul trailer."

"It's silly for everyone to go, anyway," Mildred sighed, sliding her hands in the pockets of her slacks. "It's my problem. It doesn't exactly take five people to look at a house. Just one. Me. I should call that lawyer and—"

"That's it! The lawyer. Two cars. Problem solved."

Mildred slumped sadly. Her shoulders drooped into the shape of a frown. "It's nice of you to offer, but if I'm going to see it, I should just go with Gurtler, and not bother anyone else."

"Absolutely not. This is upsetting you. Isn't it? You've got a big decision to make."

Mildred paused, shrugged in agreement.

"Well, then, you need moral support. Isn't that why we all moved to the Ridge? So that somebody would always be around? And I don't mean for Bingo."

"I can think of one person who's been roped into this thing who's not the least bit interested in being my moral support."

"Oh, Norma's fine," Jim assured her. "Growling's just the way she talks. It's not necessarily a warning that she's about to bite you. Besides, she's been after me to get this—red thing—out and take her for a ride," he chuckled.

Jim tugged the tarp from the front of his car. As the sunlight streamed in through the open door, his eyes landed on the dings the old Ford had collected. The marks that had been left from his life with Sarah: The backseat stitching that had gotten pulled up by the teeth of Jim's Levi's in the midst of the first sweet, fumbling, awkward, glorious time he and Sara had made love—1970. The dimple in the passenger door created by the runaway cart Sarah'd failed to catch in the Smitty's Grocery parking lot—1974. The crooked bend in the front bumper that had appeared after Carl knocked the can of paint off the very garage shelf he was not supposed to touch—1982. The crease in the grille Cherry's kid had added for good measure.

No other 1965 Mustang looked exactly like his. No other car had aged in exactly the same way. The wounds and the imperfections had made his old car truly unique.

Jim glanced up at Mildred's worried expression, and it hit him that maybe he and Mildred and Norma had all collected their own dings. The passing decades had littered their bodies with a unique pattern of sunspots and scars, markings of heartbreaks and triumphs. Their faces had acquired a slew of wrinkles that, at this point, said more about them than the creases in their hands. A fortune teller could read their faces better than she could read their palms. Oh, who was he kidding? It didn't take a fortune teller. Anyone could look at Norma and know her particular set of dings had turned her into one tough cookie. Know that Mildred's had turned her into a timid thing who liked the safety of her books. And Jim's had turned him into a creature yearning for one more big adventure.

"We all become one-of-a-kind just by surviving, don't we?" Jim mumbled under his breath.

"Say what?" Mildred asked, leaning toward him. "I didn't hear you."

But Jim only shrugged. "I was just saying this old thing hasn't been out in a while—poor thing's really just barely been surviving here in the garage. Almost like an animal in a cage. She needs a good trip."

"She? Don't tell me her name's Sally."

Jim laughed. "Nice," he said, appreciating the dig. "Old Mustang Sally here hasn't been out in a while, but I know her well. Her heart's still good, and she can make the trip."

"Her heart? You're not going to break into a

rendition of 'Long May You Run,' are you?"

"You're endearing yourself more to me every minute, Mildred. You and Norma have more in common than you think."

"That's kind, but I don't think it's true. She doesn't care for me."

"She's testing you. Didn't you have students who did that?"

Mildred's shoulders relaxed slightly.

"Just outside of Iowa City, you said?" Jim asked, shifting the subject before Mildred had a chance to argue with him, offer definitive proof that he was wrong about Norma.

"Apparently, it's an old house on some land. Thomas—I mean, the person who left the place to me— he was from that area originally. He was a teacher," she added softly, as though her mind had started to wander. She stepped closer to the Mustang and began to run a finger around the curve of the side mirror. "He would have liked being near the university, I think. I can see him taking a few classes, actually. Most universities offer free courses for anyone over sixty."

"You don't talk like you had problems with this person," Jim observed.

Mildred flinched, drew her hand back. "What?"

"I mean, you act like you have some good memories. Whoever this person was to you."

Mildred grabbed the front of her blouse in a fist.

"We could leave early and be back before midnight. It's about seven and a half hours from here in Missouri up to Iowa City. Made the trip many times before I retired." He made it sound like it had all been work related, but in reality, he and Sarah had made the trip to see Carl. No—that wasn't quite right. Jim had driven Sarah up to see her son. And Jim had sat at the kitchen table, relatively ignored until Jennifer, Carl's wife, asked if he needed another cup of coffee or Todd, Jim's grandson, shot him with his latest water gun.

Mildred clutched her shirt tighter. "This whole thing is moving too fast," she began, looking Jim square in the eye. "This isn't some joyride. Not for me. This person, this *jerk*, who left me his place—it's complicated. It's embarrassing. It's honestly something I've tried for years to forget. He was someone who barged into my life when I was young."

Jim nodded. "One of those."

"And just when I've decided to start a new life with new friends and new experiences, here he is all over again."

"Well, that's a relief," Jim admitted.

"What is?"

"I didn't think I was going to make it that long behind the wheel for such a long stretch. Bad back."

"Bad liar," Mildred corrected. "Did you hear anything I said about the pitch of a lie?"

Jim shrugged. "But it is the kind of lie everyone else will believe. Blame it on me and my bad back, Millie. Make me the reason for not rushing straight up and back. We'll drive up, spend the night at a hotel in Iowa City. Give you time to catch your breath, get your head together. After a good meal and a night's rest, we'll get you out to the property, let you take your look. Sound good?"

Mildred nodded slowly, hesitantly. "Aren't you going to ask me to tell you the whole story? You'd be going up there without knowing anything about the situation. Doesn't that make you feel strange?"

"Nope. It's your story to tell. You'll tell it when you want to. If not, that's okay, too. I just can't stand the thought of you up there in your room slamming the phone down every time it rings for the next twenty-five years."

"Me, neither," Mildred sighed.

"Call that lawyer," Jim said. "Two cars. Tell him we all have to go. I mean it. And you don't have to tell him you need moral support if you don't want to. You still need to help Hannah. I've got to give that Bryan character a few more of my sage quotes for that paper of his. And I really need to get this thing out and moving again," he muttered.

His eyes blurred a moment when he glanced into the reflective finish on the red hood. In the smear of colors, he saw Norma's face staring back at him. Norma's—not Sarah's. And he had to stand still a moment just to catch his breath.

Friday morning, Jim dressed in his luckiest golf shirt and his whitest sneakers. He raced to the parking lot, where he raised the garage door, an overnight bag in his hand. He tossed the bag in the trunk, then leaned in through the driver's side, removing his vials of pills from the glove compartment. He plucked the picture of Sarah from the rearview mirror, too, and placed it all inside a small gray lock box. The top wouldn't latch quite right with the vials inside, though. For a minute, he wondered if he'd have to sit on it, like the suitcases he'd packed quickly in hotel rooms in his eager rush to get home to Sarah.

He sighed with relief as he finally slid the closed box beneath the front seat. He'd have to be a bit of a magician to get his pills out from under the seat without anyone seeing. But it was the safest place he could think of. He'd been on enough vacations to know that somebody was bound to pop that glove compartment looking for a map or extra sunglasses or a snack.

The engine grumbled like an animal being roused from sleep, unsure yet if the creature responsible for waking her was friend or foe. "Easy, Sally," Jim cooed as he pulled toward the entrance of Granite Ridge. The entire group was already waiting, standing like the accused in a lineup. But the crime, Jim suspected, had yet to be committed.

"Murder," he mumbled, staring at Norma's hard face. That, he knew, could well be tomorrow's headline: *Murder of Ms. Mildred Sudbury.* Mildred seemed to know as much, having chosen a spot as far from Norma as she could get, on the far left of the line of strained, confused faces. Were it not for the look of pure fear she wore, she could have doubled for an ad for a travel magazine, in wrinkle-resistant navy slacks and a wildly patterned scarf, a bun big enough to cast shade across her forehead. She slipped on a pair of large sunglasses that gave her eyes a bug-like appearance.

On the other end of the line, Norma looked both perturbed yet practical in khaki slacks and bright yellow sandals, a lime green T-shirt beneath a long-sleeved floral blouse, and a sun-blocking yellow ball cap. Bryan and Hannah stood—almost protectively, it seemed to Jim—between Norma and Mildred. Bryan in his usual high-top black Converse, walking shorts, and a *Catch-22* T-shirt, and Hannah in a white sleeveless blouse and a not-quite-right-for-an-Iowa-City-journey multi-colored gauzy skirt that kept snapping in the summer breeze like the sail on a boat. An outfit chosen to catch Bryan's eye, Jim figured. At that point, though, the only thing skirt was managing to catch was Bryan's left calf.

Jim pulled behind a still-running Honda CR-V.

The taillights died, the door popped open, and a man exited the SUV wearing an expensive-looking pale green button-down shirt and khakis. He had the look of a man whose life was well ordered: no wrinkles, no stains, perfectly combed steel-gray hair, clean-shaven face. He was the kind of man who had never collected complications. Some people just went through life like that—breezing from one day to another, meeting each challenge like it was something they'd seen before. Others, Jim knew firsthand, went through life with dilemmas and problems sticking to their bodies like static cling.

"Gurtler," he introduced himself in a friendly tone, extending a hand through the Mustang's window.

Jim nodded, shaking his hand with confidence. He glared at the lawyer's car as he stepped into the parking lot. He hadn't planned on an SUV. They could all fit in Gurtler's vehicle with room to spare. Getting his "red thing" out was looking more and more unnecessary.

"Okay," Jim announced, clapping his hands before anyone else could make the same observation. "Me, Norma, and Bryan in my car, and Mildred, Gurtler, and Hannah in the other."

"Uh," Hannah yelped, holding up a finger. "I thought—couldn't we—divvy the seats up in a different way? Maybe Norma ride with Mil—"

"Nope," Jim insisted. "Only way it works out. This is business, not pleasure. Two papers to finish. We have to make sure you get plenty of one-on-one time with Mildred along the way. Bryan's got a whole notebook of fantastically condescending questions for me, don't you, Bry? Too many voices, too many conversations going on at once means nothing substantial gets done."

Hannah wrinkled her face into a wordless *shoot*. Bryan adjusted his glasses; the eyes behind the lenses pleaded with Jim to let him ride with Hannah anyway. And Jim felt for the kid, because he was in the same situation. Because what he wanted was time with Norma. More than anything. More than he wanted to help Mildred. More than he wanted to finally find a purpose for the Mustang that had so easily come roaring back into his life.

Jim shrugged apologetically. "Plenty of leg stretching bound to take place along the way. And don't forget, we're all staying the night in Iowa City. All sorts of trouble there we can get into."

Hannah nodded reluctantly before hoisting the strap of a backpack over her shoulder and picking up an enormous textbook—*The Complete Shakespeare*—from the sidewalk beside her feet. Bryan clicked his pen and climbed into the backseat of the Mustang while Jim loaded Norma's bag in the trunk. And suddenly, they were off in a mini-parade, Gurtler's SUV rumbling ahead of them all.

"No GPS," Bryan said, jotting something in his spiral notebook.

Jim didn't answer. He was too busy sneaking glances at Norma. She looked awfully stiff there in the passenger seat.

He squirmed, the leather seat squeaking underneath him; Jim felt as out of sorts as Norma looked. He hadn't driven on city streets in two years; forty miles an hour was uncomfortably fast. The steering wheel wobbled strangely, feeling looser than he remembered. The hum of the tires was higher pitched, louder—almost like a scream. And even though he'd wanted Norma in that passenger seat right from the very moment the idea had popped into his head in the dining room, it was odd to find someone other than Sarah beside him. Odd, too, that they'd begun this new outing without a single daisy with a red ribbon tied around the stem. Norma didn't seem the type. And besides, this wasn't exactly a date. Though Jim wished, silently, that it was. And wished, silently, that they were back at the Ridge at the same time. This was silly. The whole thing. And strange and—what was he doing?

And while he was at it, what did Norma want? Was she going to spend the entire trip with her arms crossed over her chest? Was she not going to speak to him at all for the next two days? How was he ever supposed to get her to soften toward him with that Bryan kid in the back?

Yet again—what in God's name was Jim doing?

"Are you using a map?" Bryan persisted. "A paper map? What's the reason for that choice?"

"What's GPS stand for, anyway? Graduated Policy Sales?" Jim tried to joke. "All those fancy mapping things seem pretty useless, frankly. And as I'm sure you already know, considering the age of your own wheels, the 'Stang didn't come with GPS. Way after her time. And the more miles you rack up, the more you realize mucking with add-ons just leads to all sorts of unnecessary problems."

"Do you, now?" Norma muttered. "Could have fooled me. This whole trip is mucking with somebody else's stuff, isn't it?"

Jim grinned. She was talking to him. That was a start.

Before he had a chance to make much use of it, though, Bryan blurted, "Are you the Mustang's original owner?"

"Yup," Jim said proudly.

Norma tightened her arms around her middle. And she shrank—just a little; Norma wasn't exactly the wilting type. Still, though, Jim saw it—a definite shrink. A droop of the shoulders, a drop of the chin toward the chest. It made him remember the way Norma'd behaved sitting beside her own daughter that first evening Jim had joined her for dinner.

He pulled in beside a gas pump at a Shell station on the outskirts of town. "Why don't you go get us some beef jerky?" he asked Bryan.

"Pulls out my fillings," Norma grumbled.

"Well. Beef jerky and Super Glue, then," Jim said.

Bryan's eyes darted back and forth between the two front seats. "Oh!" he finally said, blushing. "Sorry, I'll just—" He motioned toward the convenience store and scurried to climb out of the back.

"What's *your* beef, Normal?" Jim asked, once Bryan was halfway across the lot, out of earshot.

"I'm in your ex-wife's car while on a trip to see your new girlfriend's house. What do you think?"

"Good grief, woman. Mildred is my neighbor. That's it."

"For now. Until you can upgrade. Then *I'm* your neighbor—and that's it."

"Oh, come on. This thing was my excuse to have an adventure with you. Not Mildred. Okay? After all that teasing on your end, I couldn't exactly get this old car out for just anything. Some trip to Walgreens wasn't going to cut it. Did it honestly never cross your mind that I'd been waiting all along for some special moment to get my 'red thing' out? Hmm?"

Norma only turned toward the window.

"And while we're at it, at our age, lives are crowded. Okay? Neither one of us is a blank slate. We've got kids and grandkids. Your late husband. My late wife. Everything that happened to you up to the point you moved into the Ridge. Even without clueless Bryan, without Mildred and her problems, without that lawyer what's-his-name, without shy little Hannah, this trip would still be crammed. Wouldn't this car still be full if it was just you and me driving around?"

Norma unfolded her arms—for the first time since Jim had pulled away from Granite Ridge—as Bryan climbed into the backseat. He eyed the two of them. "I could go get some barbecue sauce for the jerky, if you need me to."

Norma shook her head. "Naw. Don't want to wear you out, Peter."

"Peter?"

"You must have a Peter Pan complex. Isn't that why you're so fascinated with us old people?"

"Interesting diagnosis, doctor," Jim said.

"And while we're at it, you know, I worked with computers and networks at the end of my career, too. Actually, I'd been watching them grow more compact and efficient for decades. My husband and I didn't exactly sell abacuses. When, exactly, do you become a 'geron'? Sixty-five and retired? Sixty-three and still employed? Fifty? Fifty-five?"

"Well, I—" Bryan tugged at his lip.

"She's about to put you in your place, son," Jim warned.

"If you're going to write a paper, write a damned paper," Norma thundered. "About real 'gerons' using real technology. Not about wrinkly farts falling and pressing the buttons on necklaces that call nurses to come put them back in their walkers, stick a fresh pacifier in their mouth."

She swiveled to shoot him a glare; Bryan started to grow red.

"Don't tell me that was actually what you were going to write about," she grumbled.

"Well—I wasn't—exactly. Mostly. Well. Yes."

"Kid, give me that notebook," she announced, snatching it out of Bryan's hands before he had a chance to save it.

"But—see—I was just getting started—"

"That's exactly right," Norma agreed, tearing pages from the spine. "You're getting started right now."

Jim was laughing as he popped the door and began to circle around to the passenger side.

"What's up with you?" Norma asked, handing the notebook back and wadding Bryan's scribbled-on pages in her hands. "Think I'm being too hard on your kid back there?"

"Nope. I think you're just the right person to get us all where we need to be." He opened Norma's door and motioned her toward the driver's side. "Scoot over."

"Scooting's for nineteen-year-olds. What are you after?"

Jim tossed her the keys. "You get behind the wheel. I don't know when I've ever seen the world from this side of the car."

"You know where we're going, though."

"I'll help navigate. But you choose the roads. I have a feeling the trip will be infinitely more interesting with you behind the wheel. We'll still meet up with Mildred's crew in Iowa City tonight. But how we get there is up to us. Isn't that right, Normal?"

She grinned as she pulled herself out of the car, pushed past Jim, and circled to the driver's side.

Jim laughed from the base of his gut when Norma left black marks pulling out of the parking lot.

17.

"So Prospero was a big fat quitter," Hannah grumbled from the backseat. "He broke his staff and couldn't be a magician anymore. He quit."

"Well, you see, Hannah," Mildred stammered, "When Shakespeare wrote...When he included... Prospero symbolized..." She squirmed, wishing she'd taken a seat next to Hannah in the back. It was uncomfortable being so close to Gurtler. Mostly because it made her feel like she was a student teacher whose performance was being evaluated. He knew she'd been an English instructor. And rather than inspiring Hannah, so far, she was only making her sink deeper into complete Shakespearian hatred. Mildred was developing the whole horrible-piano-recital feeling; her clothes scratched, she started to sweat, and everything she tried to offer Hannah was one wrong, sour note after another.

"You're going to break your own staff soon," Gurtler chimed in. "When you graduate. Right? Just like Prospero. You won't be a student anymore—but you won't be quitting, either. You'll just be moving on. To a new part of life."

"Huh," Hannah muttered from the backseat.

Mildred shot him a look from the corner of her eye.

Gurtler shrugged. "I taught in grad school. The lit thing, you know. Before I went to law school." And he smiled. A sickening smile, Mildred noted. Smug.

As she continued to stare, she realized he had on a new shirt. It had that department store crispness to it. And that was possibly a new haircut, too. He was out to impress, but why? And why was it so important to her that she looked capable in front of him? Why did he make her so nervous?

Hannah's phone went off. She raced to answer, as if anxious for any excuse to change the subject. When she saw who'd called, her voice turned instantly high-pitched and shaky, betraying any attempt to cover her own nerves.

Mildred's fingers flew to her throat as she wondered if she had sounded the same just a moment ago, trying to impress Gurtler as she'd talked Hannah through her paper.

Of course not! she told herself. Around her, the car fell silent as Hannah paused to listen to Bryan. *I'm not trying to wow him. I'm trying to show him he's wrong about me. I'm no hot number. Thomas was a red beaded dress, something I wore once that's giving this Gurtler character the idea that I'm some sort of sexy siren. That's all. I do not have a schoolgirl crush. Of all things! At my age! Ms. Sudbury doesn't do crushes.*

Gurtler raised his salt-and-pepper eyebrows

at Mildred. *Bryan*, he mouthed. And placed his right hand over his chest, thumping it quickly (and softly, so that only Mildred could hear) to imitate a rapidly beating heart.

Mildred found herself grinning in agreement. And liking, despite herself, that Gurtler was teasing her. Or smiling at her. Or sharing his thoughts with her. Whatever that little exchange had just been, Mildred had liked it.

"Okay, um, I—" Hannah leaned forward, sticking her face into the space between Mildred and Gurtler. "They're choosing their own route to Iowa City," she said. "Jim's car. We won't see them on the road, but they'll meet up with us at the hotel tonight." Her voice was thick and low with utter disappointment.

"That's nice of him to call," Gurtler offered.

"Yeah." Hannah brightened a bit. "It is."

She leaned back, continuing her conversation with Bryan—quieter now, as though she didn't want Mildred and Gurtler listening in.

Gurtler glanced in the rearview. "Now that Hannah's occupied, I've finally got a moment to give you this." He pulled a fat business envelope from the pocket in the door, the space usually reserved for wet umbrellas and muddy gloves.

Mildred clenched her jaw as she eyed the envelope, yellowing around the corners, her name in ink in the center. "What is that?" she asked hesitantly.

"It's from Thomas."

"Damn him," Mildred snapped.

Hannah jumped, leaning forward. "Ms. Sudbury?" she asked, wearing a fearful expression. "Is everything—?"

"Fine, fine," Mildred said, waving her away. She tried to wave Gurtler away, too, but he pressed the envelope closer toward her.

"Take it. You're going to see his house. You shouldn't see it without reading that, too."

"What kind of mission are you on, exactly?" Mildred hissed. "Why do you care?"

"Why did anybody care about Romeo and Juliet?"

"I'm sorry to disappoint you, but we weren't Romeo and Juliet, and ours was not a great love story."

"I beg to differ."

"Look, Mr. Gurtler—"

"Ouch. Mister stings a bit, coming from you. Aaron. Please."

"You've got our—whatever it was—completely wrong. You've romanticized the whole thing. I read something into it that wasn't there, too. That's easy to do, especially for people like us, who love our books, our stories. I'll give you that. But you've got to stop thinking that this was something glorious, something beautiful. I was lied to and made a fool of. And I feel as though I'm being made a fool of all over again. I can't help but think this is some kind of joke."

"Why would you think that?"

"Why wouldn't I? Why would he do this? Who was I to Thomas Clyde, other than a moment of pure recklessness? I feel like he planned on one more good practical joke before he died, and I'm the brunt of it. I can't help but imagine that when I get there, the only thing I'll find is a giant jack-in-the-box that'll pop up and shout, 'Gotcha!' To add to the complete and total humiliation of this whole thing, I'll have to endure it in front of an audience."

Gurtler just kept poking her arm with the pointed corner of the envelope. "Take it."

"No."

"I mean it."

"So do I. Quit making me act like I'm eight."

Mildred turned her face toward the window.

Gurtler sighed. "Prospero had a magical staff that he wielded. But maybe, sometimes, we also wield a grudge like a sword. Or anger. Anger can be used the same way. We just go into the world, waving it around, wreaking all kinds of havoc. Sometimes, breaking a 'staff' isn't sad—more like a release." He slid the envelope into Mildred's lap.

She stared at Thomas's handwriting, still familiar after all these years. Her first instinct was to roll down the window and toss the envelope out. The same way her first instinct was to refuse anything Thomas Clyde wanted to give her. But curiosity clamped hold of her, and instead, she slipped it into the front pocket of her purse.

Hannah rattled on quietly in the backseat, still engaged in what was becoming an increasingly longer—and apparently emotional—conversation with Bryan. The kind of conversation that came complete with a couple of whispered sentences and a barely audible, "Yeah, it'll be good to see you, too, when we all get there..."

"Young love," Gurtler sighed wistfully.

18.

Norma loved driving Jim's car. It felt awkward at first, but cars always did—each one of them had their own set of wobbles and quirks. Still, though, the basic dials on the dash, the old-fashioned slim steering wheel all reminded her of the early cars she'd owned with Charlie. Or the Caddy her father had owned when he taught her to drive. And it took her all the way back to the sixteen-year-old Norma. The Norma she'd been behind that Caddy's wheel. The Norma she'd been in Charlie's Dodge Dart, sitting in the center of the bench seat just to be closer to him.

And that made her wonder about how Jim's Saturday nights had played out in this car. She imagined him and Sarah at movie theaters and burger joints and even her own parents' country club—because they all seemed interchangeable somehow. Oh, sure, Jim and Sarah were college sweethearts who'd met after Jim had returned from his stint in the military (she'd dug that much out of him over their dinners), and Norma and Charlie were a little younger when they'd begun exchanging smiles and flirting over high school locker doors. But weren't the dreams of youth always identical? To pass algebra. Kiss the boy. Cross the city limits of a childhood hometown too small for two stoplights. Choose your own life. Press the gas pedal down as far as it will go. Maybe youth itself was always the same repetitive story churned out on an assembly line—just like all the 1965 Mustangs that had rolled across the factory floor.

Yes, Norma knew exactly how Sarah had once felt in that Mustang—no different than it had felt to be Norma in Charlie's Dodge. And Jim had surely felt no different than she'd hoped Charlie had, when she'd first become part of the excitement glowing there in his bright-as-a-movie-screen eyes. Jim had harbored dreams of his own, dreams of Sarah. And some of them had come true and some of them—well. It wasn't that they didn't. They just came true in the way of reality, which was always far less flashy than what you had originally imagined. Families and pay raises and new houses—they never really did have that red carpet impact you'd pictured. Probably, though, even the real red carpet, stretched out for the world's biggest stars, just felt like a plain old rug—with a bunch of dirty footprints on it.

Jim snapped her picture as they flew past another one of those green mile markers (what they were actually measuring, Norma'd never quite figured out). She flinched against the flash. "Listen," she snapped, "you don't go just taking a woman's picture after a certain point—no more than you ask her about her age. Especially when she's behind the wheel."

Jim laughed and snapped another.

"Sunglasses," Norma barked, cringing against

the flash. "You want me to run us off the road?"

While Jim leaned forward to dig her glasses out of her purse, she raised his old thirty-five millimeter and snapped a picture of him.

"Hey!"

"What's good for the goose..." she said, taking her sunglasses from him. She had acquired what felt like fifty pairs of glasses—reading glasses, sunglasses—half of them had already been strewn across the dash as she'd used them to consult Jim's road maps during various rest stops.

As she finally got the sunglasses seated on her nose, she glanced up into the rearview at Bryan, silently staring down at the blank top page in his notebook. Now that Bryan's list of questions were wadded up in Norma's pocket, all he could do was listen to Jim and Norma rattle on, one anecdote bouncing to the next, with rarely a single thread connecting them.

"Whole world feels as impersonal as a cold call," Jim said, more to Norma than to Bryan. "Just a bunch of clicks on a keyboard. Never did know how you could get anything real done on a blog. Even the word—*blog*. Sounds like a disease. Wash up after you shake his hand. He's got the *blogs*."

"Face-to-face sales worked for us, too," Norma chimed in, glad that her ball cap was keeping her chin-length hair from blowing into her eyes. She shifted into third gear seamlessly, no hesitations or jerks from the motor. "Had a few salesmen who would come to the store, show us the latest and greatest office machines. When it's your own store, you always have so much to do, you take the best things that fall in your lap—and then recommend them to your customers. But only after you've tried them out. Charlie always insisted on trying our products out ourselves. Encouraged trust. Meant we always knew how to use the latest and greatest."

168

In the backseat, Bryan began tapping his pen against his notebook.

Jim glanced behind his shoulder. "You look worried, son."

"I don't think we're helping his thesis," Norma agreed. "He wants to write about technology, and we're telling him it's the face-to-face time that works. As much as he claims to be old-school, he still believes in the superiority of gadgets."

"Maybe he should write a paper about senior women being at home behind the wheel," Jim said and winked.

"Think I'm doing okay?"

"Looks great from over here," he said.

Norma tried not to beam like a headlight. But the chuckle that slipped from Jim told her she hadn't quite succeeded.

She was getting hungry, though. And they really had made pretty good time. She'd shown the boys that she could hold her own in the fast lane. Time to try something a little off the beaten path. "You trust my decision-making capabilities, right?" Norma said.

"Absolutely," Jim said, settling deeper into the passenger seat.

Norma grinned and veered toward the off-ramp, past another green highway marker—this one indicating she was taking them toward Fulton.

"Whatever happens in Fulton stays in Fulton," Jim joked.

"Just go on and laugh," Norma warned him as she slipped down the ramp. "A real woman knows where to find the action anywhere. And she doesn't need an app for it, either," she added, tossing her eyes into the rearview mirror just in time to watch Bryan shake his head and slump with disappointment.

The Mustang eased down the streets at the speed

of a teenage cruise. This, too, felt achingly familiar. Norma had loved those Saturday nights that she and Charlie had joined the rest of the kids lining the streets, idling at drive-ins, hanging out in parking lots. What the teenage portion of life called for was being seen, after all. Being out on the weekend meant you were somebody. Sidewalks were no longer littered with saddle shoes but pretty flats. Hands no longer held the softballs and earthworms of childhood but wove between a boy's fingers.

Just like her childhood days when she was expected to be home by dinner, or her teenage days when she was expected to be in by eleven, there was still a curfew of sorts. A place she—and everyone else in the Mustang—had to be at sundown. People who were expecting her. She had a check-in. But right now, these hours were hers, all hers—just as they'd been when she was young. It made her feel electric.

She drove along slowly, squinting at the line of downtown businesses in ancient turn-of-the-century buildings. At the far end of the street, Norma saw the darkened glass of the restaurant. A bar, actually. With a couple of semis, a motorcycle, and a small assortment of beat-up old cars out front. One missing a back windshield. A few so dented, they looked a little like crushed soda cans.

"Uh, what are we doing here?" Jim asked as she steered into the lot.

"We're going to lunch," Norma said simply. "Looks like the perfect place for barbecue. Says so right there." She pointed at the Pappy's neon sign hanging just beside the advertisements for Coors and Bud.

"I bet, after dark, there's a sign in the front window that flashes 'No Fat Chicks,'" Jim teased.

"You are so old-fashioned. Nobody's fat, and no one calls women chicks anymore. Do they, Bryan?"

170

Norma asked, leaning backward slightly. "Surely there are far more colorful demeaning terms for girls these days."

"Well, but, see, I think this place is actually—" Bryan started.

"Oh, please," Norma groaned. "You two aren't afraid of a little bar, are you?"

The two men exchanged glances. "It's just that I saw plenty of places like this on the road. And I knew enough to avoid them," Jim grumbled.

"Yeah," Bryan chimed in. "There are bars and then there are—you know—*bars*. I don't want to walk into the middle of a fight."

Norma gathered her purse and tugged herself out from behind the wheel. "I'm starving. And you can't deny this place smells great. Bet they've got a bunch of ribs smoking right now." She threw her shoulders back and raced toward the entrance.

Behind her, she could hear the doors of the Mustang reluctantly clicking open.

Inside, it took a minute for her eyes to adjust to the darkness. Once they finally did, she realized there wasn't another woman in sight. Only several tables of casually dressed men. *Casually dressed*, she kept repeating in her mind, as though these guys were all in khakis, stopping by for a drink before heading back to the office. The reality was obviously far darker— danker. She got that danger-approaching ripple that usually accompanied after-dark alleys.

But she ignored the feeling and took a few of her signature purpose-driven strides straight for the bar where a man was wiping down glasses.

As she slid onto the stool, she realized he was actually far younger than she'd thought at first glance—a rough late-thirties. In the sunlight, she figured he'd have maybe only one or two long wiry gray hairs in the brown mop that stretched down to his shoulders—he'd grown it out, she figured, in an attempt to detract from his widening belly. Ten years ago, he'd probably been sexy-dangerous. But now he seemed to be settling into the idea that the sexy portion of his life was behind him. Glasses clinked as he stacked them behind the bar.

He snorted a laugh when he saw who'd just taken up three stools in front of him.

"We just—we're on the road—" Bryan offered nervously.

The bartender grunted, crossed his arms over his chest.

"Lunch," Jim muttered.

"The special?"

"What's the special?" Bryan squeaked.

"Pulled pork. Fries. Beer on tap."

"Rack of ribs," Norma corrected. "Fries. Soda."

"Two," Jim said.

"Got some baked beans?" Bryan asked cautiously, like he was still expecting to feel a fist on the side of his head at any moment.

The man nodded slowly, but his eyes never left Norma. "Nobody orders ribs."

"You have them, don't you?"

"Yeah," he said quietly.

"So?"

He paused, finally uncrossing his arms to slip into the back. In the darkness of the bar, Norma, Jim, and Bryan fell into relative anonymity. But when the bartender banged through the swinging doors carrying three paper plates piled with ribs, fries, baked beans, and half a loaf of white bread, Norma felt like he might as well be shining a spotlight on them.

Norma took a bite, moaning as she chewed. "It's much better than it smelled," she told the bartender, who beamed.

On the two stools to her right, Jim and Bryan scarfed their lunches, heads down, as though racing to finish before they were assassinated.

"You do a lot of barbecue business?" Norma asked.

"Some. Enough to keep a barbecue sign out front. Guys who come here are mostly interested in cheap beer. Sandwiches do all right."

"They're missing out," Norma said, her eye falling on a nearby dartboard. She grinned, remembering the way that Charlie had begun to wave his hands in defeat when she'd come to him wielding her darts, challenging him to another round.

She glanced over at Bryan, a plan beginning to form. *Take your business to the highest level,* Charlie had always taught her. Time to show Bryan how they used to do just that...and how a senior mind and body still functioned.

"Catering?" she asked.

The bartender threw his head back and howled with laughter. "Oh, yeah. Sure. Me catering."

"Why not?"

"I'm not exactly the type for white tablecloths and wine glasses, if you didn't notice." He turned to grab an empty mug from one of the men seated at the bar and tugged at a beer tap, providing a refill before being asked.

Norma elbowed Jim. "Isn't there some sort of summer festival at the Ridge?" she asked quietly.

"Fourth of July, I guess. But it's not really much of a festival. They just kind of put some chairs out in the parking lot and we suck on watermelon and watch the fireworks from the country club."

"That's too soon. Fourth of July's next week already," Norma mused, wiping her mouth.

"I heard Linda—you know, the activities

director—wants to do something for Labor Day. The kind of thing you could invite family to, let the grandkids run wild—if you like that kind of thing." He rolled his eyes.

"A picnic," Bryan chimed in.

"Something like that," Jim said. "She's always looking for Ridge events that turn into recruitment days for more paying residents."

"Hey!" Norma shouted at the bartender. "Play you for lunch."

"Play me what for lunch?" he asked, thunking the mug back down on the bar, in front of what was apparently a perpetually thirsty patron.

"Three bullseyes," she said, pointing at the dartboard. "If I hit three bullseyes, we get free lunch. The three of us."

He wheezed a laugh.

"Don't think I'm the type?"

He shrugged.

Norma peeled herself from her stool. Heart beating hard enough to shake the collar on her shirt, she tugged the darts from the board, backed up behind the line drawn on the tile floor. *Don't look over your shoulder*, she scolded herself. *They'll be watching.* All of the men in the place—not just the two she walked in with. If she looked behind her shoulder, she'd wobble. She squinted, aimed, and let go of the first dart.

Bullseye.

But Norma didn't relax or celebrate. Instead, she held her body steady, kept her eye fixed to the same spot on the dartboard. She threw the next two darts one after another; they thunked against the board.

Bullseyes.

She walked calmly to her stool accompanied by a spattering of applause.

"And now, I'm out three free meals," the

bartender complained.

"Nope," Norma said. "You've got your first catering gig."

"Lady, what're you talking about?"

"We're from the Granite Ridge Retirement Community in Springfield. We need some good food for an end-of-summer picnic. You're a bullseye. Trust me. I know bullseyes. I know types. You're the barbecue type. The cook type. The *catering* type."

"I have to think about it."

"Thinking just means you lose any guts you had in the first place," Norma told him.

He offered a half-grin, leaning against the counter.

"But—you guys are residents," Bryan protested. "You don't have the ability—"

"I can call the place right now," Jim offered, pulling his phone from his pants pocket. "Linda the activities director owes me, since I took you on," he reminded Bryan. "She's always trying to get me to participate in something. Ball-throwing, jumping ridiculousness. Charades." He cringed. "She's asked me a hundred times to come to resident meetings, feed her some new input. Well, now, she's going to get it."

Norma grinned as Jim dialed the Ridge, asked for Linda. He launched into a spiel of his own, explaining where they were and what delicious barbecue they'd stumbled upon. He held his phone toward the bartender, who paused, considering.

He tucked his hair behind his ear before finally pressing Jim's cell against his head. "Labor Day," he said. "Yeah, actually—yeah," he agreed, staring at Norma. "I can do that."

"And that," Norma announced, leaning around Jim to get Bryan's attention, "is why old-fashioned face-to-face encounters still work—and why so many of us feel no need for your silly technology."

Bryan stopped chewing, the light of inspiration sparkling in his eyes.

19.

Gurtler pulled to a roadside rest stop just outside of Columbia. Thumped the wheel. Started to undo his seatbelt. "Nope," he said, latched the belt, and pulled back out of his space—all before shutting off his engine.

"I thought we were going to stop," Mildred protested. "I'd really like to stretch my legs."

"Yeah. This place looked perfect," Hannah said, sticking her face between Mildred and Gurtler again. "I need to get some thoughts down for my paper. I brought my laptop. I thought I'd grab a picnic table, write awhile, and then Ms. Sudbury could read it."

"Not here, though," Gurtler insisted. "Totally wrong setting. I mean, we're in a college town. We're all literature people here, talking Shakespeare. Surely there's a better spot for us than this. Bet Hannah back there would prefer a nice coffee shop where she could get some work done and a bite to eat, too. And I'd like to treat Mildred here to a walking lunch."

Hannah perked. "That'd be great," she agreed.

Rather than chiming in, Mildred crossed her arms over her middle. She was feeling off-kilter and frankly annoyed. Mostly, what was making her feel so strange was the envelope she'd shoved into the front pocket of her purse. What did Thomas want to tell her? Did she want to hear it? Would his words only tear her open, make her heart beat more furiously than it ever had out there on the street, in the rain, with the headlights of Thomas's car trailing her?

Gurtler steered them all toward downtown. But the vibe was more small-town yesterday than modern college city. The kind of place with hundred-plus-year-old stone buildings lining the street. Quaint. Quiet.

Gurtler parked in front of a brightly painted coffee shop, and Hannah instantly gathered her things, scrambling to get out of his car.

"Aren't you guys coming?" her muffled voice asked.

Gurtler rolled his window down. "Walking lunch, remember?"

"Oh." Her face fell, like a child being ditched on the playground, told she couldn't play with the rest of her class.

"You don't need us interrupting your work," Gurtler told her. "You need time to concentrate. Besides, there are no cars here—you're sure to have the whole place to yourself. Like working in a library."

Hannah brightened. "Meet you guys back here in an hour, then?" she asked.

He gave her a thumbs-up.

"Good luck, Hannah!" Mildred called out. "Can't wait to read it."

Hannah paused to turn a strained smile toward Mildred and hold up two hands' worth of crossed fingers. As she raced for the front step of the coffee shop, a summer breeze grabbed hold of her flimsy, voluminous skirt and threw it into her face.

"I feel that way most times," Mildred said, watching Hannah struggle to untangle herself from the fabric.

"Don't we all," Gurtler laughed. "Come with me."

They began to walk quietly—in step—side-by-side. The air was getting hot. Not really oppressive, not a scorcher, but hot enough to make Gurtler's walking lunch idea grow uncomfortable quickly.

The summer she'd spent with Thomas had been mild, Mildred remembered. Almost like one long giant sweet spring—until autumn came along and whacked her upside the head with its cold hand.

"Do you think Bryan will reciprocate our fair Juliet's feelings?" he asked her.

Mildred took in a deep breath, grateful that Gurtler was yanking her away from her memories—grateful, too, that he was comparing Romeo and Juliet to someone other than her and Thomas. "Probably. They just seem like such an odd match. Don't they?"

"Which is what makes them perfect," he said.

Mildred shook her head in disbelief as he pushed her into a fast food joint to buy two plain hamburgers and two iced teas. "The thing is," he told her as he forked over a whopping four dollars and sixty-nine cents for their meal, "two people who don't really fit in anywhere else wind up taking solace in each other. Forging a connection that's almost stronger than two people who make perfect sense together. I mean, they're so surprised to have found each other. Sometimes, utter surprise connects people, too."

Gurtler led her back outside. Together, they peeled the wrappers from their hamburgers and sipped their teas as they window shopped. Or, more accurately, as Gurtler window shopped and Mildred watched him. He was timid about nothing: His first bite took out more than a third of his burger. Each step took similarly enormous bites out of the sidewalk. He hummed as he walked, expecting neither to trip over any flaws in the cement or find an overly strong onion on the patty. He seemed to enjoy everything. More than that—he acted as though he expected the world to keep on offering him beautiful things to be appreciated. He had probably thoroughly liked Thomas. Of course he'd liked Thomas. He was, in fact, quite a likable person. She had liked him herself. Though "like" was also a watered-down version of what she'd felt for him.

There it was, in all its ridiculousness—in just a few short weeks, she'd fallen for him. Hard. Fallen for his cleft chin and the way the skin in the corners of his eyes crinkled when he smiled at her. For the way he held her while she read poetry to him. For the daydreams he sent popping to life inside her, like a string of shiny soap bubbles. And this, too, came back to her in an uncomfortably hot, violent gust: She'd loved the way he'd gone after her. Loved that someone like Thomas— so polished and collected and adult—had pursued her. Loved how much like a woman that had made her feel.

It was an awful thing to think: The way Thomas had pursued her had made her feel womanly. It was like a line from some ancient misogynist text—but it was also a hundred percent true.

"What'd you stop for? Mildred? Hello. Mildred?

She blinked herself back into the present. She'd quit walking. There she stood, mid-chew, holding the straw of her iced tea cup an inch from her lip.

She swallowed, took another few steps forward.

But her thoughts had made her feet wobbly. She was unsteady, and she staggered.

"You okay?"

Mildred nodded, taking another bite. The pickle was especially sour, and the burger had a lot of charcoal in it—but somehow, right then, the slightly bitter tastes were good, too. Or fitting, at least. Matching the slightly bitter twinge of her own thoughts.

Gurtler waited for her to catch up before he rattled on, "I bet these sidewalks are packed with students when regular Mizzou semesters are in swing. I'm sure that the literature students walk this way. It's just got an aura about it, doesn't it? There's got to be a bookstore around here somewhere. Right?"

His excitement spewed out of him, spraying the sidewalk and the closest plate glass windows and even Mildred. It made Gurtler seem far younger than his actual years.

"Ahh!"

Mildred flinched; she wasn't sure if Gurtler had merely lunged toward an awning-covered doorway or if he'd just been abducted.

But she sighed with relief—and chuckled at herself—when he grasped hold of a door and shouted, "I knew there'd have to be a bookstore in this town somewhere!"

The interior had that lovely, hypnotic smell of books—used books, which possessed completely different scents than new volumes. These pages had been turned before—they'd absorbed someone else's perfume. They'd known hands; they'd been caressed before.

Mildred watched the eager way Gurtler mindlessly shoved his greasy burger wrapper into his clean khaki pocket and attacked the nearest shelf.

"Why did you quit your lit studies?" Mildred

asked. "Give up on teaching?"

"I didn't," he said simply, turning a surprised expression toward her. "It's all still here, Mildred. The love. It didn't go anywhere. Even if I did choose something else to do for a living—something that would allow me to make more money. I didn't have the excuse of a family to provide for. Wasn't taking care of anyone but myself. I could certainly have afforded to make a different decision. But the love of literature didn't go anywhere. True love never does, does it?"

"You never married?"

He shook his head.

"Wasn't important to you?"

"No—the opposite. I took it seriously. Probably way too seriously. Was never going to marry if it wasn't a have-to thing. Wasn't going to be something I did because I'd suddenly gotten to be the right age for it, or because the rest of the world told me it was something I was supposed to do."

Mildred nodded.

"I like that you took it seriously, too," he said. He held her eye, telling her with that look that he meant it. That it wasn't an empty compliment. Mildred was actually starting to wonder if he'd ever given anyone an empty compliment, ever said anything that was even slightly insincere.

"Maybe too seriously," Mildred whispered.

He shrugged. "Romantics are that way," he conceded. "Aren't we?"

Mildred wasn't sure what she thought of his label.

"I also just didn't like listening to the sound of my own voice all the time," he went on, picking up with his browsing again, pulling a few volumes from the closest shelf to get a look at the covers. "Most people love to pontificate. I couldn't stand the idea of foisting my ideas onto a bunch of kids. Making them agree with me. I mean—no offense. Not every teacher is like that. You weren't, in the car back there with Hannah."

"I was losing her."

"No, you weren't. She was thinking. Really questioning the play. What Shakespeare meant. That's the point, isn't it?"

"What really snagged her attention was your graduation analogy. You would have been a good teacher. I'm sure you *were* a good teacher. When you were a grad assistant."

"You think?"

"I think your love for it had to have been infectious."

"In grad school, I got the feeling that if I made it my full-time job, it would officially change colors. It was already starting to. It wouldn't be love anymore, it'd be my obligation. It would change things."

"A purist."

He shrugged in agreement. "I didn't want to take the thing I loved most and make it about money. Other people do it just fine. I thought it would change something in me."

"That's why I don't want to read that letter," she blurted.

"Thomas's?"

She nodded.

"A reader who doesn't want to read?"

"It'll change something. You know it will."

"It's your story, Mildred. I'm not telling you how to interpret it. I'm just saying you owe it to yourself to read every single line in it. If you quit reading *Pride and Prejudice* halfway through, you'd have a different interpretation of the whole thing. Right? Don't quit reading halfway through. Especially when it's your own story."

Talking to Gurtler made her feel like a desert plant in the midst of a rare rainstorm. Like his sentences were raindrops, and she was trying to drink it all in, but it was coming down so fast, she could barely swallow one drop before two more were hitting her face.

"I know it's not easy," Gurtler said. "Dredging all this up. Never does go anywhere, those kinds of feelings. Yep, love—it's always still there," he added in a whisper.

"Maybe emotions are a habit, too," Mildred said. "And when you don't rehearse them every day, they fade. You get rusty. And maybe falling in love—maybe that's the same way. Maybe, after a long time of not having done it, you don't know how anymore."

Music began to play—so faint, it could have easily been overlooked. At first, Mildred just thought it was the radio playing softly in the store. But Gurtler raced to look through the plate glass window, then lunged back toward her.

"Hurry," he barked, grabbing her hand.

Before Mildred could protest, Gurtler was dragging her outside, where the music grew louder. A guitar player and a singer—both Hannah's age— had parked themselves on the sidewalk near an open guitar case. The song they'd chosen tickled the back of Mildred's mind. The melody was vaguely familiar— maybe Simon and Garfunkel. And Gurtler's hand was suddenly in her own, the other resting lightly in the small of her back. And they were dancing.

Every man in the Ridge had danced with her at the candlelight dinner, but this was different. Something stirred inside of her. It startled her, the waking of this forgotten part of herself. She felt her entire body go stiff with surprise.

But, no—there was no need for the stiffness, she reminded herself. Not with Gurtler, who understood everything, it seemed at that moment. Even what had happened with Thomas. Understood it in a way that was already making her view it in a different, softer light.

She relaxed into his arms.

"See?" he murmured into her ear. "It's still there, Mildred."

20.

The Mustang took a bullet shortly after three in the afternoon.

That was what it sounded like, anyway. A bullet straight to its guts. Only, judging by the way the steam started to spew out from underneath the hood, the more likely scenario was actually a rock to the radiator.

Norma yelped, clutching the wheel tighter. But wasn't that what we all did, Jim thought, when we were faced with a situation we didn't like? Didn't we all just try to squeeze tighter, hold on? And what good did holding tight ever really do anybody? How did it ever fix anything?

"Ah, the obligatory car trip malfunction," Jim said through a laugh. "Of course."

"And we were making such great time, too," Bryan grumbled. "I wish I knew more about cars. I don't know anything. Other than where the gas goes."

Slowly, Norma's hands relaxed. "In all honesty, I'm not exactly heartbroken about this." She edged the wheel toward the right.

"Now, now," Jim said, grabbing hold of the wheel himself to prevent her from steering onto the shoulder. His fingers brushed Norma's, though, and the warmth of her skin was so delicious that he paused, letting his hand linger.

"I may not have read the driving manual in a while, but I know the shoulder's the perfect place to go when you're in the midst of a breakdown," Norma teased.

"Unless your passenger knows that a welding shop is around the next bend," Jim said, finally lifting his hand to point through the windshield. "Or it was the last time I came through here, anyway."

"Just when I thought we might actually be able to escape old Dreadful and her problems," Norma muttered.

"Dreadful?" Bryan asked from the back.

"Yeah—Mil*dred*. Dreadful." She tossed a look at Jim. "Hey, if you can call me Normal, I can call her anything I want. In private, at least."

Jim chuckled. "Still aren't entirely convinced, are you?"

"That I should like her? Not really. She makes me feel like I need to raise my hand to go to the bathroom."

Jim laughed again, sputtering even louder than the Mustang as he pointed once more, this time toward the Lowery Auto sign.

The Mustang belched and spewed across the lot.

Jim reached across Norma's lap to honk, bring the owner outside. The moment he did, though, he remembered the hundreds of times there had been a similar leaning-over in this very seat. Sarah leaning into him, him into Sarah. And how that leaning had always ended in a kiss. And he felt it, suddenly—the urge to kiss Norma.

She glanced up, into Jim's face. They held each other's eyes.

He wanted her. He had from the moment he'd sat at her table back at Granite Ridge. But now, coupled with his new intense urge to do something about it, doubts were crowding in, too. Maybe that was the way of urges like these—maybe doubts grew in the same increments that wanting someone did. Maybe wanting someone was the seed of fear.

Regardless, Jim was suddenly unsure if he would make it to the finish line with Norma. And while he was at it, what *was* the finish line, anyway? He didn't want to get married again. Rolling around in the sack seemed so overrated—especially at his age. And especially compared to the joy of just being close to somebody. But how did you navigate whatever it was that was left, at this point in the journey? That was the problem with movies and love songs—they only navigated matters of the heart for first-timers. Bryan knew the steps. Jim didn't. No one talked about this dance, right here, the one he was doing just looking at Norma, leaning into her, in his car. How to begin again, at yet another starting line after having already run a marathon, with a bad heart that still was full of so much longing.

"Somebody's coming," Bryan said, making Jim lean away from her.

He cleared his throat and waved, stepping out. The man who greeted him was slightly older than Bryan, with a patch on his coveralls that read, "Craig." Jim frowned in confusion.

"You look like you were expecting my dad," Craig said, extending a hand. "People still do, even after me and my brother took over a couple years ago."

Jim nodded limply. He was disappointed. He did want to talk to this kid's dad. More than that, he didn't need another reminder of how much time had gone by. But he shook the kid's hand, anyway, surprised to find that the grease didn't transfer to his own fingers. The stains probably weren't even new, Jim mused. More of the permanent variety—the kind of stains that had every bit as much chance of rubbing off as a tattoo.

"We're about fifteen minutes from our destination, if you can believe it," Jim said with a shrug. "Busted the radiator."

"No sweat," Craig said. "Get you all patched up. New fluids, too."

Jim nodded gratefully as Craig slipped back inside the shop to open a bay door.

"Another frequent stop for the salesman?" Norma asked.

But the world was spinning after that almost-kiss in the front seat. Jim was a little dizzy and his pulse sounded like a hundred mallets were attacking his eardrums. He wasn't thinking when he blurted, "No, my son lives near here."

"Your son? Really?"

Jim shot her a look, hoping it said that he didn't want to talk about it. Hoping he shut her down in the nicest way possible.

Craig came back out, pointing toward a bay, chattering the whole time. Something about getting them right in to work on it. "You could put historic plates on it, you know. Might help you out, insurance-wise."

Jim flinched and turned toward the car, which was still spewing fluids all over the lot. The same way his own heart was still spewing fear and hope and love. Even now, after all this time. And he'd almost just kissed another woman, and hated that he hadn't, and he wanted another shot at it. But did a person ever stop wanting another shot? Did anyone ever feel like they were really finished? Even at a hundred and ten years old, wouldn't he still wish there was more left? And with all of these thoughts and desires and fears coursing through him, it only made Craig's "historic" hit him like the world's greatest insult.

"No way," Jim told Craig, in a voice far more emphatic than it needed to be. "We're not done making history yet." The moment he said it, though, he hated himself for it—for the "yet." Every bit as much as he resented Craig's "historic."

"Ever," Jim corrected himself. "Not done making history ever." Because he knew he never would be—he'd never be done. A man didn't retire from life, after all. A man never stopped wishing for one more kiss.

21.

Norma pointed through the windshield at yet another roadside hotel. "How about that one?" she asked, just as she'd been asking for the past hour or so, pointing at everything from bed and breakfasts to mom and pop motels to Best Westerns. She glanced at Jim, raising an eyebrow over the rim of her sunglasses, waiting for him to shake his head no at this suggestion, too. Just as he'd shaken his head at every single one of her hotel suggestions, ever since they'd crossed the Iowa City limits. Actually, he'd been acting funny since the auto shop. And Norma didn't know why. The mention of his son, maybe? Seemed a prickly subject. Was he worried that another malfunction for his beloved Mustang was in their immediate future?

"We really ought to pick a place soon," Bryan said. "Already a quarter after four."

"Dinner's in full swing back at the Ridge," Norma pressed.

Jim only shook his head, as though that, too, was silly.

Bryan leaned forward, grasping Jim's seat. "I mean, we ought to tell Mildred's car where we're going. Right?"

Finally, a grin started to etch its way across Jim's cheek. "You mean Hannah's car?" he corrected. "Don't want to go the whole night without seeing her, eh, Bryan, old man?"

Norma's eyes lifted toward the rearview in time to catch Bryan in the midst of an embarrassingly stiff shrug. The kind that betrayed his flimsy attempt to seem nonchalant. The type of shrug that indicated he cared very much about whether or not he was going to be seeing Hannah.

She took a new turn, winding away from the business district, away from the Pizza Huts and the Subways and the Motel 6s. If they didn't pick a place soon, they'd be outside the city limits and back on the interstate. She sighed, tilting the steering wheel toward yet another turn onto yet another new street full of hotels that Jim would surely never want to stay in, either.

"Whoa!" Jim shouted. "There."

"Are you sure that's a hotel?" Bryan asked as they all squinted at a yellow Victorian three-story house. Turn-of-the-century gingerbread detail fringed the large wraparound porch. A quaint white wooden fence stretched out from the side of the building.

"According to the sign, it is," Jim said.

"And according to that sign," Norma announced, "it's also got garage units available in that neighboring lot over there. Why don't you just drive this thing inside? Park it in the lobby? Or do we need a king-sized bed for it?"

"Sally's not used to outdoor parking," Jim

insisted.

Norma snorted a laugh as she tapped the brake. Bryan scrambled into his pocket for his phone.

The gravel in the parking area had barely stopped popping under the tires when the front door flew open and a man lurched onto the porch. He was a tad overweight and middle-aged, his face shadowed by a ball cap, his ancient T-shirt bearing a Hawkeye Football logo. He raced down the steps, waving his hands in a *no, no, you can't do that* manner as he hurried toward their car.

"No vacancy?" Norma guessed when he panted to a stop beside her door.

"Got a few places for humans, but—" he stopped mid-sentence to adjust his ball cap and whistle. "Look at that beauty!" he marveled, gesturing at the Mustang. "Those garage units are full, but never fear—you can use mine in the lot behind us." He reached into the front pocket of his jeans and pulled out a garage door opener that he tossed at Norma. "I'll be sure to tell my wife at the counter inside. There's no way that car should ever be left in a parking lot."

"I knew this was the place," Jim said, nudging Norma. "Show us where to park and we'll get our stuff," he told the owner. "We're meeting up with some friends who'll be staying here, too. But they won't be needing a garage."

"Don't travel in such style, do they?" the owner beamed as Norma began to roll forward again.

As they gathered their bags from the trunk, Jim hummed a melody that sounded vaguely to Norma like an old tune that had been played at her parents' country club. "Perfect place," he announced again, leading the way around the building, toward the front door.

Finally, she thought, *he's starting to come out of whatever funk he'd fallen into back at the old auto shop.*

She sighed with satisfaction as they all banged through the Victorian's front door. "Yes," she agreed, getting a good look at her new surroundings, "just perfect." The sitting-room-turned-lobby had been filled with an assortment of antique wingback chairs and landscape paintings in gold frames that put Norma right at home. Jim, though, began to scratch the back of his neck, just like a little boy in a wool sweater.

"You've done a beautiful job putting it all together," Norma told the owners. "Duncan Phyfe, isn't it?" as she pointed to a table placed in the center of the room. A table that had also been filled with welcoming tidbit trays bearing wrapped candies and even a small silver calling card tray that now held a small stack of business cards, the calligraphy letters proclaiming, simply, "Welcome to The Goldfinch."

"State bird," the woman behind the counter explained proudly as Norma fingered the card. "That's the reason for the yellow paint out front, too."

"It's utterly lovely," Norma said honestly. "I'd jump at the chance to come work here every day."

"I'd jump at the chance to drive that car every day," her husband announced. As he turned to explain the garage situation to his wife, the door flew open and Gurtler and crew arrived, feet clomping against the hardwood floor. They paused in the lobby to drink in the interior of The Goldfinch.

And then—nothing. Not a single word. Road fatigue had definitely set in, Norma thought. And maybe Hannah and Bryan were a bit intimidated by the furnishings. They'd been so interested in crossing paths—Bryan had wanted so desperately to see her that evening, and now, they didn't seem to quite know what to do with themselves. Bryan acted interested only in his notebook and Hannah seemed unsure of where to put her hands since her skirt was without a single pocket. Maybe, at their age, they would have been more comfortable with bean bag chairs and concrete block bookcases.

But Hannah and Bryan weren't the only two contributing to the strained atmosphere. Jim was staring off into the distance, looking uncharacteristically downcast. Mildred was about to hug that purse of hers so tightly that she was in danger of squashing her pennies. And no one was talking—not one of them.

Up to you, Norma, she told herself. As it always was. *Make it a game, make it all fun.* She smiled, she shouted a welcome, and she asked about their drive.

"Fantastic," Gurtler announced, breathing a relieved smile as Norma rattled a quick anecdote about radiators and rocks not being able to get along.

There was laughter then. The kind that meant they'd officially arrived. The kind that meant Bryan could lean toward Hannah and murmur, "We went to a biker bar."

"Man, I knew I should have been in your car," she whispered.

Norma smiled. She'd done it. Again.

"And now we need two rooms," Gurtler shouted, lunging for the counter.

"One for the girls and one for the boys?" Norma teased.

"Like summer camp," he agreed with a nod.

She grinned. Maybe, she thought, Gurtler might actually help her keep the enjoyment alive during this stretch of the trip. She put a hand on his arm in appreciation.

Norma glanced behind her shoulder as Mildred hugged her purse still tighter to her chest. She had such a strained, worried look on her face that Norma felt compelled to ask, "Did you lose something? Your billfold? Mildred?"

Mildred shook her head, hugged her purse tighter, and backed away from the counter.

"She's been like that ever since we hit Iowa City," Gurtler hissed at Norma. "Talk to her, will you?"

"We don't really know each other," Norma started.

"Please," Gurtler whispered. "I had seven hours with her, and I don't know if I did much good. Maybe if she talks to another woman..."

Norma frowned. Was she now going to be required to be warm to Dreadful? Forced to befriend the woman? She sighed, called out, "All right, girls, let's get cleaned up." She gathered her bag and followed the owners' directions, up the stairs, second floor, room four.

Norma unlocked the door. "Home sweet home," she announced.

A suite. They'd gotten a suite—or what passed for one in the Victorian. Their unit had three rooms: a bath, a bedroom with twin beds and cast iron headboards, and a living room of sorts that contained a vintage overstuffed sofa, an old ice box being used as a TV stand, and a coffee table that wordlessly invited them to enjoy a cup of tea, as it offered them a delicate looking porcelain pot and Limoges-style bowls containing a variety of tea bags and sugar cubes. Gone with the Wind lamps cast a soft glow across the rose-patterned wallpaper, giving the entire area a sweet, comfortable ambiance.

"Hmm," Norma muttered. "Not bad."

"Not bad at all," Hannah agreed. She pointed at the couch in the living room, announcing, "I'm actually cool with that. You guys can take the beds."

"Thanks," Norma said, still trying her best to be as chipper as possible as she and Mildred dragged their bags into the bedroom.

Mildred tossed her purse onto her quilt. Pulled out an envelope and tossed it onto the bed, too. Stared at the slightly shaky masculine handwriting across the front.

"He likes you," Norma said.

"Who?"

"That lawyer. He likes you."

Mildred grunted, still staring at the envelope. "I can't imagine why people do it more than once," she said softly.

"Do what?" Norma pressed.

"The love thing."

Norma felt a chill run down the length of her body. Was Mildred talking about her and Jim? Was she making a snide comment, the kind women made at weddings, rolling their eyes at a bride who'd worn white for the fifth time?

Mildred picked the envelope up, flipped it over, stuck her finger under the flap. But she stopped abruptly, throwing the envelope back down on the bed and taking a step back. Acting like it was tied to explosives.

The envelope was older, Norma noticed. Yellowed. And the front bore Mildred's name.

She's talking about herself, Norma thought suddenly.

"Is it an ex-husband? The one who left you the property?"

"First love. He was married, but not to me."

For once, Norma honestly tried to put herself in Mildred's place. "I don't know what I would have done if Charlie and I had parted ways, and I'd had to watch him marry someone else," she murmured.

"He was married when he was with me," Mildred confessed. "I didn't know it at the time. I've also never said that out loud to anyone. Ever. Gurtler—he knows what went on. Thomas told him. But I've never said it."

"How's it feel finally just letting it out? Freeing, I would suspect," Norma said, sitting on the edge of her bed.

"Disgusting, actually. Like eating concrete."

"How long? You and this Thomas person."

Mildred sighed, sitting on her own bed, a good two feet from the envelope. "Couple of months. Forty years ago."

"It must have been really powerful."

"Yes—no—I don't know anymore. I just could never bring myself to do it again. And now, the fact that I didn't also makes me mad."

"How so?"

"Because he believed he was the love of my life. Thomas. Obviously."

"Was he?"

"By default, I suppose. There was no one else."

"*Nobody* since this fellow?"

"Nobody," she sighed. "It's strange. I know it is."

"No—it's—beautiful, actually."

"I never thought it was. I thought it was embarrassing—the way we always think the things about us that make us a little different are embarrassing. The only consolation for me was that no one knew. Not even Thomas. At least, I didn't think he was aware that there was no one else. But now, this inheritance has shocked me senseless. I don't understand it. And it turns out, the affair itself wasn't exactly top-secret—I mean, Gurtler knew about it, and now, everyone who's on this trip will know. Here I am telling you about there being no one else—and I suppose everyone will probably find out about that, too. Every last one of you, and it will change what people think of me."

"So what? Who cares what everyone else thinks?"

"Other people knowing defines me in a different way, and maybe I'm afraid that will change what I think of myself."

Mildred put her head in her hands. "How do you do it?" she blurted. "You and Jim? How do you just jump into another time?"

"I'm not sure we are, actually," Norma muttered. Something had almost happened between them back at the station—that pre-kiss eye-hold. But then—nothing. Maybe, she'd thought, getting so close to it had made Jim realize he didn't want to kiss her at all. That he'd been dancing along the edge of a giant mistake.

When Norma looked into Mildred's eyes, the woman was just so hopeful, so desperate for some nugget of wisdom she could hold to that she blurted, "My husband and I had eight cats."

Mildred shot her a look that said, in short, *Yuck— and what's that got to do with anything, anyway?*

"Not all at the same time," Norma went on. "Well, usually two at the same time. But eight total. The thing is, with an animal, you know when you get him that you're going to see his end. You're going to have to deal with his death. You fall in love and you take care of this creature who, in the end, is going to die. You know the whole thing's going to end in heartbreak. But you do it anyway. Eight times, we did it. And it was okay, because the joy of having them was never outweighed by the pain of losing them."

"I don't know what you're trying to get at." Mildred propped her elbows on her knees, stared sadly at the floor.

"Two months loving someone is nothing, Mildred. You've endured far more pain than joy over the past forty years—a heart and mind full. That's why you didn't want to try again. It doesn't usually go that way. Maybe Gurtler's your chance to finally know the

199

opposite—what it's like to feel more joy than pain."

Mildred's head popped up. Norma wasn't sure if the look she was offering her was horror or elation. Funny, Norma thought, how the two expressions looked nearly identical.

22.

Mildred wanted to punish the clock on the nightstand between the two twin beds. *Quarter to nine,* she wanted to say with the same *oh, come, now* tone she once used on students who tried to pummel her with thin excuses for not having their homework done. She wanted to send that clock to the principal's office. She wanted to make it write sentences on the board: *I will not tell Ms. Sudbury it's far later than it really is.*

But, no—clocks didn't tell student-style flimsy lies. It really was already a quarter to nine. And Mildred had been trying to read Hannah's paper for more than an hour already. Two large pizza boxes were still open, bearing little more at this point than a pile of discarded crusts and dark wet grease splotches. The TV in the other room was blaring with no one watching, Norma was stretched out on her own bed, pillows propped behind her back as she sipped the last of a soda, and Hannah was stretched out on her side at the foot of

Mildred's bed, picking the pepperonis one-by-one off her last sliver of the supreme Jim had ordered and had delivered.

"Is it really that bad?" Hannah asked, gesturing at the laptop Mildred had propped on her thighs. "That battery will die before you get done reading."

"I'm—thinking, that's all," Mildred muttered. That wasn't really a lie—her brain was, in fact, speeding crazily from one thought to the next. But none of it had anything to do with Hannah. Or Shakespeare. Or essays.

Well. It did have something to do with writing, Mildred reminded herself as she looked at the envelope she'd placed on the nightstand beside the clock.

The moment she got done critiquing Hannah's paper, she'd be forced to finally pick up Thomas's letter.

And she didn't want to do that. And she did. And she didn't.

Mostly, Mildred was afraid to read Thomas's letter and find out that it would have been okay to remember him fondly. To learn that she didn't need to harbor so much anger. To realize that she really should have made another decision—the same kind of decision the rest of the world seemed eager to make: willingly jump headfirst into some other love. Go soft in another man's arms. She was afraid, in short, to discover that her mistake was not loving Thomas, but the way she'd behaved afterward.

Then again, she reminded herself as Hannah's typed words blurred once more, it wasn't as though she'd lived a life of pure self-denial. She hadn't moved into a cloistered convent. There had been Christmas parties in her own home. Vacations with other teachers—albeit usually other single women. A special club of ladies who understood each other. She'd even gone to England once, with her mother and a fellow literature instructor. Seen plays at the Globe. She'd relished good food and laughed and enjoyed her books and her music and in reality, it had been lovely. Every bit as lovely as her childhood had been.

She had simply never felt it again, the all-encompassing emotions that had flowed through her when she'd met Thomas, threatening to make every vein explode.

Or was it simply that you didn't let yourself feel it? she asked herself. *Did you erase the possibility?*

"Wonder what the guys are doing," Hannah mused.

"Sleeping," Norma muttered. "They're worn out."

"Bryan might not be," Hannah muttered.

"If you want to see him, just go over there," Norma said. "He's next door."

"I don't know," Hannah moaned. "What do you think? Ms. Sudbury?"

Mildred flinched. She had no idea, at that moment, what sort of advice to offer. Go for it? Don't be like me? Or don't let Bryan twist you around his finger? Which?

Her eyes returned to the envelope. Her answer was in there. But did she want it?

A knock rattled their door. Hannah jumped, racing out of the bedroom to answer it.

"Hey." A young man's voice slithered through the living room into the bedroom, barely audible over the TV.

Without getting out of bed, Norma leaned forward, closer to the doorway, as though it would help her listen in.

Mildred didn't need to crane her neck, cup her ear. She knew it was Bryan. He'd come for Hannah. And she knew exactly what it had done to her: Made

Hannah's heart race. Made her start to sweat. Made her gloriously elated.

They chattered nervously. With lots of pauses.

"Why don't the two of you just go down to the pool?" Norma thundered.

"Pool?" Hannah squeaked.

"The white picket fence at the side of the building. There's a pool behind it. Didn't you see the sign?" Norma turned to roll her eyes at Mildred.

"It's still warm out," Bryan encouraged. "Did you bring—?"

"A suit? Yes! I thought maybe I was being silly, but now I'm glad I've got it. Give me a minute to change. Meet you down there."

Hannah lunged into the bedroom, letting out a mini squeal as she slammed her bag on Norma's bed—a move that reminded Mildred of a professional wrestler tossing an opponent onto a mat.

Hannah tugged her swimsuit out and dipped into the bathroom. The door flew back open in record time. "Hey," she whispered. "Does this look okay?"

"Beautiful," Norma whispered back. "Just beautiful."

"Are you sure?"

At that moment, Mildred's heart went out to Hannah again—just as it had in that library at the Ridge. In truth, Hannah was wearing a one-piece in an unflattering olive green, with modestly cut legs and a shelf bra that smashed her flat. Mildred thought of all those lessons her mother had given her about emphasizing the best parts of her own figure—her slim waist, her broad shoulders. And then she began to think of all the times her mother had grabbed her shoulders and pulled her out of a slump, how she'd insisted on proper posture. Not because it was good manners, but because a physical expression of pure confidence—head up, shoulders thrown back—could keep the rest of the world from ever noticing the small stain on a cardigan after lunch or a run in a pair of stockings.

"Listen," Mildred murmured, "you're the one he wants to see. Not the suit. Right? He came over here."

"I'm afraid I'll mess it up."

"It's not a class," Mildred whispered. "Look— take the thought that somehow, you're second best in your hand. Hold it like a staff. Now imagine breaking it."

Hannah grinned. Her back straightened and her eyes started to glitter.

She'd just started to race back toward the suite's front room when Norma hissed, "Hey!"

Hannah turned.

"Grab a towel, girl. And be cool," Norma advised.

Hannah nodded. She snatched a towel from the bathroom. Just before entering the living room again, she held her hands out from her sides, as though to remind herself to calm down. She inhaled a deep breath and sauntered forward.

Now that Hannah was out of sight, Mildred held her breath and felt herself crossing her fingers—just as the girl had before dipping into the coffee shop earlier that afternoon.

"Ready?" Hannah asked in a husky, relaxed, Kathleen Turner-style voice that made Norma open her mouth into a kind of wordless laugh.

As the door clicked shut, Norma let out the cackle that she'd been fighting to hold back.

"I don't know what that staff stuff you were spouting was all about, but it worked," Norma said.

"It had to do with her paper. Just shows that Shakespeare remains applicable in the modern age. The pool was a good idea to get them alone," Mildred added somewhat wistfully.

"Oh, I had a kid," Norma said with a dismissive shrug. "I knew Hannah'd never come up with a decent idea on her own. Elaine never could think straight with her high school boyfriend standing in front of her. Mostly, she just kind of foamed at the mouth. Hard to concentrate when your mind's spinning a hundred miles an hour, isn't it?" She pointed at the envelope.

"Yeah, it is."

"Maybe you need to go to the pool, too," Norma suggested.

When Mildred forced an awkward laugh, Norma said, "I'm actually being serious."

"I could stand to get out for a minute," Mildred agreed. She picked up the envelope, slid it into her pants pocket, and walked down the stairs, through the front door of the hotel.

She stood on the porch, staring through the spaces in the gingerbread detail, up at the stars that were starting to glitter. The same stars were glittering above Thomas's house. She'd arrived. She was in the right place. The city of her destination. Why didn't that in itself feel triumphant? Like an accomplishment?

She pulled the envelope from her pocket, running her finger along its edges. She tugged at the flap a few times. Her heart beat so hard it hurt.

Splashes and squeals stole her attention. She used the noise as an excuse to shove the envelope back into her pants pocket and edge her way toward the white wooden fence at the side of the building.

Bryan and Hannah had the entire pool to themselves. She stood at the gate, watching as they splashed each other, squealing with delight. The moonlight bounced against the water, reflecting their dance. The age-old dance of young lovers wrapping the dark sky around each other, making sure no one else in the universe existed.

Mildred had herself never had such a night. She would have left them to it, but suddenly, Hannah was breaking away, climbing the ladder, water gushing off her body. And she was running from Bryan, down the length of the pool. *Don't run away*, Mildred wanted to scream. *Slow down.*

In less time than it took Mildred to gasp, Bryan grabbed his glasses and Hannah's hotel bath towel. He raced after her, snagging her in a white cotton lasso.

Their squealing and playing died. Completely. Bryan slid his glasses back off as Hannah tilted her face upward. A pause, then, as they held each other's eyes—as Bryan asked her, wordlessly, if this was what she wanted. Hannah answered immediately, saying wordlessly and without question that it was. Bryan lowered his face to hers.

Mildred touched her own lips—which had not been kissed that way in four decades. She closed her eyes and pictured what it felt like.

She jumped, letting out a strangled yelp when a pair of hands circled her shoulders.

"Shhhhh," she heard, the hissing sound echoing in her ear.

When she turned, Gurtler's smile was maybe an inch from her mouth. "You going for a swim?" he murmured.

Mildred shook her head. "And interrupt that?" she whispered. "I wouldn't dare."

"Good. Because I found us a place," he said, drawing her away from the pool. "You'll like it."

He hummed as he led her toward the sidewalk, then down the street. Mildred slid her hand into her pocket, holding onto her envelope. Afraid it might fall out. Afraid it wouldn't.

"There," he said, pointing at a neon sign above a door.

"It's—a bar," Mildred said.

"A jazz club," Gurtler corrected. "That's what it says out front. Saw the sign when we passed by on our way to the hotel. And I instantly started to fantasize about getting you in there. Plus, I just took a walk to find out what it was like inside. Had to see it for myself before I took you. And I'm telling you, you're going to love it."

"Pretty seedy," Mildred muttered.

"Better than the Handsome Diner," he told her, tugging on her arm and grunting in a way that let her know she was fighting him, digging her heels in. And he was not going to accept a no.

"Is this a piano bar?" she asked.

"Oh! No, no, no. Would I take you someplace with bad singers belting standards out of tune?"

Mildred still wasn't sure about this idea. So many cars in the parking lot indicated the place was crowded. She had liked Jim's original idea of spending the night, enjoying a bit of calm before heading out to the Clyde house. And now, here, with Gurtler, in a crowded and noisy bar, hiding Thomas's letter in her pocket, it was all too much. Sensory overload.

But Mildred Sudbury was not one to argue or protest. She allowed Gurtler to push her through the open doorway. And it was as though she had just done a cannonball dive into an ocean of music—bubbles of saxophone and guitar notes dancing all over her skin.

Gurtler led her toward the bar. "You after another couple of boilermakers?" Mildred asked over the noise of the crowd. "Or you think I need one?"

"I thought you'd like the atmosphere."

"Anything's an improvement over the Handsome."

"Mildred, I'm not talking about the décor."

She frowned, not sure what Gurtler was talking

about, frankly.

"Two vodka and cranberry juices," he ordered.

Mildred almost spoke up that time. She'd never liked the taste of cranberries. They were too sour, too tart. Lemonade had always hit her the same way. Did anyone ever really quench their thirst in the summer with lemonade? Sour drinks always made her thirstier than she'd been before. And as far as the vodka went— she had no intention of getting drunk.

But she did want to get to the bottom of what Gurtler had meant about the atmosphere. She glanced around, trying desperately to see through Gurtler's eyes. But all she could see were plain wooden tables and the soft light emanating from out-of-date sconces. *Not the décor*, she reminded herself. Slowly, she stopped looking at the tables and started noticing instead who was seated at them. She took in an abundance of gray hair. Wider middles. Crow's feet.

And they were laughing. Flirting. Dancing between the tables. A long silk scarf slipped to the floor; a man snatched up the fabric and wrapped it around a woman's neck, drawing her close.

Mildred shivered; they looked at each other exactly as Bryan and Hannah had just a moment ago. It was an identical dance, the very same game. And she understood, all in a gush, why Gurtler had brought her here. Maybe some of these people were still married to their first loves. Maybe their first times around had never stopped. But these couldn't all be first times. Some had to be with loves they met later in life.

Gurtler put a drink in her hand. This time, when she took a sip, she found that the cranberry juice tasted slightly sweet.

That happened with acquired tastes, Mildred surmised, glancing at Gurtler. Sometimes you had to try things over and over again until you realized you actually liked the taste on your tongue.

23.

"**A**lone again," Norma muttered with satisfaction, flopping onto the couch in her suite's living room. She leaned forward, snatching a remote from the coffee table, and grinned when she found a printed TV guide beneath it.

"Ah, antique people," she sighed. Anyone who gravitated toward vintage furniture generally just liked an older way of life. A slower way, quieter way, a way of fewer gadgets. There would probably be printed newspapers in the lobby tomorrow morning, too.

Norma squinted, holding the guide at arm's length. But her arms weren't quite long enough for the tiny print. Her glasses—she'd left her glasses on the Mustang's dash. And the keys, she realized, were still in her pocket. And the garage door opener was on the coffee table, where she'd tossed it shortly after her arrival.

She shuffled down to the garage, cringing

against the way the door squealed and screeched all the way up. It sounded especially awful in the dark, in the quiet. She couldn't shake the feeling she was probably waking the entire block—even though it was still relatively early.

The keys were already in her hand the moment the door hit its zenith. She lunged into the unit and unlocked the driver's side. The dome light popped to life as she swung the door open—but the dash didn't hold a single pair of her unending streams of glasses.

"Where'd they go?" she grumbled through a frown as she ran her hand in the creases of both front seats. Still nothing.

She squatted, patting the floorboard. Her fingers zipped beneath the driver's seat, banging against some springs and the metal landscape of the Mustang's body—and the pointed corner of a box. A metal box, wedged beneath the seat. Curious, she tried to slide it forward, but it was jammed so tightly that she had to fight to wrench it free. She grimaced and grunted until the box finally popped out, flying across the floorboards like it had been launched from a catapult. The lid popped, too, causing the contents to spill out as the box tumbled forward. Norma hissed a string of swear words as she placed the now-empty box in the seat and scurried to scoop up the contents. She picked up a picture and chased some objects rolling toward the pedals.

She tossed it all into the lock box—the kind that she and Charlie had used to hold their own Social Security cards and property tax receipts. "Stupid, stupid..." she muttered, though she wasn't sure if she was talking about herself or the latch that had failed.

She went to flip the lid shut and stopped abruptly. Stopped moving, stopped breathing. These were medicine vials. With Jim's name on the label. A statin, a beta-blocker...

Jim had a heart problem. Just like her Charlie.

"I can't believe it," she whispered, leaning away from the seat. Her legs felt floppy, threatening to give out beneath her. So she sat on the ground, the cool concrete floor bleeding through her slacks.

She sat for several minutes, trying to decide what she should do: Admit she'd sneaked a look into Jim's private business? Tell him she knew? Forget she'd ever seen the pills? Not mention them, but refuse any more of Jim's advances—if there would even be another advance, another attempted kiss? Be his friend? Not be his friend? Go through this again?

Finally, she sucked in a deep breath and returned the box to its place beneath the front seat. Her reading glasses—and her sunglasses—were both in the glove compartment next to Jim's map.

Numb, she locked the Mustang, lowered the garage door, and staggered back to the front porch of the hotel. She sat on the front step watching a band of fireflies and listening to the cicadas in the trees.

Somewhere off to the side of the porch, hinges squeaked and a wooden gate flopped open. She watched, full of jealousy, as Bryan and Hannah emerged, towels tied around their waists. Holding hands. She envied them their blank slates, their hearts that had yet to be broken.

Slowly, then, Norma began to think about her cats.

24.

Jim wasn't going to be the only person left in his room. Sitting alone. Staring at stuffy, frilly wallpaper. Not when he could be out on the town with Norma—not just eating ice cream and playing in swings. Really out, for once. Just the two of them.

He changed his clothes and combed his hair. He shaved. And he sauntered down the hall and knocked on the door. "Normal?" he asked, knocking again. But no one answered. Jim's stomach tightened, as he wondered if she'd run off with Gurtler and Mildred. He should have asked where Gurtler was going. But he'd been too anxious to get rid of him, waving goodbye when he left shortly after Bryan.

Jim hurried downstairs. "Did you see—the woman—with the reddish hair—"

The male half of the partnership that owned the old hotel hiked his ball cap up higher on his forehead and glanced about the lobby. He pointed at the screened front entrance, asking, "Isn't that her?"

Jim signaled a thanks as he hurried out the door. "Hey, there, Normal," he said, stepping out into the moonlight. "Wondered where you shot off to." He sat down beside her, patting her knee.

He expected a slightly-weary smile. Maybe even a sigh. Her confession that driving had utterly exhausted her. And in return, he would tell her he'd be the one doing the driving tonight, taking her out where the two of them could be alone. It would probably be their only chance on the trip to indulge in a little solitude. The scene at the auto shop swelled in Jim's mind again. And part of him also wanted to say that he felt as though Norma had a welding torch, and had mended something inside him—just as quickly as that mechanic had mended the Mustang. Did that sound stupid? Would Norma want to hear it? She didn't seem to be the mushy sort.

"Let's get out of here," he declared. He wanted another shot at it, the kiss. The rest of it—all those great proclamations? He'd feel it out as the night went along.

The look Norma turned his way startled him like the sound of a car backfiring. It was a look unlike any he'd seen her wear before—wide eyes, pale cheeks, a slight nervous twitch around her tight lips. That was fear, pure and simple. Jim didn't think a woman like Norma ever got afraid. Oh, sure, fear came for her—the same as it came for anyone. But he'd assumed she was the sort that squashed fear anytime it showed up, smashing it like an ant on a linoleum floor.

Before he could ask what was wrong, her phone went off. As she answered, her voice cracked.

"Where are you? Mom?" The woman's voice stomped through the phone so loudly, Jim swore she could have been sitting right beside them on the front porch.

"Elaine?" he asked.

Norma shrugged in agreement. "Why are you at the Ridge this time of night?" she asked her daughter.

"Because! We all went to dinner. And I tried to call you. And you weren't answering the phone in your apartment."

"I had my cell with me."

"Why would I think that? You never use it. I didn't remember you even had one until about two minutes ago."

"When you came by to check up on me."

"Well, it certainly seems as though it's a good thing I did. Why *aren't* you in your apartment this time of night?"

"I'm in Iowa."

"Mother! How is that possible?"

"You told me I was supposed to get out with the rest of the residents. So I did," Mildred answered simply.

"Why didn't you at least tell me you were leaving? When will you be back?"

"Not sure—in a couple of days, I guess."

"Couple of days! But I—but Barbara—I—"

"It's fine. I'm fine, Elaine, really. Take care. See you—"

But the voice on the other end continued to chatter on, making all sorts of high-pitched demands.

"Really, Elaine. I'll see you soon. Bye now. I'm hanging up."

Norma pulled the phone from her ear, ended the call, and turned the phone off.

"She panics when you're not around," Jim observed.

"Unfortunately. Barbara's even worse about letting Elaine out of her sight. Seems so strange to me. Really. They should want to get out on their own. Test the world. Shouldn't they?"

"Maybe you always felt that way," Jim said, nudging her. "But not everybody's as tough as you are."

The eyes that turned toward him were now a different shade of shocked.

"Don't get me wrong; I'm not saying people who aren't tough are *weak*. They're not—they're soft. Like Mildred. She's the kind of person who's nice to be around because it makes the world seem like a gentler place. But you, you're—"

"Gorilla Glue?" she whispered. It had a funny ring to it—almost hopeful, it seemed.

"I was thinking more like stone. Some material you can use as a foundation. Or a retaining wall. Something that supports everything, keeps the world around her from sliding apart."

Norma didn't hug him as much as she threw her face against his chest. She wrapped her arms around his waist and squeezed.

Jim felt a warm rush of emotion—but that was the way pure affection had always hit him. Like swallowing a shot of whiskey. He laughed, wrapped his arm around her neck and hauled her even closer, murmuring, "I love you."

Norma kept her arms around his waist, pulling her neck back just far enough to look up at him. The new expression swirling across her face was a mix of part happy surprise, part *can't be*, part total confusion.

"Well, so what if I do?" he asked. "Who needs all the stupid folderol? The prancing about and pretending, as long as you can, that you're indifferent? I love you for being obstinate and honest. For being fearless—like you were back there in the barbecue joint. I love the way you charge through. Your wanting to be with me—the fact that you're willing to go for a crazy trip in my old 'red thing'—it makes me feel tough, too. By association."

Norma stared at him. "Is that all?"

"What do you mean 'Is that all'? Right now, I'm sitting here with you, and this night is particularly gorgeous and memorable, and tomorrow, we're going with Mildred to find out what this inheritance thing is all about, and who knows what will happen after that."

Norma's face darkened for a moment.

"You want to go out someplace? See what this town has to offer?" Jim held his breath, waiting for her to answer.

"No," she said. "I want to stay right here—right now—with you."

And then it happened once more, just like it had in the Mustang—the quiet pause, staring into each other's eyes, leaning forward. This time, though, Jim leaned all the way into Norma. Jim kissed her. As soon as their lips parted, he only wanted to kiss her again.

Norma sighed in contentment as she leaned against him.

"You act as if you've settled in for the night, Normal."

"I'm planning to stay here as long as I can."

There was something about the tone of her voice—it insisted there was no need for further discussion. It was final, like she'd made a bigger decision, even, than just about how she intended to spend the night.

25.

Mildred woke before her current roommates. She used a small hotplate in the living room to heat water for tea. She sat in the bedroom's window seat as the sun rose, her heart continuing to beat increasingly harder.

She felt as if, after all this time, she was going to see Thomas—not his house, Thomas himself.

"You okay?" Norma asked in a sleep-filled voice.

"I don't know," Mildred responded as Norma pulled her face from her pillow and propped herself onto her elbow. Her chin-length reddish hair swirled wildly about her face. She rubbed her eyes, still so far from fully awake that her face looked squishy to Mildred. Like maybe Mildred needed to warn her not to press to hard against her features, or they'd all cave in, like a wad of Play-Doh.

"You want me to go in your car?" Norma asked. "With you and Gurtler?"

"I don't know what I want right now, honestly. But I appreciate the offer."

Norma nodded, swung her legs out from under the covers. "Look," she said, "I haven't been the most welcoming person in the world, but if you want to lean on me, you can."

"What brought this on?"

Norma shrugged. "I just—life's short. Too short to spend it being a jerk."

"And in return—what? Do you have a paper you need help with, too?"

Norma chuckled. "No, but I'm going to need someone to talk to—someone other than my daughter, who I'm sure will never want to see me with someone other than her dad."

"Are you talking about Jim?"

"The L-word got thrown out last night."

Mildred turned her face back toward the sunlight streaming into the bedroom window. She'd never heard it, she realized, not once. Not from someone who wasn't a relative.

They dressed while Norma chattered on, working overtime trying to pep Mildred up. But her voice didn't sound excited to Mildred as much as it sounded nervous. And if even Norma was nervous for her, that made Mildred feel ready to run right back to the Ridge. Cancel the entire thing. Did she really want to do this in front of a crowd? Would it ever stop feeling like they were merely an audience and start feeling like support? What about Gurtler? He'd seen this house before—hadn't he? Had he visited Thomas there? Was there something out there that he especially wanted Mildred to see? Some other surprise?

Too many unknowns buzzed around Mildred's head. She wanted to shout, "Shoo! Scat!" and stomp her feet until she frightened everyone away.

But Norma was right—life was too short to be a jerk. And besides, her mother had raised her to be tough by example, hadn't she? The way she'd huddled over her work at all hours of the night, her sewing needle hammering away. Oh, her mother—what would her mother have said about all this? About Thomas?

Or had she known, in the way mothers always knew about their children? She'd never asked questions when Mildred had changed schools, left the classroom to be a librarian. Had she known even then? Maybe, Mildred thought, her secret wasn't quite as secret as she'd thought it was. This, too, was embarrassing—like looking down to realize she'd spent the last forty years with her skirt tucked into the back of her pantyhose.

Mildred dressed hurriedly in a pair of light gray slacks and a white tailored blouse. She gathered her purse into her arms and one last deep breath into her lungs. "Okay," she told Norma, though she wasn't sure she was really that okay at all.

Downstairs, Hannah was seated at the lobby's Duncan Phyfe table, her computer before her as she waited for the rest of the crew.

"I thought—maybe Bryan and I could ride with Norma and Jim. Unless—I mean—you had something you wanted to say—about my paper." Hannah chewed on her bottom lip, waited for Mildred's reaction.

In truth, Mildred wanted to jump for joy. She had yet to read a single full paragraph of Hannah's paper, and if Hannah rode with Jim, that would also mean there'd be one fewer person in Gurtler's car watching her reaction as they pulled up to Thomas's house. She could have hugged Hannah, kissed her cheek, squealed with delight. Instead, she simply cleared her throat and agreed, "I think that would be best—you go ahead and ride with them. We'll have time to finish talking about your paper on the way back."

"It's okay if you'd rather not talk about the paper until we get back to the Ridge," Hannah assured her. "The hard part was getting the words down on the page in the first place, and I never would have gotten started if you hadn't helped talk me through it yesterday. We've still got plenty of time to get it fine-tuned. Besides, my paper's not exactly the only thing going on right now." She stood, flashing a kind smile. But Mildred knew the offer wasn't completely selfless. Hannah was hungry for a little more time with Bryan. Maybe, Mildred thought as Bryan entered the lobby, they'd tossed the L-word around, too, the night before. There was definitely something different going on between the two of them. Less awkward, it seemed, as Bryan approached the table. Gentler. Softer.

Hannah closed her laptop and stood, smiling at Bryan as she wiped her palms on her dress—one of those loose-fitting T-shirt shaped sundresses, this one in a dark red, almost maroon. *No*, Mildred corrected herself. *Cranberry.*

And she smiled, remembering the drink she'd had the night before.

Mildred kept having to remind herself to breathe as Gurtler steered toward a well-cared-for white cottage in the midst of manicured fields, its front yard enclosed by a picket fence. She glanced into the rearview mirror, at the red Mustang following along behind them. From the front seat, Norma give her a thumbs-up. Mildred wished she had her confidence. Instead, she was trembling. And trying not to—which only made the trembling worse.

"What's all that growing over there?" she asked, pointing to the rows of tall green stalks dancing in the slight summer breeze.

"When Thomas got older, he leased land to a neighbor," Gurtler said.

"So that's still being farmed?"

"Yes, but there's far more land that belonged to Thomas lying fallow."

He pulled into the drive. They idled. Mildred's chest heaved.

"It's all yours, Mildred," he said. "The house, the hundred acres, the cars, the furniture—the bank accounts. Lock, stock and no strings attached. No debts. No liens. Free and clear."

She pulled herself from the car and stared up at the house as though waiting for it to turn into something recognizable—as though the house could somehow swivel on its heel, like a fellow passenger traveling on the same train she'd just boarded, and show her its face. Show her they'd met somewhere before.

It didn't, though. It stood immobile, a mass of wood and stone. Hard to believe she'd been so intimidated by the thought of it. It was just a house. Not unlike the house she'd lived in her entire life. Behind her, car doors opened and slammed shut.

She turned; the five people who had come to support her stood waiting for some direction, all of them wearing concerned expressions. "You want company?" Norma asked.

"No. Give me a minute, guys. I need to go in by myself."

Gurtler reached for her hand.

"No—really," she said, pulling away. "I need—" But she stopped when she realized he was trying to give her the key.

She took a few tentative steps up the walk, onto the porch. Inserted the key. Unlocked the door.

The smell in the house instantly provided the familiarity she'd been waiting for. An odd mixture of male aftershave and soaps and even faint cooking scents made it somehow feel as though Thomas were standing in front of her, extending his hand, welcoming her inside.

The feminine touches provided by a wife were still evident—rocking chairs in the living room, patterned throw rugs, sheer curtains. Slowly, Mildred walked through the living room, down the hall. In a small back bedroom, she discovered the only space that she felt was pure Thomas: here, the furniture consisted of a single twin bed, a small upholstered chair, and a bookcase filled with nonfiction books. History books. Not a single ceramic knickknack in sight.

She opened the closet door, expecting to find his suits, that blue seersucker jacket of forty years ago. But what she found instead were casual slacks and well-worn jeans and colored T-shirts. Funny—in her mind, Thomas was frozen in time. These clothes made her picture, for the first time, how he had aged. Maybe his hair had gone white. Maybe he'd gone bald. Been arthritic. Had a hearing aid. Forgot to take his vitamins. Hard to believe that age had found him, too—the young Thomas she'd always carried around in her mind.

She tugged an out-of-date long woolen gray winter coat from the closet. *Ah, yes*, Mildred thought, *his coat*. The second-skin he'd worn for who-knew how many years. She placed it in the chair, draping it in such a way—collar high on the back, sleeves on the straight wooden arms—that she could picture Thomas actually sitting in the chair. Slowly, she pulled the envelope from her slacks and sat on the edge of the

224

nearby bed. She unfolded Thomas's letter. It hit her suddenly that here she was, with one more essay from a boy. Ms. Sudbury had always listened to boys—more than ever, her mind needed to be open now. Quietly, through shallow breaths, she began to read:

Mildred,

I am not a wordsmith, not like your favorite writers. Bear with me.

We all get one lightning bolt in life. Most of us get it when we're young. First love. My first love—my wife—was my best friend. I loved her. We were a good match. But my lightning bolt came later. That was you. That's not a lie, and it's not an old man looking back fondly on his younger years, attaching meaning now where there wasn't any to begin with. You were my lightning bolt.

But I was already married. I was committed. Maybe breaking ties doesn't really mean much these days, but it did to me then. I had given my word. I said my vows. I suppose I broke them, when we were together. But I couldn't sever them completely. It was a different time, and we were different people. I was, anyway.

Life rolls on—at times good, at times miserable, at times plain boring. And the memory of you was with me always. You got me through it all. In that way, you have given me much through the years. So I wanted to give to you, too.

Thank you, Mildred. Thank you for being my warm memory. And for being my lightning bolt.

Affectionately,
Thomas

Mildred's cheeks were wet and her hands

trembled as she lowered the letter into her lap.

"Are you okay?"

Mildred glanced up, finding Gurtler standing in the doorway.

"I didn't mean to snoop," he said. "I was just worried. I didn't know how you'd take it."

"I was his lightning bolt," she said, waving Thomas's letter. She sniffed, wiping her face.

"I know." Gurtler took a step into the room and paused. "Do you believe it?"

Mildred took a breath, glancing through the window. Hannah and Bryan were outside, walking through the backyard. *Did* she believe Thomas? What had he known about her—what had he learned, in only two months' time? Had she ever known him, really? Had they fallen for the ideas of each other? Mildred squinted at the screen, watching as Bryan wrapped an arm around Hannah's waist. Maybe, she began to suspect, that's all young people had to offer, and all they ever needed to know about one another: their surface-value. Maybe she and Thomas *had* fallen for each other—for everything they'd been back then. Maybe, she thought, falling later on was richer, because the person doing the falling was richer, too—more developed, seasoned.

"Mildred?" Gurtler pressed, sitting beside her on the bed.

She glanced down at her letter again. In Thomas's mind, she had never aged, either—and the initial, undeniable fire had never cooled. Each time he'd thought of her, she was young and stealing glances at him and meeting him in the park and unable to stop touching him.

She finally spoke. "I do. Maybe it's being here. But yeah. I believe him."

"You look relieved. What did you think he was

going to tell you? Didn't you expect this?"

"I expected—pity," Mildred said. "I expected this to say, 'Poor Mildred. We had an affair, and she read so much into it. She let it bother her too much. Let it mean too much. Lived her life the way she shouldn't have.'

"But it truly was important, wasn't it?" Mildred went on. "My reaction wasn't stupid. I didn't overreact. Didn't overthink it. It wasn't something Thomas did simply because the opportunity presented itself. It really was powerful—maybe even as powerful as Romeo and Juliet. I was his lightning bolt. Little quiet bookish Mildred Sudbury."

"I'm glad you read it," Gurtler said.

"I'm glad you made me."

He just continued to sit beside her, not speaking, not urging her to get up, put the letter away, come to any final conclusions. And perhaps because he wasn't, her mind spun on overdrive and she made several decisions, one after another.

"I want you to break your staff," she told him.

"What staff?"

"The one that's made up of what you think of me. What Thomas's confession made you think of me. I'm not a homewrecker—I'm no shriveled up old maid, either. But I'm also not—" she paused, rustled Thomas's letter again. "I'm not lightning in a bottle. I'm not pure excitement. I'm just—"

"Mildred Sudbury," Gurtler finished. "Don't you know I've already broken a hundred of those staffs already? I broke one when you hung up on me. I broke one the first time we met at the Handsome Diner. I broke one when you showed up with a hundred strange people to bring along on this trip. That's life, Mildred. Nobody keeps the same idea of a person all the time. Tomorrow, I'll break the staff I'm holding right now—because you'll show me a different side of you. And

227

the thing is, I don't think I'll ever quit breaking them, because I don't think I'll ever get to the bottom of you. That does make you lightning in a bottle. And quiet and bookish. And hundreds of other things, too. Things I want to unwrap. See for myself. *That's* what I find exciting. Seeing all the different parts of you."

Without thinking, Mildred leaned forward. Gurtler's hand raised to her cheek. And for the first time in forty years, a man lowered his face toward Mildred's. A man brought his lips to hers.

But this was not the kiss that Hannah and Bryan had shared the night before, out by the hotel pool. This was a mature beginning, a beginning that all at once tasted both sweet and sour. A beginning that was as warm as the first stream of sunlight after a hard winter.

Mildred knew—even before Gurtler had lifted his lips from hers and tilted his head back an inch to stare into her eyes—this was her inheritance. What Thomas had truly given her. A second chance. The rest suddenly didn't feel like anything she had a right to call her own.

And right then, Mildred made another decision. The kind that made her smile and wrap her arms around Gurtler, squeeze him in a joyful hug. "Come on," she announced, standing and tossing Thomas's letter onto his coat. "Everybody's waiting."

Mildred's traveling band had dispersed a bit, but the sound of the front door flapping open made them all race to congregate in the front yard.

"Are you okay?" Norma called out.

"Absolutely," Mildred said, weaving her hand in Gurtler's.

Norma noticed that motion—she might have been the only one who did—and she smiled softly.

"So you're keeping it?" Jim asked. "Moving from the Ridge?"

"No."

"Mildred!" Gurtler shouted.

Mildred untangled their fingers, held up her hand to silence him. "I'm not going to keep it for my own. But that doesn't mean I'm not going to accept Thomas's inheritance. I think we can make another arrangement—one that would please Thomas *and* his pushy lawyer," she added, trying to lighten the atmosphere. "I'm going to sell the property and the contents. An auction would be the easiest way. We could sell a portion of the land to the neighbor who's currently farming it—or if he can't afford to buy it outright, continue to lease it to him. Whatever works out best. I want to use the proceeds to establish a scholarship for high school seniors planning a career as an English teacher. There should be enough to last for years—what with proper investment interest. You can help me do all that, right?" she asked Gurtler.

Gurtler nodded. "I can."

"It's a good idea, Mildred," Norma agreed.

They stood a moment, everyone waiting for everyone else to break the silence, to make a move, a suggestion. "Are we ready to head back, then?" Jim finally asked.

"I'd really like to stay a few more hours and get going on Mildred's project. We have an entire lifetime to dispose of," Gurtler said. "It's a big job."

"The rest of us can head back to the Ridge, then," Jim started.

"No," Norma insisted. "You and I have an errand of our own to run. We'll be back here later on today, find out how things are going with Mildred."

"All right," Jim said with a shrug. "Hannah and Bryan, let's—"

"No," Norma said, her voice as final as the click

of a lock. "Just you and me. "

26.

"**C**all your son." Norma handed Jim her cell as Mildred and Gurtler walked back into the house. She crossed her arms over her chest in an effort to show him there would be no arguing with her.

"I don't think so," Jim said.

"Do it. You said he lived here, didn't you?"

Jim sighed. "That really doesn't matter. He doesn't want to hear from me. Hasn't for a long time."

"Why not?"

"Because—he's still got resentments piled on top of resentments. I was on the road most of the time he was growing up. When I was around, I didn't take time to find out who he was. He has a right to be angry about that."

Norma pushed her phone closer to Jim, remembering the brown vials. Mostly, she was banking on the fact that when a woman invaded a man's heart, she had some control over him. Not completely. But a bit of the kind of influence he couldn't ignore. "Call him. Now."

Jim eyed her a moment, sighed, and began to dial. He turned his back to her. He spoke a minute.

"No, no, if he's not there—"

"Who is that?" Norma asked, tugging on Jim's shirt.

"His wife," Jim muttered, holding the phone away from his mouth.

"Tell her we're stopping by."

"Why—?"

"Tell her."

Jim sighed in surrender, spoke again in a series of grunts. And then handed Norma's phone back.

"We'll be back to the funny farm soon enough," Norma urged, her voice light as she pretended this, too, was a game—something as simple as hopscotch, maybe, with plenty of skipping feet and laughter.

They drove away in silence. The wind attacked Norma through the open convertible top in the same harsh way she was sure Jim wanted to. The wheel was in Jim's hands, and Norma knew that in reality, he could have driven anywhere. Pulled over to the side. Turned around. Elaine had done something similar, she remembered, with her girlhood piano lessons. Norma had driven her to the piano teacher's house, Elaine had waved goodbye, and then she'd gone to a friend's house two doors down. Jim could have gone that route—agreed to drive to his son's house, then steered instead into the parking lot of a diner, asking Norma if she wouldn't just prefer a few all-she-could-eat pancakes.

He didn't, though—which Norma took as a positive sign. A green light. Fifteen minutes later, Jim pulled into the drive of a redbrick ranch house—the sort everyone in the Midwest bought to raise their family in. Norma finally exhaled. He'd arrived; Norma'd been right; this was a good idea. Something Jim wanted to do, and didn't quite know how.

Bicycles were scattered like the carcasses of dead animals through the front yard. The sounds of play trickled into the Mustang as two little boys tied firecrackers to G.I. Joe figurines.

Norma pulled herself from the seat. "Well?" she said to Jim, who sat motionless.

He hesitated; Norma bristled. *Get out, Jim,* she thought, repeating the words in her mind. *Get out, get out, get out...*

Jim popped the door and climbed from the car, calling, "Hey there, boys."

They eyed him with shock. No open arms and racing to greet him. No slapping their hands into his like Barbara always did when she saw her own grandmother. And it absolutely tore at Norma's heart. Which only made her shove Jim a step closer to the boys.

"The one with the punk in his hand is Todd, my grandson," Jim informed her.

Todd kept his deer-in-headlights expression on both of them.

"And his friend over there is—"

"Rick," the other boy responded.

"Right. Rick. Nice meeting you," he said in a stiff, uncomfortable manner.

Norma cringed. *Nice meeting you?* she thought. *He's not forty, and this isn't a cocktail party, Jim.*

Todd continued to watch silently, confusion smeared like fruit punch stains across his face, as the front door flapped open. A woman Elaine's age burst onto the porch, drying her hands on a well-used dish towel and blowing a lock of black hair from her face.

"I called him," she said. "He should be here

soon. Come in—I've put some coffee on."

Jim eyed her in the same way the boys had just stared at him. Completely unsure of how to proceed. What to say. He looked as though he'd forgotten how to make his legs move.

Norma gave him another shove, and he stepped into the house mumbling something about how much Todd had grown. But it didn't sound to Norma like an empty way to fill an uncomfortable pause. It sounded sincere—like Jim really was shocked at the change in his grandson. They hadn't seen each other in some time. And that tore at her heart again.

Inside, Jim and Norma pulled chairs back from the kitchen table. His daughter-in-law apologized for her own appearance and introduced herself to Norma as Jennifer. The distant sounds of boys playing continued to filter in from the yard. The garage door screeched as it rolled up.

Jim fidgeted while Norma made small talk, tugging at the edges of their conversation like pizza dough—spreading it wider and wider with each toss. "We're here with some friends. Drove up in Jim's old car—the Mustang. I've never been in this area before. It's really pretty..."

The man who entered the kitchen through the garage door had Jim's build, but the face was all wrong. Norma never would have pegged him for Jim's son— but as she continued to stare, she realized how much he looked like the photo in Jim's lock box.

He nodded uncomfortably toward his father and acknowledged Norma with a bland "Yes, Norma, hello" when introduced by his wife.

"I laid your things on your bed," Jennifer said, playing with the handle on her coffee cup. She was speaking to Carl, but clearly eyeing Norma. "Next to your suitcase." She emphasized that last word. And

Norma winked back, instantly understanding.

"Are you two taking a trip?" Norma asked, following Jennifer's lead as Carl carried his own cup of coffee to the table and took the seat beside his wife.

"Just Carl. The company sends him out all the time. On-site computer network development."

"On the road. I can relate to that," Jim mumbled.

Norma smiled at Jennifer, who reciprocated.

"I wish you'd spend some time with Todd before you go," Jennifer told Carl. The way her pupils dilated in fear as she glanced up at Norma said that she was on dangerous ground—the kind of thing that could possibly spark an argument. Even here, among the kind of relative strangers that meant manners were a must. "Maybe you two could hit the driving range. He's always wanting to go with you," Jennifer quickly added.

"The driving range?" Jim perked.

"The kid's obsessed with golf," Jennifer explained.

"So is Dad," Carl said quietly, tracing the pattern on the table cloth with his thumb.

Carl met Jim's gaze straight-on for the first time since he'd stepped into the kitchen. The look was as loaded as any Norma had ever seen: a heavy, brutal mix of hurt feelings and hatred for the years of silence that had created such thick walls between father and son—the kind of walls that can only be built when two people stop reaching out to each other. Those, Norma thought, were the toughest to knock down. She began to wish someone would invent a sledge hammer for the job—it would, she mused, have to be the strongest tool on the planet.

Your thoughts are running a bit toward the melodramatic, aren't they? Norma asked herself. But her dry mouth and her pulse and the knot in her stomach insisted she wasn't.

She flinched as Carl cut into the growing silence to ask, somewhat hesitantly, "Did you enjoy the drive, Dad?"

"Yeah—I did." Jim's voice was surprisingly soft.

"It's nice here in the summer," Carl said, his voice equally soft. They both sounded to Norma as if they were dangling a hundred feet off the ground, on a tightrope with no net. Like one slight breeze would send them falling to their deaths.

"Fall's beautiful around here, too—you probably remember that, though," Carl said. "Maybe you should come up—spend some time with Todd."

"Maybe he could come up when you're here. Spend some time with you, too," Jennifer offered.

Norma sat silently, ears perked. She swore she could hear a few cracks hitting the air. The wall between the two men was starting to fracture—wasn't it?

"Yeah," Carl muttered, eyes glued to the table. In that moment, Norma could see him, barely seven years old, with a cowlick and muddy feet; a boy desperate to get his father's approval. "That'd be nice, too."

"And all of you should come down to see us," Norma announced, her voice bursting too quickly, too loudly. It smacked against the kitchen walls, startling everyone at the table. But she couldn't help herself; this was too wonderful, and she couldn't take it all in silently anymore. "The Ridge is having an incredible Labor Day celebration. We have lots of extra rooms for guests and a golf course next door. Should have lots of great barbecue, too," she added, nudging Jim with her elbow.

Jim burst out laughing—his own too-loud voice tangling now with Norma's. "That we should," he agreed.

A loud pop from the yard drew everyone's attention, and they all stampeded toward the front door. Carl and Jim burst through, side-by-side, asking in unison, "What's Todd up to?" Only now, it didn't seem at all like small talk.

The hours rolled along; Jennifer's coffee turned into salami sandwiches crammed down between Todd showing off his putting skills to his pleased grandfather and Carl sitting beside his father on the porch swing, the two rocking gently as they talked—about Carl's work, maybe, Norma mused. Or the return of Carl's childhood car, or missing Sarah, or what had been on TV the night before—who knew for sure? What business was it of hers? And what did it really matter, anyway? They were talking. That was all.

Late that afternoon, long after Todd's friend had returned to his own home, after Jim had taken Todd to the nearby driving range to purchase his grandson a yearly pass and a respectable driver from the adjacent golf shop, Todd returned to the front yard and the task of winding Black Cats onto his G.I Joes.

Jim nodded in approval. "I think you've got it down now," he said.

"I still don't like this idea," Jennifer muttered.

"Oh, no boy can resist the Fourth of July," Jim laughed. "Now this one knows how to get the best bang action without losing fingers. Right, Todd?"

"Ah, the great wisdom passes down another generation," Norma mused.

"You'll send some pictures, won't you?" Carl asked. "Keep us up-to-date around here, let us know what you're up to?"

"If you don't mind getting them in the snail mail," Jim said.

"You don't still have that old thirty-five millimeter, do you?" Carl teased.

"Until they rip it from my hands."

At which point, Norma felt her eyes beginning to tingle. Because even though he'd said "it," for a split second, she'd heard "you."

And maybe Carl had heard it that way, too. Because without thinking, he hugged his dad. And Jim hugged him back. It was a hug that said Carl got it—an admission that he was on the road every bit as much as his father had been. That said he understood how providing for the people in his life kept ripping him away from their lives, forcing him to spend time apart from them. It was a hug that said his anger had been juvenile. That he'd been jealous, hating the fact that every single time his father had returned, he was suddenly on the outside of two people who were a real love-match. Odd man out, the one no longer getting every last drop of attention. And now, here he was in the same kind of household he'd grown up in, only in a different position—here he was, living his father's life. That hug said he'd been thinking these things for a while, even, but hadn't been able to be the one to reach out first—he never would, because no matter how old Carl was, in this relationship, Jim was always the adult and Carl was always the son.

Norma grinned; she read everything that hug had to say, and it made her proud for pushing. Proud for responding to her gut instinct, for making Jim be the one to reach out, for believing that it would be okay to drag Jim out here.

They waved, they said their goodbyes. The scene was punctuated by the bang of a firecracker and the high pitch of boyhood laughter.

Norma and Jim laughed happily, too, as they crossed Carl's front yard and headed toward the Mustang. Jim opened Norma's door for her. But before she slipped inside, Norma reached for Jim. "I loved meeting your family—especially Todd. And maybe, just maybe, I sorta love you, too. Despite the fact," she added, whacking his hip with her own, "that you wear white sneakers."

Jim smiled. Leaning down, his lips brushed hers. "Know what, Normal?" he whispered in her ear. "This time of my life is just fine—all because you're in it."

27.

Jim was on a high after seeing his son. And hearing Norma's first "I love you." He couldn't help it—an honest-to-God high. And he was itching to celebrate.

He and Norma piled into the car—the lovely, wonderful car that truly had come to him for a reason: to insist it was easy to reclaim the parts of your life that you believed were lost forever. Of course that was the reason—hadn't the Mustang been telling him so, right from the start? How easy it had been to find the old car—right in the very same place he'd left it. And so, it turned out, was Carl. So was love—right there in the passenger seat.

But Jim never would have realized it without Norma. Sometimes, he thought, it takes another person to show you how to connect the dots of your own life.

He parked the Mustang in the driveway of Mildred's recently acquired farmhouse, jumped out, and began waving at Hannah and Bryan, sitting together on the front step—so close, in fact, that Hannah was practically in Bryan's lap.

"We need to get going," Jim shouted, waving his hand. *What's wrong with you?* He wanted to cry out. Why were they just sitting around? That was the trouble with young people—they thought that there was no need to hurry, that youth was somehow certain to be the longest period of life, old age just a blip toward the end.

"Oooh!" Hannah yelped, twisting Bryan's wrist so that she could see the face of his watch. "How could it be so late?"

"I got so caught up," Bryan agreed, smiling at her.

Yes, yes, caught up in each other, Jim thought. *That seems so magical right now, but just wait, the entirety of your lives will go every bit as fast as this day has. You'll suddenly look down and wonder where the time has gone...Get moving, get moving...*

"Mildred! Gurtler! Where are you?" Jim forced Hannah and Bryan to lean away from each other, making space for him as he stomped onto the porch. He threw the front door open hard enough to give it whiplash.

"Hey!" Jim yelled, finding the living room empty.

"In here," Mildred called, her voice lassoing him and tugging him into the kitchen.

"Hey," he said again, his tone softening with surprise. Mildred and Gurtler were seated at the small kitchen table, separated by a scattering of papers. But there was nothing about the scene that indicated they were simply in the midst of filling out legal documents. Instead, the way they were leaning toward each other reminded Jim of the way Hannah and Bryan had been sitting on the porch—so close, their thighs and shoulders had been touching. So close, the slightest breeze would have sent Hannah's hair rippling across Bryan's face. Mildred's hand was in Gurtler's. A soft pink smear lay on Gurtler's bottom lip—the same dusty rose shade that Mildred gravitated toward. Evidence, Jim thought, of a kiss.

"We definitely need a break," Gurtler said, clearing his throat. But Jim suspected a break from what had been happening in that kitchen was the last thing either of them wanted.

"No—we can flat-out leave. We're done here," Mildred said, her voice calm and controlled.

"Don't you want to go through the contents of the house—list everything to be sold—make sure you don't want to keep anything—" Gurtler started.

"No. I mean it—I want to hire an auctioneer. Everything that can be sold should be. If there's anything left, I'll pay for a cleaning company to come scoop it all out. I don't want to personally go through his things."

Jim paused a moment; he'd had a similar thought just a few weeks ago, about how Carl would handle his own belongings. Now, though, the idea didn't sting. Probably because it wasn't a real possibility anymore. Just like that—his life had changed. Usually, dramatic changes were tragedies. Like the morning he'd rolled over to instantly find himself a widower. Or gone downstairs at the Ridge to suddenly be told, by an empty chair, that he no longer had a best friend. Usually, the good changes—like climbing the corporate ladder, losing weight, building a nest egg, knowing the woman at your side would be your wife—those things took time, snuck up on you. Now, though, the abrupt change was a happy tune Jim could tap his feet to. His son was back. Love was back. Norma had *said* it.

"We need a celebration!" Jim shouted. He

shouted it a second time when he realized Norma had slipped into the room behind him.

"We certainly do," Mildred agreed, smiling at Gurtler.

"Millie, my dear, you're absolutely beaming," Jim observed.

"So are you," Mildred agreed. Her eyes darted past Jim's shoulder as she smiled at Norma. Jumping to her feet, she tugged at Gurtler's arm. He scooped his papers up and followed her out.

They drove in a mini parade, the SUV behind the Mustang. They stopped for dinner at a Chinese buffet, where Jim kept tapping his fingers against the table thoughtfully—then impatiently. It seemed to him that beneath the soft veil of twilight, as they'd driven to the restaurant, he had seen something that had made him smile. And the more he thought about it, the more what he'd seen turned into regret, a *should've stopped*. As the dessert dishes were emptied and the check was paid, it turned into an itch, a *gotta go back*.

He rushed everyone outside, telling Gurtler to follow, no questions asked. Jim drove, feeling a panicky sensation rise inside him as he wondered if he would drive right by it, the thing he'd seen. If he'd even be able to find it again. It would look different now, in the dark. Or maybe he'd simply mistaken it for something else. Maybe he had it all wrong, and here he was, losing time on their trek back home because he was trying to get back to something that had never even existed in the first place. A mirage. A trick his mind had played on him.

His eyes widened with relief as spots of light popped on the horizon. He flicked his turn signal and pulled onto the shoulder beside a gate. Gurtler pulled behind him.

Engines died; car doors swung open and

snapped shut again. Utterly confused expressions swiveled toward Jim, who chuckled happily. "There it is," he announced, pointing under the cover of a thousand twinkling stars toward a distant outdoor celebration, a party surrounded by brightly glowing Japanese lanterns. Music wafted softly; muffled voices trickled; staccato shouts bubbled; long streams of laughter gurgled.

"It's a dance!" Mildred announced.

"And here you are not wearing any red sequins," Jim teased.

Mildred slapped his arm.

"It's a wedding reception," Norma corrected. She pointed toward a billowing white dress floating through the center of the gathering.

"This looks like a private country club," Gurtler said.

Jim grinned. "Even better."

"Jim's the expert at sneaking into country clubs," Bryan told Hannah, reaching for her hand in a way that requested she prepare for just such a break-in.

"We're crashing a wedding?" Gurtler asked, grinning.

"You're up for it, aren't you?" Jim asked.

Gurtler turned his gaze toward the distant gathering, edging still closer to Mildred. It was a motion Jim recognized—Gurtler's sly grin revealed he was looking at that reception and imagining his own possibilities. At the same time, Jim glanced at that party as he wrapped an arm around Norma's neck and drank in the contentment of everything in his life falling into place. As for Hannah and Bryan, they were staring at the young couple and feeling the joy of having found someone themselves—the kind of joy you wanted to broadcast, just like those two happy newlyweds.

Didn't weddings do that? Didn't everyone at

a wedding find some reason to see themselves in the happy couple? And wasn't the joy of a wedding something everyone wanted to experience?

Jim raced forward.

"It's all about your level of confidence," he instructed, waving them forward.

They followed along—all five of them. "No slumping, no crouching," Jim hissed, tossing the words toward the crowd behind him. "Shoulders back, heads up. The key to sneaking in is looking like you're not sneaking in at all."

They all sauntered up to the edge of the gathering, playing their parts perfectly. So perfectly, in fact, that no one at the reception bothered to look twice at the way they were all dressed—in what was closer to picnic garb than clothes appropriate for a formal wedding. Norma and Mildred chattered as if discussing afternoon tea. Gurtler and Bryan appeared deep in serious discussion, pointing at the club house. "Hey, there," Jim said, slapping the closest man on his back.

The man turned a surprised face toward him. "H-hey?" he muttered.

Norma waved. "Brought the kids tonight," she announced, pointing at Hannah and Bryan. "On break from the university."

"Th-at's nice," the man said, waving at the younger couple.

Mildred threw her head back and giggled as Gurtler took her into his arms and started to spin her across the floor. Bryan did his best to imitate Gurtler, but the awkward way he tugged Hannah into his arms only made Jim laugh. They were such novices. Jim was a pro—and so was Norma. They wrapped each other into an embrace in one fluid, lovely motion.

"Hey," he said, tapping a nearby man on his

shoulder. "We're still having fireworks later, aren't we?"

"I—think so," the bewildered man replied.

Jim nodded. "All momentous occasions deserve fireworks," he said, and hugged Norma again.

28.

Norma's feet throbbed as she danced—more than they ever had after an entire day of running and playing in the old saddle shoes of her childhood. They throbbed as she glided across the floor, and as she wondered if there would ever be another trip as surprising and eventful as this one.

She glanced over at Mildred and smiled. She actually liked the girl.

"Thanks, Norma," Hannah murmured, as she and Bryan swayed past her and Jim. She winked, as though Norma's suggestion that she and Bryan go swimming back at the hotel had somehow changed everything. Norma laughed at the happy squeal that spilled from Hannah as Bryan lowered her into an awkward dip.

Hard to believe that just a few weeks ago, Norma was the woman hiding in her room, eating dinner on the couch. Resenting Elaine and wishing for something more.

Jim tugged her still closer, and she responded by hugging him back. At that moment, she didn't care one whit about tomorrow. There was only tonight, a right now—this place she had traveled so many miles to finally reach. Only new friends and warm summer air, strangers who'd decided to let them play their silly game, dance at their wedding. Only the music of love and triumph...and her Jim.

Mile

41,633

Two Months
Later

29.

A *giant* "Welcome to Labor Day at Granite Ridge" banner stretched across the front of the parking lot. Voices bubbled against the late summer air, though not in the same wild, celebratory way they had when Jim and company had crashed the outdoor country club dance floor. Today's get-together had the feel of a playground during daily recess. Or a park bathed in bright Sunday afternoon sunshine. Of knowing that the summer was coming to a close, which was okay, because fall brought its own magic. There would be long drives to see the leaves shift to bright reds and yellows. There would be trips to pick plump pumpkins straight from the patch. New sweaters and cider. Life would keep rolling leisurely forward, just like the tires of the Mustang, no need to press the gas pedal so hard.

Barbecue scents wafted through the outdoor picnic area, making Jim's mouth water. Or so Jim had said about six hundred times. Four hundred of those times to Todd. "Doesn't it smell good? Get your appetite ready," he announced, pointing at the smoker branded with a giant Pappy's logo. The same weathered face that had greeted Jim, Norma, and Bryan in Iowa City was now red and covered in sweat as the cook doled out slow-cooked ribs and pulled pork sandwiches.

Not that Todd cared. He was more interested in the nearby golf course.

"Grandpa, isn't that it?" he kept asking, pointing toward the closest green.

"Don't you want a sandwich first?" Carl asked, attempting to usher Todd toward the picnic tables with red and white checkered cloths. "Something to drink? Lemonade?"

Todd's shoulders slumped as he let out a frustrated "Uugh."

"What boy can eat with a challenge like that waiting for him?" Jim asked, pointing in the country club's direction.

"But he needs to eat something."

"What he needs is to get a few long drives under his belt. Then you'd be able to eat, wouldn't you, son?" Jim asked.

Todd shrugged, trying now to act cool, like it didn't matter to him one way or another. But Jim knew better.

"My sticks are right over there," Jim said, "at the table with my girl." The words slipped out, surprising him like a patch of ice under a foot. But he didn't stumble; he smiled up at Carl, owning the term. *My girl.* And waited to see what the reaction would be.

Carl simply grabbed a single-minded Todd up by the back of his shirt. "Hang on, there, bud," he said, pointing to Hannah and her full tray of sandwiches. "You were about to trip her and get slimed in a gallon of barbecue sauce."

Todd apologized; Hannah assured him no harm was done; Jim was left open to race forward, straight to his table. Norma, Bryan, Mildred, and Gurtler were seated together, looking equally slimed in sauce themselves. Before Norma could realize Jim was there, he tickled her behind her ear. She squealed, making Mildred laugh. And because Mildred had laughed, Gurtler joined in, trying to wipe his mouth even as the chuckles continued to pour.

"Gal, you've got so much sauce smeared on your face, you look like a competitive eater," Jim teased.

Norma flinched, reaching for a napkin.

"You're not bugging Norma, are you?" Hannah barked at Jim. "I might just have to take you down. Us girls stick together." She winked, this time carrying a tray of bacon-wrapped appetizers toward another picnic table surrounded by full-time Granite Ridge residents and their guests.

"When do you get off?" Bryan called out, wiping his sticky hands on a paper napkin.

"I've got clean-up duty," Hannah started.

"No you don't," Linda interrupted. "I'm pulling rank and putting on my yellow gloves. You're out of here."

"Why would—" Hannah started.

"Oh, someone might have persuaded her," Norma said with a shrug. "Because she also might owe me for my barbecue idea."

"Come on, come on, your food can wait," Jim said, tugging Norma to her feet. "Let's play. You and me versus Carl and Todd."

"I don't know how," Norma started to protest.

"That doesn't matter," Bryan told her. "Not if you're with Jim. He has the same way with scorecards that he does with country club fences."

"—makes the game more interesting," Jim finished.

"Grandpa!" Todd shouted, already halfway to the course. "You're too *slow*."

"Looks like we've got another fence-jumper in the making," Bryan laughed.

Norma wove her fingers between Jim's, allowing him to pull her along. Todd was sprinting now, and Carl was calling after him, asking him to slow down.

Carl threw his head over his shoulder, shouting back at his father, "Can you believe him? Can't get away from me fast enough."

"Oh, that sounds like someone I used to know," Jim called out. It came back to him—those years when he felt he'd tried to reach for his young son and only filled his hands with empty space.

He smiled now, in no hurry, knowing he'd catch up to both of them. And he drank it in, the feeling of his life rolling on at a comfortable pace.

Jim's hands were full, indeed. He squeezed Norma's fingers. She squeezed back—just like he knew she would.

30.

"They're great together, aren't they?" Mildred asked, watching the group approach the golf course.

"Norma and Jim are definitely a pair," Gurtler agreed.

"No—I meant Jim and Carl, actually."

"Yeah, them too," Gurtler said—even now, Mildred thought of him as *Gurtler*. It fit him better somehow, the same way his button-down shirts seemed to fit him better than T-shirts, even on the weekends.

They listened for a moment to Jim's and Carl's distant laughter bubbling up the hill toward the back patio. It was a fantastic sound, the kind you wanted to pause your whole life for just so you could drink it in for a moment—like the unexpected trill of a bird singing at your window or the sudden rush of the tide tickling a beach.

Norma turned and waved. Mildred waved back.

But her view of the golf course was interrupted as a VW puttered by. Hannah stood up in the passenger seat, waving her arms through the sunroof. "Ms. Sudbury! I just got a text from my prof! All those revisions we did these past few weeks paid off! It's an A!"

"What'd you expect?" Gurtler shouted. "You and Bryan going to frame your matching A+ term papers?"

Bryan didn't appear as though he heard, though—how could he, with Hannah squealing and the car gaining speed, sputtering around the corner of the building toward the exit.

Gurtler laughed. "Oh, I remember that feeling— the pure ecstasy of finishing the job. Lasts about a minute and a half before the real world comes to grab you by the jugular. Fleeting but fantastic. Like so many things." He paused, cocked his head to the side. "You'll miss her, won't you?"

Mildred nodded. She would. Hannah would go her way—a new job, a new chapter. Another coming and going, like all those students through her years of teaching. Another fracturing off—one more brief piece of Mildred's life gone.

Funny, though—she didn't think of the constant fracturing-off of life as a sad thing anymore. Or even as all-or-nothing breakings of one's staff, like old Prospero. She saw it instead as a constant sculpture in progress—one chip after another, each whack turning the current piece of artwork into something else entirely. A frightened face could be chipped at to become a smiling, relaxed face. A face refusing to look back. An *-ed* becoming another *-ing*.

Gurtler reached for her hand. Without thinking, she squeezed back affectionately. When she relaxed her grip, though, she realized he was circling her ring finger in a funny way. *Is he trying to measure it?* she wondered.

She must have stiffened, because Gurtler caught her eye and said, "You know, I've been thinking about that obligation thing."

"What—obligation—thing?"

"Like we talked about on the road trip. How I said I was afraid of the thing I loved the most—books and literature—meaning something else when it became an obligation. And I was thinking—you know, sometimes, signing on the dotted line, making something your whole life *isn't* an obligation. It's just knowing that something is permanent. That it's never going to change. That the love isn't going anywhere."

As Mildred's mind spun faster than it ever had, Gurtler took a breath, said, "I think that VW's going to become their Mustang. Hannah and Bryan. Because I also have a feeling that's going to be a permanent thing, too."

"Hmmm," Mildred mused. "Sounds like a novel in the making to me."

Without hesitation, he squeezed her ring finger and agreed, "Looks exactly like a novel in the making."

Mile

43,401

Nine Months Later

31.

Norma walked down to the garage unit—a trek that had become something of a daily routine. She opened the door and tugged at the edge of the tarp along the front fender—just as she'd done before every adventure she and Jim had enjoyed together the past few months: Thanksgiving at Iowa City. Christmas in Kansas City, just the two of them—to the dismay of all their kids and grandkids—shopping on the Plaza beneath the holiday lights and eating turkey in their hotel room and laughing like teenagers sneaking away together. Antiquing in Eureka Springs. Vacationing in Puerto Rico, sipping daiquiris and letting the ocean wash over their legs. They'd made sandcastles—Jim's recognizable, hers a lumpy pile with foot-sized dents she claimed were windows. And they'd laughed. Good God, had they laughed.

She unlocked the driver's side door and squatted to pull the gray metal box out from under the seat.

She used the small silver key from Jim's key chain to unlock the box—she'd learned it was the small silver one just by watching him. She sniffed, mumbling, "You learn so much about a person just by watching. So much they never really wanted you to. All because you kept them in your peripheral vision." She pulled out a small faded photo of a woman sitting in the Mustang's passenger seat. "But you know that, too, don't you?" she asked the image.

Norma returned the metal box, climbed in behind the wheel. And she put the picture in the corner of the rearview mirror.

"Jim slipped away on a Tuesday morning," Norma told Sarah, her voice breaking. "After a day of golf with your son. After an evening with me," she whispered.

"Maybe you already know that. Maybe the two of you have reunited. Maybe when the time comes for me, I wind up with Charlie again. But I just wanted to let you know he was a good man. And I'll miss him," she added, a tear in her eye, "just like I know you've missed him these past few years.

"If you have any awareness at all of us earthlings," Norma added, "I'd appreciate a few prayers or good thoughts or whatever good energy you could direct my way. I know I can count on you, because you know exactly what I'm going through, don't you?"

Norma put her head on the steering wheel and cried. Tears ran; her shoulders shook; the muscles in her stomach began to ache. She cried until she heard a familiar high-pitched voice. She raised her head, wiping her cheeks dry.

"I'm in here, pretty girl," she called out to Barbara. Because she knew Barbara would never be walking about the Ridge all on her own. Elaine was sure to be close by.

Norma slammed the door of the Mustang, and put on a pair of sunglasses to cover her bloodshot eyes. She threw back her shoulders and sauntered out of the garage unit. Because, regardless of what stage of life she was currently in, that's what a Gorilla Glue woman always did.

32.

"This is bullshit," Norma said, flopping back into her chair.

"What is?" Gurtler asked. He raised an eyebrow, looking at Norma in a way that said her tone had hurt his feelings.

"This whole thing," Norma continued unapologetically. "You and Mildred have each other. It's like Jim gave you that. Because he insisted that we all go with Mildred to see that stupid house. No trip, no you two. And Carl and Todd got the entirety of his wealth—as they should, I'm not saying they shouldn't." She paused to gesture at the will on Gurtler's desk. "And I—" Her words began to fail her. She let out a strangled sound as she fought a round of tears.

"You know," Gurtler offered, "I always admired Jim. How he went from a low-paid road salesman to regional manager to a VP. But I learned a lot more about him just by drawing up his will. His sense of humor will stay with me forever—especially that golf grant to the country club he never joined." Gurtler paused to smile. "He acquired quite a small fortune. But Jim honestly thought the best part of it all was what he left you."

"My Jim's gone," Norma said, her voice cracking. "You and Mildred have your new life. Hannah and Bryan are both off in their own adventure. Newly engaged. Their Christmas cards will trickle off in the next few years. There's a stranger in Mildred's old apartment, and Jim's apartment is empty. The painters will show up soon, get it ready for someone else. Erase Jim."

Gurtler shook his head, leaned back in his own chair. He drew his hands in toward his chest, began to spin a wedding ring around his finger.

"Everybody's won," Norma proclaimed. "Everybody's got something. Even the Ridge. You know Jim saved some sort of tomato seeds? Grown by his old neighbor? Thanks to Jim, the Ridge is now growing a variety of tomatoes that've been around for almost two centuries. And what've I got? A used car. I repeat: that's bullshit."

She scooped the Mustang keys off Gurtler's desk and started to race out of his office.

"Hey, wait," Gurtler called. He picked up a business envelope and held it toward her. "Jim wanted you to stick this in the rearview."

Norma rolled her eyes, snatched the envelope from his hand, and stomped out.

"Thanks a lot, Jim," she grumbled, getting behind the wheel of the Mustang.

She started the engine, sighed. "Oh, stop being such a grumpy old lady and open the envelope, already," she scolded herself.

She peeled the flap back, and found one of Jim's thirty-five millimeters. She recognized it instantly— the crazy blur, that open-mouthed laugh. She'd taken this. On the trip to Iowa City. Before tears could find her again, she stuck the picture in the rearview. And put the car in reverse, backing out of the parking space near Gurtler's office, still fuming.

Why was it that the world had made a habit of giving her a traveling partner only to snatch him away again? She was tired of this awful hurt. She hated that she was disappointed by Jim's inheritance, that she couldn't see why Jim and Gurtler had thought it was so special. Mostly, she was tired of being the one person who did not have that one *thing* that was purely her own. The kind of thing that could have helped carry her through this hurt—redirected her thoughts, given her something warm and comforting to fall back on. The kind of thing that could have soothed her soul.

She was also, quite frankly, tired of being the one person expected to be there for everyone else, the girl expected to shoulder the universe. The girl who was left with a used car while the rest of the world got their shiny new everythings.

She drove aimlessly, one highway bleeding into another. Until the green highway sign that pointed toward Finley. She had already passed maybe fifty like them—just some plain sign pointing toward a tiny little Missouri town. But this time, she grabbed the wheel and veered toward the off ramp. She felt compelled to— didn't she? Why? Maybe she was tired—or hungry—or just in need of something new to look at—something other than gray stretches of highway.

She drifted toward an old-fashioned small-town square surrounded by 1900-era buildings. The car started to rattle a bit; glancing at the dash, she found the gas gauge aiming for "E."

Norma growled. "A used car with no gas. Thanks twice now, Jim."

But hadn't the tank been full when she'd started

out? Had she really driven that far?

She coasted to a stop in front of a brightly painted little shop. Were fluids spewing everywhere, just as they had on that first road trip? Is that why the car had no fuel? She pulled herself from the Mustang, squatted to glance underneath it. No puddle—no smell of gas.

She sighed and began to slam everything: the car door shut, her feet against the walk, her hand against the store entrance. The series of angry bangs and whacks did little to brighten her mood. Only made her feel increasingly sour.

"Hey, there," a pleasant voice called out from behind the counter.

Norma grunted a greeting. "There a gas station close by? Or a phone I could use?" she added, still wondering if the old car had a problem more severe than being a little thirsty. "I might need a tow." She groaned, wondering how far she'd actually driven. This tow was going to cost her a fortune. *Thanks three times, Jim.*

The woman leaned against her glass counter— filled with glittering displays of jewelry.

Norma raised her eyes to look around, her frown easing as she took in the framed art and vintage clothes and furniture. She'd walked into an antique store. Of all things—just the kind of place that could actually lighten her mood.

"Not having much good luck today, eh?" the owner asked. She pulled her reading glasses from her nose, letting them dangle on a rhinestone chain. She ran a hand through her frizzy gray hair and shook her head.

"Bad luck has my name, number, and address. Always has," Norma grumbled. It wasn't true, really. But she still felt like saying it.

"You look like you could use a breather, hon. Why don't you grab a soda from my cooler over there." She pointed at an ancient red Coca-Cola cooler.

"That works?" Norma asked.

"As good as I do," the woman said. "We're actually the same age."

Norma laughed and continued to stare around the place. So much stuff. The place needed some better displays. Needed to be fanned out a bit. Hard to believe many customers could see individual pieces enough to find something they wanted to buy.

"Go on, hon. No charge. Have a sit." The woman pointed at an old church pew near the counter.

Norma nodded a thank you. She pulled a soda from the cooler, twisted the cap, and sat, her slacks slippery against the varnished wood.

"My husband'll be back in a few minutes. Making a furniture delivery. He'll give you a hand with your car. One look and he'll know exactly what you need. He's pretty handy."

"This is nice of you," Norma said. She meant to sip the soda, but realized, as soon as the liquid hit her tongue, just how thirsty she really was. She gulped, like Elaine after one of her childhood softball games.

"Well, we do what we can for our customers as long as we can," the woman said, leaning her elbows against the counter.

"As long—?" Norma asked.

"Yeah, we're retiring."

"I did that once," Norma muttered.

"You act like you didn't like it."

"I don't much. Not these days," she added, thinking of the Ridge, void now of both Mildred and Jim—which meant it also seemed void of the promise of future fun.

"I'm afraid of that."

"So you're closing up shop," Norma said, mostly just as a way to continue their polite chitchat. Small talk. Empty. Safer that way. It steered her mind away from Jim—from her latest loss. That wound was fresh; it hadn't scabbed yet.

"Yep. Closing as soon as we find a buyer," the woman said. "Won't be long, I hope. Price is reasonable."

Norma's mind began to spin. "For the shop?"

"The shop and the apartment upstairs," she said. "We've been here a long time, me and my husband. All of us with businesses here on the square live in lofts right above them. It's a real community, all of us spending so much time together. Working on marketing together— getting people out to the square, you know. The people here—I'll miss them more than working."

Norma's scalp tightened. Her entire body tingled. This was no coincidence. It couldn't be. Being drawn to this city, the car shutting down here, in front of this store, and now this—an opportunity like none she'd ever found, falling into her lap. She glanced through the front window, at the Mustang in the lot. She swore, for a moment, she saw him in the passenger seat—Jim, waving at her through the windshield. She swore she saw him cup his mouth, swore she heard him shout, "Do it, Norma! Go for it. This is it—your thing."

"I'll buy," Norma blurted. "As long as there's a garage for my red thing," she added.

As she stared, Jim's image faded. Norma smiled, swiveling to face the front counter again.

"Got a double-car garage out back." The store owner's frown deepened with concern as she asked, "Are you sure? A store—on impulse? Do you—know antiques?"

"Yes. Besides, I am one," Norma quipped. "And I ran a business for decades—my husband's business. But this would be mine." She grinned. "My own thing."

266

"You sure you won't miss that retirement of yours?"

"No way," Norma said, the sadness of loss slowly growing smaller in her rearview. A new feeling greeted her in its place—the joy of starting an engine, feeling the rumble beneath the seat and knowing a new adventure was beginning.

She grinned. "I've got miles left yet."

NORMA *has just rolled into the town of Finley...*

and the town has plenty of secrets. In fact, word has it that the spirit of Amos Hargrove, the town founder, is still at work, granting second chances, making dreams come true, and playing Cupid by uniting hearts meant to be together. Has he somehow granted Norma's wish by calling her to Finley, giving her this new chapter?

Find out—and meet a delightful new cast of characters—in the short story collection *Forever Finley*.

Check **HollySchindler.com** for availability.

HOLLY SCHINDLER

is a critically acclaimed, award-winning author of books for readers of all ages. She believes storytelling is like the never-ending road trip: you never know ahead of time where the stories will lead, but you always know each new tale is destined to be an adventure.

View the full list of Schindler's publications, find links to purchase or download her latest reads, subscribe to her newsletter, or send her a message at:

HollySchindler.com

BOOK CLUB
Discussion Questions

1. Books for younger readers are called "middle grade" while books for teens are called "YA" (young adult). Books for and about people of retirement age have been referred to at times as "Boomer Lit" or "The Second YA." What would you call books in this age category? What term sums up this time of life?

2. All three main characters (Norma, Mildred, and Jim) seem nearly identical from the outside: they're older, retired, and they've had successful lives (have good savings and are able to retire at a luxury retirement community). But when you dig deeper, they're all strikingly different. Have you been thrust into a situation with others (for example: dorm life) when it seemed you should all be so similar, and yet, once you got to know each other, you were shocked to learn how different you all were deep down?

3. Mildred is misinterpreted by the Granite Ridge residents during their candlelight dinner. Have you ever been misinterpreted? How?

4. Relationships with children are complicated in *Miles Left Yet*. Do you think Jim would have eventually connected with his son had Sarah lived? Or do you think that it took someone (Norma) with her own complicated mother / daughter relationship to help Jim find his way back to his son?

5. The Mustang means different things to Jim at different points in his life. Have you ever kept a sentimental object long enough that its meaning changed as time went on? How so?

6. Mildred and Norma both receive inheritances. But in each case, they receive far more than just stuff. (Mildred receives assurance that her relationship with Thomas had been special, and Norma receives the promise of yet another fresh start from Jim.) Have you ever received an inheritance like this, in which the true value had nothing to do with dollars and cents?

7. Mildred is suffering from one-love-affair-itis. Do you think it's possible for one brief experience to make such a profound, decades-long impact?

8. The three older main characters express a wide variety of strong emotions: jealousy, love, hope, shame, distrust, etc. These emotions are every bit as strong, perhaps even stronger, than those expressed by the two younger road trip characters (Hannah and Bryan). Do you think our emotions cool as we age or get stronger?

9. Which character do you relate to more than any other? Why?

10. Humor can be a window to the truth. At different points, Norma, Mildred, and Jim reveal truths wrapped in little slices of humor. Was there ever a time in your life in which you felt the only way you could explain or express yourself was through a joke, a funny observation, etc.?

11. Where do you imagine Norma's Mustang is? Does she still have it? Or have new friends, a new town, and a new business all filled the void left by Jim?

12. What does it mean to you to have "miles left yet"? What are the miles you'd like to travel yourself? Do you have a few places you'd like to visit? A bucket list? A person you'd like to reconnect with? Would you like to try something brand new? If you could start an adventure today, what would it look like?

Made in the USA
Middletown, DE
24 July 2020

13615290R00156